ALLINGHAM: DESPERATE RIDE

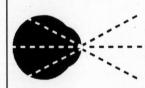

This **Large Print Book** carries the
Seal of Approval of N.A.V.H.

ALLINGHAM: DESPERATE RIDE

JOHN C. HORST

THORNDIKE PRESS

A part of Gale, Cengage Learning

GALE
CENGAGE Learning·

Farmington Hills, Mich • San Francisco • New York • Waterville, Maine
Meriden, Conn • Mason, Ohio • Chicago

GALE
CENGAGE Learning®

LIBRARY OF CONGRESS CATALOGING-IN-PUBLICATION DATA

Horst, John C.
    Allingham : desperate ride / by John C. Horst. — Large print edition.
        pages cm. — (Thorndike Press large print western)
    ISBN 978-1-4104-8002-6 (hardcover) — ISBN 1-4104-8002-X (hardcover)
    1. Large type books. I. Title. II. Title: Desperate ride.
PS3608.O7724A794 2015
813'.6—dc23   2015007948

Published in 2015 by arrangement with John C. Horst

Printed in Mexico
1 2 3 4 5 6 7 19 18 17 16 15

For Mary Ann

Man is the cruelest animal.

— Friedrich Nietzsche

CONTENTS

9

CHAPTER I:
NORTHWEST ARIZONA
TERRITORY 1884

Ramon Jesus Santiago de la Garza rested by the fire as his men settled in for the night. They were on the southernmost part of the Scotsman's ranch, closest to their homes in Mexico. The gringos left them alone. They'd waste no time heading back home as soon as was practicable. Most would be happy to get away from the chilly northern land.

"Jefe," the old man called to the boy, his leader, his patron who was one third his age. Ramon nodded but refused the bottle. He looked beyond his old friend and trail boss toward the ranch house. The light was dimming and he wondered what was taking them so long. The pay would be good but, in cash, which he did not want. It was contrary to the deal made and he liked to keep things as planned, as his father had taught him.

However, the old Scotsman had been

13

insistent, terse and gruff, almost rude, and falsely friendly. He'd droned on about doing real business as real men, with cash on the barrelhead. The Scotsman was the kind of man Ramon did not much like, the kind of man who represented the sort of gringos Ramon generally avoided.

Now he'd have to carry cash to the nearest town with a real bank and then deposit it. It would be a lot of trouble as Mexicans, even pale Mestizos, as was Ramon, were not trusted and should not have so much cash. He'd have to explain, and convince them that he was a man of property with a proper bank account and simply wanted to conduct business without being treated like he was doing something wrong.

He worked on a reata as was his habit when he had things on his mind and when it was too dark to read his books. He watched over his men; they appeared to be happy. They'd done good work getting the horses up to the gringo ranch and in a little while they'd be headed home where it was not so cold. Paulo played guitar near the fire. This kept his hands warm while the others sat with their blankets wrapped around them, up high on their shoulders, sombreros pulled down low so that only a slit remained for them to peer through, as was their custom when it was cold.

They all watched as the gringos of the ranch arrived too quickly and a little too wildly with the horses pulled up at the last moment. It was done a bit dramatically, a way to show the vaqueros that the cowboys could hold their own. The men dismounted and sauntered up to the fire.

Not all were so bad. Most were young men from all over the states. Many hadn't even seen a Mexican before and these treated Ramon and his men well enough. They had not yet been taught to hate the dark men from the south. Some had instruments, mouth organs and Jews' harps, and soon added to the music of the guitar. It was turning into a regular little party and Ramon could relax a little. He stood up to greet the son of the Scotsman.

"Buenas noches." The young gringo nodded to Ramon and his top hand.

"Good evening, Mr. Hall." Ramon reached out to shake the gringo's hand and was ignored. He put his hand back by his side and watched as the saddle bags were pulled roughly from the saddle skirt.

The young Hall was quite drunk. He half threw and half dropped the bags into the dust at the Mexican's feet; smiled stupidly, and belched feted breath at his guest.

Ramon sat back down and opened the bags, pulling the money out and looking the stacks over carefully. He'd not count each stack but instead looked them over for uniformity in thickness. Each had a band wrapped round with the number one thousand stamped on it from the bank.

He took a deep breath as a dozen thoughts ran through his mind. He looked at the Scotsman's son who was now sitting across from him pulling hard on a bottle of rye. He checked the stacks again and then checked the bags again. He was right, they were short two stacks.

He nodded to Adulio, his top hand, who began counting each stack. These as well were short by a hundred dollars each. When Adulio finished, Ramon pushed the whole amount back toward the Scotsman's son. "Mr. Hall, what of the other twenty four hundred?"

"What you mean?" Hall blinked and tried to focus. He looked down at the money between them.

"This is the final payment and it is short twenty four hundred dollars." The men stopped playing. The party suddenly became quiet.

"Well, I tell ya, muchacho. That's what we, my pa an' me, decided your horses was worth. Ain't what we expected, ain't what we bargained for, so that's what we plan to pay, take it or leave it."

At this a young hand came forward, taller and more alert than the Scotsman's son. He nodded to the Mexicans and stood next to Ramon's top hand.

"What's this, Donny?"

"Nothin', Pierce, nothin'. Don't worry about it." The drunk waved his brother away.

"No, it's something all right. Pa never said a thing about being disappointed in the herd. He said the opposite, in fact. Said these Mexican boys brought us the best horseflesh for five hundred miles."

"Shut up, Pierce."

Ramon looked on at the more sensible man. He'd not met him before but reasoned that he must have some standing in the family. "Perhaps we should see Mr. Hall directly."

The drunken man stood up. He was becoming angry now, angry at both men and he glared at his brother. "No need to bother Pa. This is all you get, muchacho, and that's that."

"Then you may keep it and we'll take the horses back home to Mexico."

Pierce held up a hand. He was flabbergasted at the thought. He looked the young man over carefully. He could see it in his eyes, the Mexican meant what he said. He was not bluffing. The vaqueros all slowly stood up and carefully positioned themselves around their young boss. The blankets were now gone and many suddenly held Winchesters in their hands.

"Señor, please." Pierce nodded to the jefe and glared at his half-brother. "Cut the bullshit, Donny. Pa wants the horses. Come through with the cash, *now*!"

The young man smiled. "All right, all right. Jesus, you boys don't know when someone's makin' a joke." He reached into a pocket and pulled out a wad of bills. He tossed it to Adulio. "There's the rest of your cash, boys." He sucked greedily on his bottle. "Go on and count it." He looked more confident than he was. "Go on boys, start back to playin'. Get the jugs out and uncorked. Time to celebrate." He waved his hand at them, as if shooing flies.

Adulio looked up. "Still short by one hundred dollars."

Pierce looked at his brother again. "Come on, out with it, Donny."

The lad grinned again. "Jesus, boys, you're too damned crafty fer me. Din' think you Mexicans could count past ten." He came

18

forth with the last bill.

Ramon put everything in his saddle bags then turned to walk away.

"Come on back, muchacho. Come on back and have a drink with us."

Ramon knew it wasn't a good idea but said, "Only one, Mr. Hall. We plan to ride out in a few hours; we need to get back home."

"Awe, you boys oughtta stay. We'll take ya around about here. Lots to do, lots to see. Got some damned pretty whores over in Kingman. White ones at that." He winked at Adulio. "You Mexican boys like white women, I guess." He drank and muttered under his breath, "Better than them niggers you got down Mexico way."

"I guess." Ramon looked at his men and was not smiling. The sooner he could get away from the rude gringo the better. Pierce chimed in.

"We'll let these fellows alone, Donny. They got plans." He nodded to his men and they all prepared to mount up.

Donny held up a hand. "How 'bout it? How 'bout just one more drink for you and your men?"

Ramon thought it would go well to be a little civil. It was early yet and the men could stand a few drinks. It would help them sleep on the rough and cold desert ground.

Soon one led to half a dozen and the music was playing and Donny was now well beyond the point of sensible behavior. This was what Pierce hoped to avoid, as his half-brother was an idiot sober and was ridiculous and violent when drunk. He moved close to the young jefe and watched his brother intently. He liked the Mexicans, even felt a little akin to the dark men.

In short order, Donny was well in his cups. He looked at Ramon a little sideways, out of tiny slits made that way by inebriation, turning Mongoloid before their very eyes.

"How's it some a you boys is dark as niggers," he pointed at Paulo's hand strumming the strings of his guitar, then pointed at Ramon, "and some of youse are white as me?" He cackled as his men stood by. He looked around stupidly, wondering why no one was laughing.

Pierce called him out. "Go on to bed, Donny, you've had enough and your conversation's turned to pure shit. Makin' yourself out to sound a real ass."

"*Yer the ass!* Hell, yer darker 'an some of these pepper bellies. Yer almost a nigger yerself."

He stood up and began urinating by the fire, nearly in Ramon's lap. The men jumped up. Ramon nearly clobbered him, but then thought better of it. He began to walk back to his war bag. It was time to get some sleep.

"No, no, don't go run off." Donny finished and buttoned up his trousers. "Want to talk, want to talk some more. You boys, heard you're pretty handy with the knives. Show me your knife, muchacho." He pulled his own and turned it back and forth so as to catch the firelight on the gleaming blade. "This here's a Arkansas toothpick. Could cut yer' damned head off." He swept the air between them and pointed his index finger in the air unsteadily. "One swipe."

Ramon stood before him. He had had enough and was tired. He looked at the knife now pointed at his own belly. He looked at the drunk again. "Good night, Mr. Hall."

With more speed and dexterity than one would expect from a drunk, Donny reached forward and suddenly had the Mexican's knife in his hand, pulled quickly from the sheath at his side. He held it up, comparing the two as if he were deciding which one to keep.

Pierce called out. "Come on, Donny, put yer knife away. Give Mr. la Garza his'n back." He stepped forward and his brother pointed both blades at him.

"Go on and step back, Pierce, or I'll pierce ya. Hah, pierce a Pierce. Pierced Pierce."

He grinned stupidly at the men around him. The ranch hands all knew, when Donny got this way, the only thing to do was knock him out. Pierce knew it too, and had done so on more than one occasion, but Donny was not usually armed. He stepped forward again, held out his hand and was rewarded with a neat gash across the cheek.

Ramon went into action and hit the young drunk with a quick right hook. It dropped him onto his backside as Pierce reeled and held his left cheek shut, blood pouring freely between his fingers, over his hand and down his arm, dripping off his elbow in a steady stream.

"God damned nigger Mexican bastard!" Donny dropped the Mexican's knife and slashed the air between them with his great toothpick, missing the agile man by a foot, yet giving himself enough time to regain his footing. He spit a bloody tooth onto the ground next to the Mexican's daga.

"Pick it up, Mexican boy. Pick it up or I'll gut ya unarmed."

Adulio tossed his own blade to his young boss and now the two men stood, crouching, ready to eviscerate each other. Ramon sallied forth with a thrust that would have done his Castilian ancestors proud, filling the air with vaporized blood and effluent and stool. The young drunk was dead in less than a minute.

They all stood around him for several moments. All the Mexicans were now armed, pistols and Winchesters cocked, prepared to do whatever was necessary to spirit their hero and jefe way.

But as it turned out, none of that was necessary. The white men all stood around, shrugging and murmuring and then attended to Pierce. When he was deemed out of danger, they handed the young Mexican a new bottle of spirits along with his previously discarded knife.

Ramon did not like the gringo alcohol but took it, nonetheless, as a gesture of peace. He waited and watched. An old hand came forward and looked him over. He glanced at his comrades, then Pierce, then the Mexicans. "Been waiting for this day to come. Knew it would, knew it was just a matter of time."

He walked over and extended his hand to Ramon and shook it resolutely. "We're mighty sorry for the rude treatment, mister. Mighty sorry."

Pierce stood up and finally took control. He called to his men. "You boys go on back to the ranch. Go on to bed. Leave Donny where he lay. No one says anything to my pa, is that clear?"

They all nodded and agreed and headed back to the ranch.

He looked at the Mexicans. "You boys leave him where he is." Pierce pulled a blanket from Donny's saddle and covered the corpse with it. "Get some sleep and vamoose tomorrow, go on home fast as you can. I'll deal with Donny and my father."

Back at the ranch, Old Pop dabbed Pierce's cheek clean, doused it with whiskey and began sewing him up with blue thread. Pierce sat like a stone remembering to keep his tongue as far to the right as possible. He waited to hear Old Pop's plan.

"Best to just tell it like it is. Don't know that the boys would ever rat you out, but makin' up a story is a bad idea." He looked at Pierce and then continued with the next suture. "Not that you would, just sayin'."

Pierce wanted to speak but the pain was too much. He feared he'd cause more of it and risk more damage by yacking. He nodded instead.

"Your father is going to lose his simple

mind over this, for sure." He started another stitch, closer to the boy's eye. In short order he was finished. He pulled up a mirror and showed the young man his handiwork. It looked like hell.

"Thanks. This will impress the ladies, sure enough."

"Only ones who like a man of character, and they're the best of all anyways."

They sat and drank and thought of the storm of shit that would fall on the ranch at daylight.

Old Pop went on: "Them Mexicans, I liked 'em well enough. They're some ridin' sons of bitches, and I swear they're some of the best horses I've seen in all my time. Your pop had a genius idea gettin' them from Mexico instead of from the Navajos down south — and they got some good horses, sure enough, themselves."

Pierce stood up suddenly and felt as if his legs wouldn't hold him. His head reeled and he vomited into a chamber pot at the foot of his bed, barely making it in time.

"Easy, lad. You've lost a lotta blood, and the body ain't used to that much pain. Lie down now. We'll think of somethin' in the morning."

"Thanks, Old Pop."

CHAPTER II:
JEFES

They were riding by four in the morning. Ramon had a good compass and could make out a road heading south. By daylight they would cover many miles and resolved to jog southeast to Phoenix, stopping over long enough to make the bank deposit. They did not want to travel through bandit land with so much cash.

Adulio rode up alongside his young jefe and handed him a canteen of coffee, still warm. The lad drank it and felt it burn his churned up guts as if he'd poured lye down his throat. He spat the part that would not go down and drank water from his own canteen.

"The men are willing to ride straight through, Ramon. Even if it kills their favorite mounts. We've got enough in the remuda that we can ride without stopping."

Ramon nodded. It might be necessary. He suddenly felt very tired. Such a promising adventure now needed an escape plan. A feeling of disappointment washed over him. It had promised to be a good enterprise with a good plan. The Scotsman's letters and telegrams were so friendly. However, when they had arrived at the ranch, it felt different: foreboding, a foreshadowing of something bad. He drank again and spit over his horse's back, away from the old man.

"Let's see once we get to the big town. Let's see what awaits us there. Not all the gringos are assholes, Adulio." He thought for a moment and grinned uneasily, "Just most of them."

As he rode he thought about the money and how far it would go. They had three other herds to sell and one man from Texas and two from California were interested. This Arizona trip was a trial run, to see if it was profitable — doable — and it seemed that it was. The horses were beyond excellent, as his father and grandfather had honed their craft well. They raised horses even the American army would want to own. Perhaps he'd go after a contract with them next.

But the gringo getting killed was not good for business, he knew that, and no matter how innocent, a Mexican knifing a gringo was never good. Words would be said, stories would be told, and there was the old animosity from the great days of the battle for Texas and the Alamo and Santa Ana. And from the rustling that went on back when he was a child, perpetrated by both sides.

It was difficult for a Mexican to do good business in el norte, in the US. He wondered if it would be worthwhile. And then, he heard his men, his vaqueros just being vaqueros, talking to their horses, herding the remuda along and knew it was his only chance to keep the hacienda and this life — this world — going for any length of time. It was a lot for a twenty year old man to carry on such young shoulders.

He thought about his mother, now back in Spain. It had broken her heart to leave Mexico. She declared that she would not survive in the foreign land, the land of the Spaniards. She was too dark from her Inca blood and she'd not fit in with her odd dialect and customs and ways.

But it was his only recourse. There was nothing for it, she'd have ended up like his old father had she remained. Porfirio Díaz had his pan o palo, bread or stick, and his old father had fallen from grace. One of the darlings of the mestizos had made a slip-up, and slip-ups were not well tolerated in the Porfiriato.

Ramon was lucky to still hold the land. Only through some careful negotiating, and the fact that he'd spent his formative years in Spain studying law, was he permitted that.

Land he had, but nothing else, and a hacienda with land and without money, would not last. It was Adulio's and Paulo's idea to sell the horses up north. They knew that the fortune could be regained, that Ramon could do it and, it seemed now as he looked about him, that the death of the loud-mouthed gringo was not a concern among any of them. But they'd been in this fight for a long time.

All the time he played the gentleman in Spain, learning and loving and becoming a refined gentleman, even taking up the ancient art of sword fighting, which had obvious benefits, this cowboy life had never been his own. It was utterly foreign to him.

But Paulo and Adulio knew his mettle. They knew the bloodline and knew the boy to be pure of heart and spirit and mind. He would make a good Jefe and hacendado and, once his fortune was regained, he'd be back in good graces with the presidente, if only to gain the chance of one day seeking revenge. Perhaps one day he would be given the opportunity to drive a Castilian blade through the rotten heart of the bastard Porfirio Díaz and he, himself, take up the mantel of leader of the people of Mexico.

Ramon knew what the older men thought of him. He was proud of himself — humble, yet proud — and knew that he'd serve them well. His stomach calmed at the thought and he was secretly proud of his performance of the previous night. Granted, the gringo was drunk and very stupid, but deadly serious in his desire to kill him, so he was not a completely unworthy adversary. But, ultimately, he regretted taking the man's life. It would do no one any good and now they'd likely be run out of the whole territory of Arizona, perhaps in all of the US. And that did nothing toward his goal of regaining everything his ancestors had fought to build for more than two hundred years. It was a significant problem.

The Scotsman screamed and limped to the corpse of his second favorite son. Pierce was between him and his beloved boy, arms out, ready to comfort his father until the old man snarled and pushed him aside. Gathering Donny up in his arms, he cradled him like a newborn, holding his lifeless face against his cheek, he surveyed the open gut wound with horror.

He was distraught with wild unfocused eyes, the eyes of a creature suffering from some derangement. He finally focused on Old Pop.

"What happened to me boy? What happened to me boy?"

"He, he got a knife to the belly, sir; a knife."

"From who, from who, goddamn ye?" He finally looked at Pierce, finally comprehending that his half-breed son had been wounded as well. He collapsed onto the ground at the buckboard's wheel and wailed.

Thad Hall was behind him now. "It's them goddamned nigger Mexicans done it."

Pierce glared at his oldest brother. He realized there was no point in trying to reason with the old man. He looked at Old Pop and stood back, watching the two poisoned minds hash out their deadly plan for revenge.

Pierce quietly moved to the ranch's top hand and whispered in his ear: "Old Pop, we gotta get to them Mexican boys. Thad'll run 'em down and kill every one of 'em."

Old Pop watched as Thad helped the old Scotsman back to the ranch house. The

31

eldest and meanest of the sons glared back at them, then put a finger up, pointing, ordering Pierce to follow.

Pierce grabbed his companion firmly by the arm, reached over and whispered into his ear again: "Get us a couple a mounts, good ones, Old Pop. Be ready to ride."

Inside his ranch house the old man gulped scotch after scotch. Thad joined him. He looked dismissively on his youngest brother. "What the hell happened, Pierce?"

"Donny got drunk last night. I tried to stop him from actin' the fool and he cut me. The head Mexican punched him and then Donny went after him. The Mexican was only defending himself."

"That's a lie. *Liar! Liar,* bastard half-breed devil. You're just like your whore mother. *Liar!*" The old man screamed and cried out in agony, as if the same blade were penetrating him as surely as it had his son's gut. He focused and looked Pierce over accusingly.

"You did this. You and those niggers from the south. You did this and you are trying to blame me boy, me sweet good boy." He turned to Thad. "Thaddie, me Thaddie, go, take good men, as many as was with that bastard Mex. Get the sheriff, get a posse, string every greasy one of them up. Do it, boy. Do it now!"

Thad grinned as he pushed past his step-brother. "With pleasure, Pa, with pleasure."

They rode hard south, hoping to overtake the Mexicans on their way to Phoenix. It had to be Phoenix. Old Pop looked at his companion doubtfully.

"What'll we do when we find 'em, Pierce? That crooked sheriff's been in yer Pa's pocket for as long as I can remember and old Thad makes Donny look like a kid preacher. Gotta get those Mexican boys some help. Somethin'. I don't know what, but somethin' sure enough." He saw Pierce grin and wondered at what.

"I know a man who's a tougher son of a bitch than 'em all, Old Pop. Gotta find them boys and turn 'em up toward Flagstaff."

Old Pop finally got his meaning. "Allingham."

"Goddamn right. That son of a bitch of a marshal, old Allingham. He'll make it right, by God, he'll make it right."

It was a sentiment repeated often throughout the land, *By God, Allingham'll make it right;* Allingham, the terse Yankee carpetbagger from New York; the ugly copper with his city ways; the man to clean up and defeat

33

the worst end-of-the-line settlement in all the West. That was Allingham.

Even the rumors that he'd retired failed to deter anyone who'd been in need of a strong and righteous hand. Anyone who had a corrupt boss or town official, who was plagued with a bully, or anyone, really, who was in need, would seek out Allingham.

And Canyon Diablo was the place, the terrible place where Allingham had secured his reputation as the no nonsense and fair-minded dispenser of justice. Few ever knew, or ever would know, that he'd gone there to commit suicide, to beat the fates at stealing him away through cancer. And all the while, Allingham was as sound as a railroad watch. He was a most unorthodox hero.

But when the dust finally settled, and the bridge was put in, Allingham was given a new lease on life with the most stunning and desirable woman in all the Arizona land. That should have been the end of it. Allingham wanted an end to it. He wanted to live out his days with his woman, start a family, spoil his love and his children, which he hoped upon hope, would be many.

And in the meantime, he was satisfied with his adopted family: Rosario, the Mexican cook; Hobbs his right-hand man; Mr. Singh, the fearless and noble Sikh; and even

Robert Halsted, the father who could never comprehend what Rebecca saw in the ugly American.

It was all going splendidly. But that was about to change.

Chapter III:
Allingham

Rebecca Allingham reached over and soundly clobbered her husband on his bulbous nose.

"Ouch."

"Sorry, darling. Your rule."

It was. On the first anniversary of their wedding day, the rule held fast. Allingham would not let his wife see him naked. He was permitted to see her, enjoy her, marvel at her womanly perfection but, once in bed, all lights were to be extinguished. The beauty was not permitted, ever, under any circumstances, to behold the beast in his natural glory — or hideousness — depending on the perspective of the beholder.

She laughed and pulled herself onto him for another go 'round.

"Hmm . . . still love me, darling?"

"With every fiber of my being." Allingham felt himself to be dreaming whenever he was with his perfect wife.

■ ■ ■ ■

They slept in until nine. He'd become a good lover. She'd made him that way; made him human and happy and outwardly as kind, at least to her and to her family, as he always was inwardly. One year had made such a difference, and it was, she thought, despite the lack of swelling she'd hoped for by now in her womb, the happiest time of her life.

Robert Halsted, her father had finally come around, more or less, and Mr. Singh was always — as always — just plain perfect Mr. Singh. He treated Allingham well and they'd become great friends.

She stretched and felt him under the covers. There was still time before Rosario would be bumping around, anxious to make up the room. She kissed him awake and he smiled and breathed in the wonderful scent of his lovely wife. He gazed down at her over his bulbous nose. It was turning out to be a fairly perfect anniversary.

A knock at the door and the sweet lilting call of Rosario finally broke the spell.

"Ola, Señora. Capitan, there is an emergency. I am sorry, I tried to make them go away, but they are muy insistente."

Rebecca kissed him on his scars, rolled out of bed and slowly, almost maddeningly, covered her naked form. She liked to watch her husband want her. She turned her back and let him dress in peace.

She smiled coyly and called out. "All right, Rosario, we'll be right there."

It was police work again and Allingham hated it. He was, by now, used to being a kept man and liked the ease of a gentleman's life that making the grand tour had taught him to appreciate so well. He'd quickly become used to letting Rebecca have her way in all things, as well. Just as his friend, Francis, had said, "Spoil them. Spoil the women you love."

His police pension would not have covered the transatlantic journey one way, but his woman had certain tastes and requirements. He could not begrudge her any of them or insist she live on his pay. Allingham was man enough not to be a fool or prideful about such things. Rebecca had the fortune and that was that. Now the thought of police work revolted him. Every time someone came around with a new problem, he did not want to deal with it. He wanted to be left alone. He was a thoroughly spoiled and kept man.

"Oh, cheer up. It might be something fun."

And Rebecca was right about that. Allingham was retired from the marshaling business, but his genius as a detective had not gone untapped by the good folks of Arizona and Utah and even once in New Mexico in the year they'd been newlyweds. Rebecca refused to be left behind while her husband did his best sleuthing. She was excited over the prospect of this new adventure, certainly more than he was. But then again, Allingham retained a certain pride in his ability to continue to catch the bad men. He was a good man, a good citizen, and he'd never refuse an assignment.

A new man waited; a physician they'd not met before. He was an easterner, now settled in a small place a bit north of Phoenix. He dabbled in medicine but had had a belly full in the war. He, too, like Allingham, had been retired, but called out for this special case.

It was a hideous business and neither the doctor nor sheriff dared to speak of it while the lady and Allingham had their breakfast. The gruff former policeman glared at the intruder, then at the sheriff who'd escorted him to the Allingham home. "Well?"

"Ahem, it is rather unsavory, sir." The sheriff shuffled and cleared his throat. "I mean, the circumstances, not something one discusses whilst eating, *or* in the presence of a lady."

Rebecca waved him off. "Nonsense, gentlemen." She looked at the sheriff and smiled. "You two sit down, have some breakfast."

"Thank you, ma'am." The sheriff held his hat in his hand, then released it to Rosario who placed a cup of coffee in front of each. The sheriff went on. "I'm sure glad to have finally met you folks. Marshal, that was some police work you did down in Canyon Diablo, and your detective work with the princess and then the chloroform robberies down in Bisbee last winter, some fine work. I'm, I'm mighty proud to meet you."

Rebecca responded as Allingham still had the habit of slipping into terseness. Old habits died hard, despite Rebecca's constant mentoring.

"Oh, thank you, sheriff. My husband does have a keen eye."

"And that's why we're here, folks." The doctor glanced at the sheriff for approval and proceeded. "It seems we have a bit of a, how do I say, ritual murderer."

Allingham looked up from his plate of eggs. "Go on."

"It's the second of its kind in the last month, down in the sheriff's jurisdiction. Happened only yesterday."

"Has the body been moved?"

"Not the second one, but we're sorry to report," the sheriff looked forlornly into his coffee cup, "the first victim's six feet under."

Allingham sighed. "How are they linked?"

"Both prostitutes, both with red hair." The sheriff fixed his gaze too obviously away from Rebecca's auburn locks. "And . . ." He could not make himself continue in the presence of the lady.

The doctor cleared his throat and continued. "Really, Mrs. Allingham, are you certain you'd not rather spare yourself the ghoulish story the sheriff and I are about to convey?" His face reddened and now both he and the sheriff looked like a pair of school boys caught in some compromising act.

Rebecca smiled in her best motherly manner, holding up a hand. "Now that you put it such, how can I walk away, doctor? I can assure you, being around my husband and father and my dear friend Mr. Singh, I've seen my share of things that would put one of a more delicate disposition into a faint-

41

ing spell. But you are safe with me. Please, go on."

"Very well." The doctor continued with great trepidation. "Both victims were raped, mutilated and one nipple was excised from the breast of each. The rectum was intact, ruling out sodomy."

Allingham looked pensively at his plate as he thought, visualizing the scene, and attempted to recreate as much as he could in his mind.

"Where did these attacks occur?"

"That is another interesting thread to tie them together, sir. Both women were very low living prostitutes, working in the worst bordellos in town. Yet they'd both been killed at the empty residences of two prominent businessmen, the houses recently vacated as the families are on a grand tour."

"Together?"

"I'm sorry?" The physician was genuinely confused.

"Together?" Allingham fairly shouted the question at him a second time. "Did the families travel to Europe together or was that a coincidence?"

"Oh, together, yes, together. They are great friends, neighbors." He rubbed the whiskers on his chin, wondering if he'd missed a clue, then looked up at Allingham.

"Is that significant?"

"I don't know." Allingham was becoming distracted. The men were putting him off with their insignificant comments. He continued. "And have you profiled the suspect?"

"Profiled?" The hapless sheriff was out of his element. He had no understanding of the concept, had no concept of what Allingham meant.

"I, I'm sorry Mr. Allingham, no. Other than consulting Dr. Webster, I've done nothing with the case. We buried the first poor victim as we never expected much else was required other than our initial investigation." He pulled out a cigarette and thought better of smoking in the lady's presence. Rebecca handed him an ashtray and lighter, nodding kindly for him to proceed. "We followed as many clues as we could, and my investigation has continued, sir, but we pretty well concluded that it must have been a drifter. We never thought we'd have a repeat performance, and now we're convinced the devil is still amongst us."

"Which consisted of what?"

"What?"

"Your investigation, your follow up, your clues, *what, what, what*?"

"Oh, sketches. And photographs."

Allingham's eyes brightened. "That's

good. Very good, sheriff." He nodded approvingly and this encouraged the man considerably.

"Thank you, gentlemen." Allingham stood up and waited for them to follow suit. He was ready for them to leave now. "I'll be around at," he looked at his watch, calculated the travel time, "four this afternoon. Please make certain nothing is moved. Post a guard, keep a watch, but let no one tamper with the crime scene." He drank the rest of his coffee and had another thought.

"And sheriff?"

"Yes, Mr. Allingham?"

"Disinter the first victim as soon as practicable."

The sheriff swallowed hard and imagined just how much decay would be awaiting him. "Yes, sir."

The doctor, a little more animated than one would expect, responded. "Do you really suppose that is necessary, Marshal?"

"Yes." He looked the man over dismissively. "Why not?"

"Oh, call me old fashioned, it's just, just to desecrate a holy burial, for what, I, I don't know. I'd hope you'd see the photographs and sketches, all the good work the sheriff has done before resorting to such drastic and ghoulish measures."

Allingham ignored the doctor's comment as he looked over at the sheriff. "Dig her up."

He watched them mount up, Rebecca standing in the mid-morning sun, turning her hair the dark copper he loved so much. Allingham reached out and gently hefted one of the long curls. "Rebecca," he hesitated as the men rode off, "have you ever considered coloring your hair blonde?"

CHAPTER IV:
HUNTING

They got a much later start than they'd hoped and now feared the Mexicans would be too far ahead to find. Pierce's wound throbbed with every stride of his mount. He looked down the dirt road, hoping to catch sight of the men whose lives depended on him — and they didn't even know it.

He looked over at Old Pop cantering alongside. He had a deeply furrowed brow, his hawk-like features fixed on the road ahead. Pierce was glad for his company. Old Pop was the top hand on the ranch and ever so much more than that. He'd been with the Scotsman the longest and, as if by divine providence or some other intervention, become the old scoundrel's keeper. It was almost as if he had been assigned to keep the terrible man in check, to keep him from becoming as truly bad as he would otherwise be.

He was the reason why the ranch was as

successful as it was; the reason why they actually had good men cowboying for them. Without Old Pop, they'd have had nothing more than a bunch of cutthroats and thieves. Old Pop was also why Pierce maintained a foothold, however tenuous, as one of the heirs to the family fortune and land.

Old Pop looked over and smiled at the lad. Pierce had been crying over his brother and had not even realized it. The young man wiped the tears from his eyes when Old Pop made him aware of them. That was the thing the old timer loved so much about the lad. He decided that talking about it was best for his friend right now.

"Old Donny. Wondered when he was goin' to get it."

Pierce looked up and blinked more tears from his eyes. Old Pop could read a man like a surveyor could decipher a map. He smiled uneasily at the thought of his brother, the most reckless, the stupidest, but not by any means, the meanest or most evil of his kin. He wondered suddenly why he'd been crying over him at all.

"Yeah, you're right about that, Old Pop. Boys used to take bets. Every roundup season, every time Donny'd go into a decent sized town, the boys would bet on the wherefores and the why hows of how'd he buy it. Lot of money changed hands over the years trying to guess when Donny'd get himself snuffed out."

"Well," Old Pop nodded, "He don't deserve such a good man cryin' over him. Even if he was your brother, Pierce, he was the most worthless son of a bitch I've ever known."

"That ain't true!"

Old Pop suddenly wondered if he'd gone too far. He looked at his hand reining his mount.

"Thad's that."

Old Pop smiled and shrugged. "Yeah, I guess you're right. Thad makes Donny look like a choirboy, sure enough. Sure enough."

"We gotta get these Mexicanos to Flagstaff and Allingham before Thad gets to them, Old Pop. You know that, don't you?" It was a rhetorical question, as Pierce knew the old man knew it well enough. "I know them Mexicans ain't babies, and I know a lot'll get killed on both sides. Maybe that would be a good way to get rid of Thad, but it just ain't right. Ain't the right thing by a long ways."

Pierce rode along and thought about his crying over Donny. Why would he? They were brothers, but not really. Same father, different mothers. The mother was really the one to make men brothers. Same mother and there was something. And he was a half-breed. He knew that, certainly. There was no way he could ever forget that with all three of them reminding him of it all the time, every chance they'd get, every day, sometimes on the hour. Well, quarter breed, really. His mother, according to Old Pop, was half Navajo, half French, and as his Pa was half Scottish and half Irish, it made him only a quarter breed. But they reminded him of it all the same, all the time.

He was dark and looked like none of them. Thad and Donny were like horrible casts of the Scotsman. They looked like him, were built like him, even sounded like him. They were all copies of the same terrible master mold. The Scotsman was an ill-tempered, venal man, and he'd made not one, but a pair of terrible replacements for himself.

Pierce thought of something else. "Why'd you stay on so long, Old Pop? They treat you like shit. You're a good man, a man who could have your pick of the best jobs in the land, and you stayed on with my damnable damned old man."

Old Pop smiled and couldn't say it. He looked on and thought about it. The boy didn't know it, didn't realize *he,* Pierce, was the reason. He met his mind halfway. "Your mother, I suppose."

Pierce turned sideways in the saddle and slowed down. "I barely remember her."

"Yeah, well, you weren't more than four when she died." He rubbed his eyes with one hand. "Hell, boy, you're going to get me blubberin' here in a minute." He laughed and cleared his throat. "She weren't much more than a child herself." He looked over at Pierce again. "I loved that little gal. She was sweet, Pierce, and I know your father says mean things about her, but he loved her, loved her more than he did his first wife, that horrible bitch."

Pierce laughed a little. "That horrible bitch."

"Yeah, and boy howdy what a bitch she was. I could not stand that woman. But your mother, she was like a little angel, boy, and doggone pretty as you can ever imagine a woman to be, and kind and pure. A pure little angel."

They came upon a ranch just off the road and stopped. A woman and an old man ran it. They were friendly and fed them and their horses and the woman was kind of pretty in a hard way. Pierce was embarrassed as she would snatch glances at his

50

blue threaded wound every now and again. He couldn't blame her. He looked like hell. He was otherwise a handsome man but the wound had puffed up a bit and was red and looked like a spare pair of sewn up lips attached oddly to the side of his head, ready to burst open at any moment and show off the insides of his mouth. He thought about wearing his scarf up over his nose, like when he was out on a cold or especially dusty day.

These same ranchers had hosted the Mexicans only the day before and reported that they'd heard the men talk of Phoenix. They were on the right track and the men from the south were not far ahead. Pierce was encouraged.

As he ate, he watched the woman as her old husband talked of the Mexicans. When he mentioned the leader, Ramon, the woman got a funny look on her face. It was pretty obvious to Pierce that she had some ideas and had wished that the Mexicanos had stayed on, at least overnight. She caught Pierce looking at her and realized he knew what was in her mind. She gave him just the hint of a smile. He was kind of glad they were moving on. He was neck deep in trouble as it was, and didn't need an angry husband hanging over him.

■ ■ ■ ■

Pierce and Old Pop thanked the couple, paid them and moved on. They couldn't be more than six hours behind. Pierce rode along at a ground-eating trot, hour after hour, daydreaming. He half thought it would have been a good idea to try bribing the ranching couple to throw his brother off. He figured he'd likely be by their place directly. Then he realized he was glad he hadn't done it, figuring maybe he and Old Pop would catch up with the Mexican boys and they'd all make a stand and he'd coolly put a bullet through his brother's head.

That would certainly put an end to it. Put an end to the nonsense. Maybe he'd go back and finish off the old man, too. Probably not, but that would work and at least he could happily fantasize about it, even if it was something his nature and decency would never allow.

He and Old Pop could run the place properly then. It would be best for everyone, even for his father. The miserable bastard needed putting out of his misery, just as one would do for a hydrophobic dog. He was pulled out of his reverie by Old Pop's declaration.

"There's dust." Old Pop was pointing a mile ahead. The Mexicans were there. He turned back and looked behind them, the same distance off. "And there's your brother and his posse."

They kicked their mounts into a gallop. Up ahead, where they'd likely meet up with the Mexicans, was a flat mesa. It would be a good place to make a stand.

Chapter V:
Descension

Rebecca tossed and turned and listened to her husband snore. Every time she closed her eyes she saw the wretched victim. It was impossible to expunge it from her mind. She listened to Allingham snore and became a little annoyed that he could have done what he'd done — poked and prodded and manipulated the corpse in such ways — and then sleep like a baby next to her, as if it had meant nothing to him.

She reached over and kicked him none too gently in the side and he turned to face her in the dark.

"Can't sleep?"

"No, of course not. How can *you*?"

"You get used to it."

"How can such a horrible thing not bother you, darling? How?"

"Oh, it bothers me, Rebecca." He sat up and, lighting the lamp, pulled a couple of cigarettes out of the package. He lit them both and handed her one. He poured her a little scotch and kissed her on the temple.

She didn't really believe him. "You seem to sleep well enough."

"Because I'm tired. But it always bothers me, Rebecca. It would bother anyone with a heart and soul and a thinking mind. That's the crime of it. It's a crime against all humanity, Rebecca, and this one's as bad as they get. This one's really a bad one. We've got to find him."

She yawned and smiled as she worked on her drink. "This is why I love you so much, you know."

He was confused as always when she declared her love for him. He still could not figure it all out.

He thought of something and went to his desk and wrote something in a book he kept with him all the time. He called it his brain, as it held all the ideas he would have about a case. He'd write in it, sketch, record measurements, even go so far as to paste photos into it. Most of it was so confusing and illegible that Rebecca was convinced it would mean nothing to anyone except Allingham.

Now he had Rebecca to help him and he'd pose questions to her, sometimes rhetorical, not requiring an answer, but at other times he needed to hear her responses. She understood that it was part of his reasoning process. The dialectic, they called it. He'd ask questions and she'd reply so that the conclusion could better come to them both. She was the best crime solving partner he'd ever known.

He didn't look up from his writing, but rather spoke into it. "What of this physician?"

Rebecca thought about it. The man seemed benign enough, but her husband would not ask such a question without good reason. She liked to listen to his arguments in such matters.

"What of him?" She often simply rephrased the question, repeating it back to him.

"Interesting, his concern for all this. I've made some inquiries. He's a real physician, trained in Pennsylvania. He seems to have an overly enthusiastic attitude toward the murders. It seems to me a bit morbid."

"Do you think him a suspect?"

"Don't know. Curious he mentioned no evidence of sodomy." He caught himself and remembered he was speaking to his wife. His face flushed and he was suddenly embarrassed.

Rebecca grinned a little. It was most

certainly new ground for her, and until that moment, she had no real knowledge of such things, despite spending considerable time around some of society's more colorful characters. "And that's not something you would have thought of, darling? I mean, to investigate?"

"No. Not really. Not really. I suppose it is useful information. The depraved often form habits, rituals, patterns of behaviors that can be linked. I won't say it was not a valid comment or investigation on his part, but it is certainly unprecedented." He shrugged. "No matter."

"Have you seen many such victims, darling? I mean, in New York?"

"A few. Our superiors never wanted us playing them up much, the serialization, I mean. Never wanted a panic or public outcry. Most people cannot, will not, accept that a person is capable of doing such a thing, not once, let alone repeatedly. They can't accept that people are out there amongst us, lurking, waiting, capable of doing such things again and again. It is just too much for many to comprehend. They did their best to keep such things quiet.

"Had one very bad one and I never caught him. Same thing, really, the prostitutes. People aren't all that concerned when it's prostitutes. As if they deserve it, as if they are asking for it. And it's not them, so it's okay as long as it didn't happen to them or their daughters or wives or mothers. You know the old story, a prostitute's life isn't worth as much as someone who is not one.

"But it was pretty well the same thing: mutilation, sexual assault, and a pattern, a sameness with a simultaneous progression in barbarity. We'll look at the first victim tomorrow." He considered her, "That is, if you are up to it."

She nodded and he continued. "And I'll guarantee she was not as badly done as this one. And the next one will be worse. That is the way with these monsters. It's never enough, they always need more to satisfy the terrible urges. And," he looked at Rebecca as he pulled something from his desk drawer, "he won't be satisfied with prostitutes much longer. He'll likely need to move on to respectable members of society." He handed her a pistol. "Keep this with you, Rebecca. Keep this with you always."

They eventually slept until five and Rebecca awoke to find Allingham working in his notebook. He had one page divided down the center, forming two columns. He had the following written on it:

S	P
Age: 30 - 45	Y
Right handed	Y
Shoe Size: 9	UNK
Height: 5'8"	Y
Weight: 160 – 175 pounds	Y
Long pinky fingernail	N
Dresses well	Y
Strong	Y
Handles blades well: surgeon, butcher, barber	Y
Handsome	Y
Scottish or Irish	UNK
In America a long time or since birth	UNK
Clean shaven	N
Chipped upper left lat incisor	N
Cannibal	UNK
Anarchist	UNK

She leaned over and kissed him on the cheek, then regarded his work. "What is S and P?"

"Suspect and Physician."

"I see. And you know all of this from examining the site and the body yesterday?"

"Hmm."

"My goodness, darling. A bit of a stretch, isn't it?" She read each entry and looked up at him doubtfully.

"No."

He wrote another note. He needed to concentrate and would have liked her to sleep another hour at least.

"Then tell me." She got up and put on a robe. She sat at his feet and smiled. She thought of something else. "Do you really think it could be that doctor?"

"Hmm."

"Darling, pay attention to me."

He stopped looking at his notes and gazed down at her. She wasn't going to leave him alone. She took the notebook from him and read the list over carefully.

"How on earth can you possibly know even a fraction of this?"

"Oh, well," he looked at the book in her hand. "Just observing. Just paying attention to what was left behind."

"And *this* was left behind? Explain."

"Oh, well, I'm imagining his age as such because of his activity. There was great exertion and likely carried out by such a man of this age range. And he'd lured the prostitute in so he was likely youngish, yet mature, and handsome and fit."

"Go on."

"Well, right handed, obviously."

"No, not obviously."

"The way he carved her up, it was done by a right-handed person. Also, he favored the right. He was stronger with the right hand, as evidenced by the bruises, and the long fingernail on the right pinky finger, right hand, right-handed man."

"Long fingernail?"

"Yes, some men will grow the nail long on the pinky finger of the dominant hand."

"Really? Why?"

"With some cultures it is a sign of high station, shows they don't do manual labor. For others, usually whites or Europeans, or the Brits, it has a more practical application."

"Really? And what application could there possibly be?"

"Nose poking, ear cleaning, general scratching, opening envelopes, picking items up from a table or floor; just practical."

"That's disgusting."

"Indeed."

She looked at the list again, and then at her husband. "You never stop amazing me, darling. You know every revolting detail and proclivity of human kind."

"Thank you." He was a little pleased with her assessment of him and felt emboldened. He continued.

"I determined his height rather easily." He nodded to the window. "Rebecca, go over and pull the curtains closed."

She complied. He followed her and nodded. "Show me where you grasped them."

She again complied. Allingham then did the same. "You see the distance between where I grabbed them and where you did?"

"Yes." She smiled and understood.

"Yes, that's the normal height; where a person would normally grab curtains to close them. Our murderer did so with bloody hands. I simply took the difference and subtracted from my own height. And now I know his height."

"You're a genius, darling."

"Hmm."

"And the others — the other things — tell me or I'll surely burst with curiosity."

"He bit the poor woman on the neck and left an impression of his teeth. The one incisor was chipped rather badly, almost half its normal size. Not missing, but definitely not intact. It should be pretty apparent when we find him. He also, when raping her, had his feet planted rather resolutely on the footboard of the bed. The impression left by the soles of his shoes indicated gaiters, not boots. He was likely well dressed." He waited for her response and was a little proud of himself. He liked to impress his wife.

He continued. "And, let's see." He looked

further down the list. "Cannibal, as he bit a good piece of her left ear off and the remains were nowhere to be found. He most likely ate it."

Rebecca swallowed hard. "That's revolting."

Allingham nodded. "Indeed. We are dealing with a monster, a monster."

"An Irish or Scottish monster?"

"Yes, well, that might not be, but it is probable. This man has a penchant for redheaded women. Both women are redheads. There might be some link, perhaps an abusive relationship as a child, perhaps his mother. Difficult to say what provokes the diseased mind."

"And a clean shaven anarchist?"

"Yes, well, he had no hair on his chin, that's pretty certain. The victim had abrasions on her face, abrasions from a man with razor stubble. The anarchist idea, well, I'm going out on a limb, but they are some of the most nefarious, many of them demented criminals. I'm thinking that the deed was carried out in mansions as a symbol. He not only raped and desecrated the corpses of the women, but he was symbolically raping and defacing the world of the wealthy."

Rebecca nodded her head solemnly. "It is

a terrible thought, darling. This is a terrible, horrible being for certain."

"Yes, and I wonder, I believe, that perhaps he's a man expert in butchery of some type. His incisions were precise. Something from a butcher or a surgeon, someone who handles a blade well. Someone who is familiar with human or, at least, mammalian, anatomy."

He looked at Rebecca and thought that he was going too far. He stood up and began dressing. "Rebecca, the next examination will be worse yet. Do you suppose you should not bother with it?"

She breathed deeply and thought what a corpse so old and recently exhumed must hold in store for her. She smiled at Allingham and nodded knowingly. "No, I think I'll be all right, darling. I want . . . I want to be there for you. I want to do what I can to help."

She began dressing as well and, as she looked into the mirror, had a thought. "So, the doctor is out?"

"Looks like it. He has no chipped tooth, whiskers that are more than a few days old, trimmed nails, which I know he could have cut since then, but that would be unlikely. He'd have had to know he left a clue from this extraordinarily long nail and preemptively trimmed it to avoid suspicion. The other items add up: he's a surgeon, he is about the same age, height and weight, and he's apparently right handed, but so are a lot of people. No, Rebecca, I doubt this could be him. I don't think it is him at this point." He shrugged. "Perhaps he's genuine. Perhaps he's just trying to be helpful."

"Darling, why were you not the chief investigator of all the police of New York? You're brilliant!" She grabbed him under the chin and kissed him on the cheek.

He grunted. "Half the time I made them furious, the other half they wouldn't believe the conclusions of my investigations. It was better all the way around I remained a humble sergeant."

"Well, humble or not, we're lucky to have you, darling. I'm so proud of you. I hope you know that."

CHAPTER VI:
THE CHASE

Pierce and Old Pop rode up hard on the Mexicans. Ramon la Garza nodded indifferently. He half expected trouble and was pleased to see this pair as they'd treated him fairly.

"Señor."

"Mr. la Garza."

Ramon nodded further at Old Pop's handiwork on Pierce's damaged face. "Good stitching."

The young man reached up and felt it, as if he just remembered the wound. "My brother is on his way, Mr. la Garza. He has a posse and a crooked sheriff with him. They aim to kill you and your men."

"I see." He was impressive in his calm demeanor. He spoke quickly to his men who pulled up around him in a half circle. They all looked beyond the two gringos, as if they expected to see the bad men descending upon them at any moment.

Pierce looked back over his shoulder and then to the vaqueros. "Not yet, but they ain't far off. Probably less than an hour."

"And what do you propose?"

Pierce looked once more back toward home. There wasn't enough time to outrun them now. They'd have to make a stand. He looked at Old Pop and then at the Mexican jefe.

"Was hopin' to catch you sooner, Mr. la Garza. There's a good man, a US Marshal named Allingham up in Flagstaff. He'd give you safe passage home and get all this mess cleared up." He looked off northeast, as if to gauge the distance it would take. "But there's not enough time. No way we'd get there without my ass of a brother catching up to us."

La Garza tipped his head. "You're right about that." He looked off in the distance and saw the posse with the mean brother heading the pack. La Garza kicked his mount's sides and spoke quickly to Adulio and Paulo as his horse cantered amongst his men, now apparently agitated at what he'd said to them in his native tongue. They pulled their Winchesters and readied themselves for a fight.

He looked at Old Pop and Pierce, tipping his hat. "It is I they want, gentlemen. It is I they shall have to try and catch. Please take my men and remuda to this Allingham. Make it right, and get my company back to Mexico." He pulled his saddle bags free and tossed them to Paulo. "I will buy you some time."

He called to his mount in a little high pitched call, almost a carcajada, but not quite. He charged toward the assassination party and at one hundred yards pulled his six shooter, firing over the men's heads. Just as quickly he veered to the left, galloping west as Pierce and Old Pop and the Mexicans stood, jaws agape.

"Jesus, Old Pop. They'll kill him sure as shit." Pierce kicked his horse into action as he looked back. "Get 'em to Flagstaff, Old Pop. Get 'em there now. The marshal'll know what to do."

They all stood dumbfounded as the young man rode away. The older men sat on their horses trying to decipher what had just happened and what they should do next.

The plan worked and Thad turned his gang west to follow his brother and his quarry. There'd be time to go back and wipe out the Mexicans. Even if he had to travel all the way down to Mexico, he'd kill them all sooner or later, maybe even in their own beds. The real prize was la Garza. La Garza's head would make his father proud.

But the Mexican and his horse were spirited and light, and faster by a long way than the lumbering posse. Even Pierce, with a renewed purpose, was leaving the bad men far behind. In less than an hour of hard riding, the posse was nowhere in sight, and la Garza slowed enough to let his horse catch its breath, and for Pierce to ride up beside him.

"Please, Mr. Hall, there is no reason for you to accompany me. Go on back to your marshal. Help my men get back to Mexico."

"No, sorry, can't." Pierce gave him an uneasy smile. He'd seen what Thad could do and knew that sometimes he — really only he — could keep his deranged brother from slipping into his most violent state. He hoped he could intervene between the Mexican and his degenerate kin.

La Garza finally stopped on a high mesa overlooking an expanse that stretched many miles before him. He could just make out the dust trail of his pursuers. They were far behind. He got down and walked his horse to cool her down. He spoke to her soothingly in his native tongue. The horse listened and periodically bobbed her head.

Pierce was impressed. The Mexicans were

horsemen through and through and he was pleased he'd taken one of the best horses they'd delivered to the ranch for himself. He looked at his own mount that had been learning his new master's language. He had renewed confidence now.

"So, Mr. Hall, what do we do now?"

"Thought you'd know that answer, Mr. la Garza."

"Ramon."

He nodded. "Pierce."

La Garza smiled and thought about it. He'd only that morning consulted his map and figured he knew fairly well where he was. "If we travel a little north west, we should hit a town called Powellville. We can cross the Colorado there and be in California. I might try my luck at a ship's passage back to Mexico, unless I can lose them by then. I'll travel by rail or horse overland if that happens. I'd rather travel overland."

Pierce nodded. "Fair enough." He looked back and could see they were still far ahead of his brother and his men. "At least we are well mounted."

"Sí." He patted his horse on the neck and looked at Pierce's new gelding. "You are a good judge of horses, Pierce. He is the best of all the ones we brought to your father."

■ ■ ■ ■

They rode until well after dark. The setting sun still illuminated a peak that they could use for dead reckoning. They'd make another five miles while the posse would have to stop for the night, for fear of losing the sign. This gave them a significant advantage.

They made a cold camp, eating jerky and tortillas with water. They didn't dare make a fire and risk being seen. They were now on a flat mesa with no cover. A flame would show for a great distance and invisibility was the best course now.

It was a bright night and Pierce could see the man quietly braiding horsehair. It was too dark for the Mexican to be able to read his book. The young gringo was impressed by the Mexican's apparent lack of concern for his predicament. He wanted to talk, but had nothing much to say. The Mexican soon obliged him.

"I am sorry for killing your brother, Pierce."

"Oh, it's okay." He suddenly had to choke back tears. It felt preposterous to cry for his brother, but still he felt like he would. He was embarrassed to cry in front of the jefe. The man was a better one than any of his kin would ever be and they both knew it. They both knew his brother had to die and it wasn't the Mexican's fault. He was just the means, more a device, to send the lad to hell. If it wasn't the Mexican, it would have been someone else.

Pierce felt better thinking this and took a deep breath. He continued. "My other brother, Thad, the one chasing you — us — he's worse yet. A real pair of, of, what's that word you all call a low down dirty bastard, penjayhoe?"

The Mexican smiled at the little bit of rope in his hands. "Pendejo, the J is silent."

"Yeah, that's it: pendejo. They're a pair of pendejos, a real pair of jackasses, as is my pa. He's the lead pendejo."

"And you are not." Ramon stated this firmly as he looked at Pierce, or where his face was. A cloud had passed over the moon and made it too dark to actually see him.

"I try not to be."

"I'm glad."

They moved out by three in the morning as Ramon had a compass and his map. By his best reckoning, they made a beeline for the town. As he rode he looked at Pierce and decided to get rid of him. It would have to sound like a good strategy to the young gringo, though, and Ramon thought hard about what to say.

"Pierce, we should part company now. I'd like you to stay back a little when we hit this rocky ground ahead. They might follow you and not me. Perhaps it would be best if you started back toward home."

"No, sir."

The Mexican smiled and waited for Pierce's inevitable rationale.

"When you get across the Colorado safely, then I'll pull out. You'll be all right then. Thad's too stupid to follow you up once you're acrossed."

Ramon let it go. They rode on and picked up the pace as the sun rose. They had another three hours on the posse. It was unlikely the bad men would ever catch them up now.

By noon they relaxed a little and saw a good flat area up ahead. It was out in the open and it would afford a good look behind them. It was only about a mile away when Pierce's mount stepped wrong and began limping just discernibly.

They stopped and both dismounted. Ramon looked the gelding over and shook his head from side to side.

"You've got to stop now, Pierce. You'll ruin the poor creature if you keep riding him."

He drank from his canteen and looked at the terrain. The Colorado was only five miles ahead, but the town was another fifteen up river. He sat down as Pierce fussed over his horse.

"I can set up here, hold 'em off."

"You plan to shoot them?"

Pierce nodded with little enthusiasm. He'd never killed a man; never planned to ever have to. Now he was contemplating fratricide and the execution of lawmen. He felt ill.

"I, I don't know." He looked at the Mexican and shrugged. What the posse was doing was plain wrong. They weren't planning to bring la Garza in for trial. They planned to execute him, take his head and put it on a stake outside his father's ranch. That wouldn't do. That wouldn't do by a long shot.

La Garza thought on it. He didn't want to put the young fellow in such a tight spot.

"Untack him, Pierce. Put your saddle on my mount. We'll walk them to the river. Let's see what we find when we get there. It might be narrow, maybe slow enough to swim across."

Chapter VII:
It Begins

Rebecca Allingham sat and picked at her food as she thought on the autopsy of the first victim earlier in the day. Her husband was right, of course. It was far worse than the corpse of the previous day. It was horrific and she could not get the stench from her nose. Everything now reeked of decomposing human flesh to her. Even the fine meal made by Rosario, she was convinced, smelled of human death. She smelled it on her clothes and on her skin. She had taken two baths. Still she could smell it. It was the worst thing she'd known in her life.

It was not so much the physical decay that was so off putting. Rebecca was truly heartbroken over the entire affair. The poor women with their faces frozen in horror, reflecting the last thing they had known on this earth: terror, and pain, and suffering. That broke gentle, sensitive Rebecca's heart.

Her trance was interrupted by her father's

hearty laugh. He sat across the table and talked and laughed and enjoyed the physician's company. He finally had someone new who was equal to his intellect, in their lives. It was nice to see her father happy. She did not blame him for his jovial demeanor. He'd not witnessed what she had.

She looked at Mr. Singh who was more reserved. He was, as always, taking everything in, processing, analyzing her own and even Allingham's, pain. Her brusque husband was right; they were victims too. They were victims of this monster's malevolent deeds as surely, albeit, not as permanently, as the two prostitutes whom he'd so violently assaulted, violated and destroyed.

But Allingham would never show it. He looked on, every bit as terse and pensive as he'd ever been. She wondered at that. He'd been amongst the animals longest. Certainly, Mr. Singh had seen his share of ugliness in the war, as had her father and the physician. They knew. The doctor had told them he'd been in the Civil war, seen his fill of it, too, but her poor Allingham, he'd not been finished with it after only a few years duration. War was horrific and violent, but, at least for these men, self-limiting. Allingham, as with all lawmen, had been living it for his entire adult life. She suddenly regretted his part in the investigation at all.

Rosario touched her lightly on the shoulder. "My dear, are you not well?"

"No, I'm fine, Rosario. I've just had a bit of a shock."

The Mexicana touched her hair. "I know, my dear. It is an ugly, ugly business."

The doctor now turned his attention to her. Ready to light a cigar, he thought better of it after observing Rebecca's blanched complexion. He held the smoke nervously in his hand.

"I'm sorry, Mrs. Allingham." He looked a little embarrassed. "This calls for a more somber mood and I apologize."

"No, no need, doctor. I'm the one who's sorry." She smiled to reassure him. She changed the subject. "What brings you to Arizona, doctor?"

"Oh, a peach orchard. I've been wanting to give up my medical practice for a while, but I'm not ready for retirement. My old father had an orchard, but the war and medical studies kept me from the land." He smiled warmly at Rebecca, and then at the men around him. "I've always wanted to get back to the land. I read about the orchards in Oak Creek Canyon and, by God, I started corresponding with a man who wanted to move on, and, well, here I am."

Allingham spoke without thinking. "So, why are you not farming?"

"I beg your pardon?"

"You seem always to be here, not farming, not tending your land. Why aren't you there, farming or doing whatever an orchardist does, instead of being here?"

Halsted looked at Allingham as if he'd lost his mind. He shuffled and coughed, but the doctor spoke up for himself. He sensed the indelicacy of Allingham's response, knew by now that it was Allingham's way.

"A valid question, marshal." He grinned and looked at the end of his cigar. "An orchard, well, one that's established, needs less care than other farming, and I've got some good workers, held over from the previous landowner. They do all the work. I'd be like a child if I had to run anything." He laughed, "I'm afraid I know nothing of the business. But I like the idea of it, nonetheless."

"More a gentleman farmer." Rebecca smiled at Allingham. He could always be relied upon to say what was on everyone's mind. They were just too polite to mention it.

"But alas," the doctor smiled again, "this horrible business with these murders . . . , well, my dear, I must say, I take my hat off to you. I thought I was finished with gruesome things, but now, here I am again, in the thick of it. I do hope you will consider your involvement in any incidences in the future."

Her father coughed, then cleared his throat. He fairly glared at Allingham. "I don't like to be a *'see, I told you so'* type, Rebecca, but I warned you." He shifted his gaze back to his daughter, then to Singh. "This is no business for you. As the doctor says, this is not something you should be involved with." He nodded gravely at the physician. "This is the job for men such as your husband, and the doctor here."

She ignored her father. "Have you been on many such cases, doctor?"

"No, no. Actually, I've never seen such a thing. I did some study back home on the deviant, and read the works of the German, Krafft-Ebing," he turned to Allingham. "Are you familiar with his works, Mr. Allingham?"

Allingham ignored him. Deep in thought, he did not hear the doctor's question. The physician continued. "But I've not actually investigated a crime." He looked at Rebecca with a father's compassion and concern. "It is a horrific business, madam. It is horrific for men the likes of us." He cast his hand

79

around the room. "And we are all men of action here. I daresay, we've all seen enough brutality for a lifetime." He smiled warmly at Mr. Singh. "I do hope, well, I mean to say, Mrs. Allingham, that I hope this is not unduly . . . No, that's not what I mean." He blew air between his lips and took a deep drink of wine. "It's, how do I say? Is the reward in your working with your husband," he looked at Allingham as one would look accusingly at a parent who'd exposed his child to unnecessary risk and danger, "worth the risk to your own mental and emotional health?"

Mr. Singh leaned a little forward in his chair. It seemed that he was the only one who understood either Rebecca or Allingham. He began to comment when Rebecca spoke up.

"It is not my husband who decides my actions, doctor. I am an adult, a grown woman and my husband did his best to prepare me. But my husband should not bear this burden alone." She looked at him and watched Allingham contemplate. She smiled at the idea that her man was oblivious to this entire conversation, unaware of the fact that the doctor and her father were lambasting him right before his very large nose. He was crime solving; calculating and figuring the whole thing out and could have been on a deserted island at the moment, he was that far removed from the conversation at hand. "My husband, as you know, is retired. He's been called out of retirement because he is the best detective in all this land, perhaps in all of this country. He'll find this beast, and I intend to be with him the whole time, every step of the way. He deserves that."

At this the doctor did something that none of them expected. He stood up a little too quickly and raised his glass. "Here, here. To Lady Allingham. And I do say lady and mean it, because a finer and more decent and loyal and dedicated lady and wife I've never seen."

"I'll drink to that." Halsted stood up as well and clicked the doctor's glass. Mr. Singh drank tea and looked at his lap.

Wine led to whiskey and eventually to scotch. Mr. Singh trounced the doctor soundly through a half dozen games of backgammon. Allingham slipped off to bed, Rebecca close behind. He had work to do and Rebecca watched him write in his notebook. An hour passed and he finally looked up at her, realizing he was not alone. He smiled uneasily.

"I'm sorry."

"Don't be. I love to watch you think." She walked over and smelled him. He didn't smell like a corpse. She was glad of that and kissed him on top of his head. "Anything?"

"Yes. The killer. He's collecting things."

"Collecting things?"

"Yes. The second victim. He removed most of her womb."

"Oh, *darling.*"

He looked at her again, remembering she was his wife and not another detective. "I'm sorry."

"No, no. Go on."

The one today, the first victim. He removed just her left nipple."

"I see. And how does that help us?"

"I don't know. But it might help build him for us. Help us find him eventually. He's likely keeping them somewhere, the body parts, I mean. For what reason, I do not know, but he likely has a cache, some single place he returns to. That might be helpful. He's not a drifter, perhaps. I don't know." He screwed up his face. "Unless . . ."

"Unless what, darling?"

"Unless he's eating them."

Rosario interrupted them with Hobbs standing by. "Capitan, there are men, many men, a white man and vaqueros here to see you."

CHAPTER VIII: THE PLUNGE

Ramon peered over the drop, down to the raging Colorado, a good hundred and fifty feet below. They were in a tight spot and he was looking back at Pierce making his way on foot when the first shot buzzed past his ear. A half second later could be heard the report. They were certainly under attack now.

He paced about and thought on it. The fall could break his neck or, if not that, he could just as likely lose consciousness and then drown. He thought about the men approaching, dirt and rock kicking up all around him. Their shots would soon enough find their mark. He'd have to act fast if he didn't want to be shot, or worse, strung up. He eyed Pierce nervously. He didn't want the gringo killed because of his indecision.

Pierce nodded gravely, pulled his Winchester and impressed the Mexican with half a dozen shots in quick succession. It slowed the posse a bit, yet he hit neither man nor beast and this was no accident. Pierce had no intention of killing any of them.

"Adiós, mi amigo." He tore off his boots and threw them to the ground between them. He tucked his map deep in a pocket and put his compass under his shirt. "Take care of my girl." He nodded to his horse. "She's the best creature, including humans, I've ever known. Her name is Alanza."

He jumped as Pierce stood resolutely between him and the engulfing posse. Thad was, in short order, off of his horse, looking over the edge. He had his Winchester ready to fire at the Mexican below as the man popped up like a cork, floating rapidly downstream. Thad fired quickly and wildly as the other men scurried to the edge with their rifles at the ready. No one else fired. Their hearts weren't in it. None wanted to shoot an unarmed man as he fought the raging Colorado for his life. He looked to be dead already anyway, as no living man would float face down without a fight or struggle to survive the angry water.

Pierce jerked his brother's arm, disrupting Thad's aim, and was soundly quirted across his wounded cheek for the effort. The lad went down. He could not move or see, but heard one of the men declare that the Mexican was dead, not from the fire of the ineffective vigilante, but from the drop on the way down.

Thad turned, disgusted, and looked at his miserable half breed, half-brother lying on the ground before him, bleeding from the newly opened wound from his whip. "Son of a bitch, bastard!" He kicked Pierce across the nose, opening up another stream of blood. He kicked him again, closing his eye. Thad would have killed him on the spot but for the sheriff, who stood uneasily amongst the band of bad men.

"That's enough, Thad. No sense worrying over it anymore. We can tell your Pa the pepperbelly's dead. He's dead, nothing more to it."

Thad turned and fairly screamed. "I want his goddamned head!" He pushed the sheriff in the chest. "You, you're nothin' but a yellow worthless ass. Wait till my father hears about you. Wait till I tell him." He looked with hatred at the rest of the posse. "All a you, all a you are worthless. Not a one a ya shot at him. Not one. You just stood there like a bunch a goddamned capons. Like ya all had your nuts cut off."

One of the young hands spoke up, "Jesus, Thad, the man was dead. Ain't no man can fall that far and live. We saw him. He was dead, floatin' face down for a long ways. He's dead. It's done." The lad shrugged his shoulders. "No sense wastin' lead shootin' at a dead man."

Thad prepared to mount up. He'd ride the river till he caught up with the corpse. Posse or no, he wanted to bring back the prize.

He turned and pointed to the men. "Don't need you; don't need any of you nutless bastards. Just go. Go back." He pointed down at Pierce lying unconscious at his horse's feet. "Take him back with you. Tell my pa how he turned his back on his own kin. Tell my pa he was right, he's nothin' but a stinkin' lying half-breed Indian. Can't be trusted, no way, no how."

The man and the woman pulled Ramon from one of the boulders placed, as if on purpose, at either shore, narrowing and impeding the river's downstream flow. He was on the smaller of the two rocks. He'd been there all night and was now blocking their passage south.

She deftly hopped from the bow of the boat and crouched over him. She was agile for such a tall woman.

"Is he dead?" The man called as he worked

the oar first left then right.

"Near so, but he's still breathin'." She gently brushed the hair from his eyes.

"He hurt, cut up?"

"Not a scratch." She took the opportunity to look him over a little more carefully, pulling his clothes away to take a comprehensive inventory. She ran her hands up and down his body, more for her own gratification than anything else. Her companion either did not notice or did not care.

"Got anything on him?"

"A compass 'round his neck." She took it from the sleeping man and put it around her own, in hopes that the skinny man wouldn't claim it for himself. She patted Ramon's pockets and found the soggy map. She liberated this from him as well. She looked back at the man. "Nothin' else."

"Son of a bitch, this is lucky. Pure luck." The man grinned devilishly as he watched the woman's backside.

She carefully pulled the man onto the boat. She didn't think this was so lucky. "How you figure that?"

"We gotta free laborer."

"What if he don't see it that way once'd he wakes up?"

"A Mexican without any means; without even any boots. What's he goin' to do about it? He owes us, anyway. If we hadn't come along, he surely wouldn't a lasted another day."

CHAPTER IX:
A JEW AND A SIKH

"A Jew and a Sikh, deputy US marshals, going to see the worst cutthroat and bigot in the Arizona territory." Hobbs grinned uneasily at Mr. Singh. "Sometimes I think the captain is just plain cracked."

Mr. Singh rode along and did not like it either. He was too far from Rebecca and did not like to be such with a murderer of redheaded women lurking right under their noses. It made him kick his mount's sides and ride all the more quickly. He trusted Halsted, knew the man could do what he needed to protect their daughter, but it made him uneasy, nonetheless. He would not rest comfortably until he was back by her side.

"The sooner we get this over, the better for us all, Mr. Hobbs."

They were an unlikely pair of enforcers and Hobbs looked down forlornly at his marshal badge stuck in the left lapel of his vest, just to the left of his fluttery heart. He looked over to Mr. Singh, who sported a copy on his suit coat.

He'd not worn a badge since the fateful day when the assassins tried their best to rub their little company out. The day he lost Francis and the day he'd help kill more men than he wanted to think about.

Hobbs half expected Singh to be wearing his badge on his turban, like he'd seen in the old photographs in Halsted's collection of memorabilia from his time in India. The Sikhs wore insignia and badges and all sorts of strange things in and on their turbans, some even sporting daggers. Instead, Mr. Singh had an odd metal ring, resting like a great shiny collar, about halfway down the saffron head covering. He nodded at it and inquired.

"It is one of the ancient weapons of my people, Mr. Hobbs. It is called a chakkar. It is used to throw at the enemy."

"Oh." Hobbs swallowed hard as he observed the razor sharp edge of the steel ring. "And, you throw it at, at what, Mr. Singh?" He had a good idea, but asked, nonetheless.

"Oh, necks, arms, legs. Depending on the distance, it will remove the head of your opponent quite easily; an arm or a leg at close distance, but a head out to more than thirty yards."

"I see." He looked at Mr. Singh and thought more about the photographs from the Sikh's younger days. His turban for war was much larger than the one he wore now and adorned with many weapons and the badge of his unit. He remembered thinking that Mr. Singh must have been a terror in battle. Even in the day of modern weaponry, firearms and cannon and shot, the Sikhs held onto the old ways, many, including Mr. Singh, preferring to fight with swords, chakkars and, of course, the kirpan, a weapon Mr. Singh carried every day. Hobbs was glad to have the Indian with him on this ride.

"My friend, what do you make of this murderous heathen amongst us? This butcher of these poor prostitutes?"

"I cannot say. It is as if the devil himself has risen from the depths of hell." Mr. Singh remembered something and continued. "When I was a boy, a similar thing happened in my village. First the villain killed only goats, he'd abuse and mutilate them. Then that was not enough and he went to the loose women, and then on to respectable women, then children, and even men."

"Was he ever discovered?"

"Oh, yes, by my father." He picked up the pace a bit more. He did not tell Hobbs the deviant's fate and Hobbs didn't bother to pry.

They stopped to eat. They'd be there by early evening and there'd be time enough to face the miserable Scotsman. Hobbs pointed to a tall saguaro and asked Mr. Singh for a demonstration of the chakkar. Singh wiped his hands clean with a handkerchief and stood thirty or so feet away. He began spinning the ring on one finger, round and round and, with a deft motion, flicked it at the lowest protruding arm of the cactus.

It sank into the flesh with a deadly thud. If it had been a man's thigh, the victim would most certainly need fitting for a peg. Retrieving it, Singh handed it over to Hobbs, who looked the weapon over with interest.

"It is superior to a knife, Mr. Hobbs, as every outside surface is deadly. With a knife, there is only one part that is capable of doing damage when thrown. With the chakkar, the whole is a weapon." He looked over at the damaged arm of the cactus. "And when it hits, it is turning, so it cuts like a saw in the mill." He placed it back in its spot on his turban. "It has a deleterious effect on the enemy."

Hobbs turned his head slowly from side to side. "As old Francis, that dear sweet boy would say, God rest his soul, *I'll be go to hell.*"

They rested awhile and Hobbs worried more about the Scotsman. He looked at Mr. Singh who seemed to never have a care in the world. But Hobbs was an old man and not a fighter and he needed to chat and make it right in his mind.

"Are there many of your kind — you Sikhs — in India, Mr. Singh?"

"No, not so many." The Sikh considered the question. "Perhaps about as many Jews as there are in the land of the Pharaohs." He smiled and Hobbs understood his meaning. But Hobbs was not a devout Jew and did his best to not even look the part. He preferred anonymity, especially in the Western territory.

"Well, I salute you, sir. To be a man who stands out in the crowd in a land that is hard enough without such encumbrances, is something to respect."

"Thank you, Mr. Hobbs." He stood up and poured Hobbs the rest of the coffee and cleaned the pot and put it away in his pack.

He sat back down and poked a little at their campfire. "It has been our way for many hundreds of years. The Guru said that we must show the world what we are, who we are. That is why we wear it, among other reasons."

"This Scotsman. He's, he's, do you think, my God, Mr. Singh, I'm all tongue-tied, I'm speechless."

"He is a profane and ignorant man, but he is just a man. We are doing God's work and the work of law, the law of the land, and the absolute law of morality. We will achieve our goal, Mr. Hobbs. We will make it right."

"Yes, well, that's not my worry so much as it might be the very last thing we do." He grinned sheepishly and had to look away. Hobbs was fairly working himself up into a terrible fright.

"When you are doing things that please God, danger and the potential for death does not matter. Remember that, Mr. Hobbs." He smiled and patted him on the shoulder. "Remember that, and you will never know fear because you will always be ready to face God."

By evening they'd reached the profane and ignorant Scotsman, lounging by his fireplace in a garishly decorated parlor like a bloated toad holding court in his great swamp. He was a self-made man. This would normally garner respect, except for the way he'd made himself and for the seed of his inspiration, which was planted when he was seven years old and living in Scotland.

He'd witnessed the terrible acts of a highwayman who'd robbed a coach and senselessly murdered all occupants, including the coach and footmen. The Scotsman watched it all as the man gorged himself on both the hideous brutality as well as the booty, which were both significant. He enjoyed every second of it.

The Scotsman always remembered that and as soon as he was big enough to handle weapons, he started. By the age of nineteen, he followed the path of many of his ancestors, escaping inevitable arrest and execution by sailing to America. He found the new land a great, wonderful, bountiful oyster, and the Scotsman plucked many a pearl from it.

By the age of thirty, he was in Arizona, and amassing an impressive fortune. As was typical with great excesses of money and property, it allowed him to perfect his mastery of the seven deadly sins, he, paying particular attention to his most favorite three: lust, gluttony, and greed.

It was the first one that, of course, resulted in his terrible and, ultimately, not so terrible spawn, as Pierce was the progeny of his last fling with lust, a little more than two decades ago. Fortunately for humanity, the old man's gluttony got the best of him, allowing him to use and abuse his body until certain parts were simply used up.

It was the fair beauty who also made him miserable from that terrible day, as he, with his inability to comprehend that something or someone could exist in the world that was not gluttonous, malicious, and malevolent, ended the life of the one who might have very well saved him from himself. He could not take Pierce's mother for what she was, and his jealousy got the best of him. The one thing that could have perhaps given him an inkling of insight, given him hope to repent and be reborn, turn into a real human being, a mensch, as the folks of Hobbsie's kind would say, was snuffed out by the venal Scotsman.

Pierce and Thad, like two opposing forces, sat opposite him, waiting for the lambasting to end. A butler interrupted the old man's diatribe on the evils of his worthless progeny.

The old Scotsman had always done this,

chosen one to hold up against the others, and now that Donny was dead, he'd have a permanent martyr to hold against his two surviving sons. They'd never reach the greatness, the mythological perfection, of the dead brother and son.

"What's this?" He demanded from the crooked and decrepit servant.

"US marshals, sir."

The sheriff appeared out of the shadows and gulped another glass of the Scotsman's whiskey. Like a trained monkey tethered to his master's wrist, he watched and waited. He wiped his mouth with the back of his coat sleeve, looking uneasy, perhaps even terrified at the thought of marshals poking about in his jurisdiction. He'd done many things over the years that would be best kept unknown to such lawmen.

The Scotsman cast his eyes over the two men. He looked Mr. Singh up and down and then, more dismissively yet, at Hobbs. "A nigger circus performer and a Jew. These aren't marshals, they're wayward fools who've lost their traveling show caravan."

Thad grinned moronically, as this brought him out of his drunken stupor. He was now pleased with the idea that someone else was present for his father to provoke and torment; he'd get a little respite from the old man's lambasting. He looked the men over and tried to think of something mean and witty to say. Instead he sat and watched his father hold court, his drunkenness adding to his slow wit and stupidity.

Hobbs looked at Mr. Singh, undaunted and unaffected by the Scotsman's epithet. With renewed courage, he found his voice. He handed a court document to the Scotsman and began.

"We're investigating the death of your son." He looked at Thad and then at the sheriff. "*And* the lynch mob that was in pursuit of Mr. la Garza. We expect, by seeing you all here that such has been wisely called off."

"He's dead." Pierce looked at the marshals with his one working, albeit watery and bloodshot, eye. "He fell into the Colorado. He's dead."

"No, he ain't." Thad grinned. "Got a report from some river rats downstream. They say he was fished out. Riding on a boat with a whore and a gambler. Headin' down to Mexico."

The sheriff perked up. He'd not known this and was worried over his own skin. He looked Thad over and then the Scotsman. "Is this true?"

"Yes, it's true and we're going back down

to overtake him." Thad stood up and was sobering up a little now. He looked at Singh and Hobbs defiantly.

"No, you are not." Mr. Singh responded in his laconic voice as Thad walked up on him and tapped him on the chest, just at the point of his marshal badge. Mr. Singh stepped back a little, squaring himself for battle. He played the attack out in his mind. He'd not kill Thad, but he'd get him under control quickly. Thad was too drunk to notice and recklessly advanced.

"And what're you goin' to do about it, dark man?"

Hobbs quickly went into action. "Mr. Hall." He stepped closer to Thad as he did not want to see Mr. Singh gut the young upstart just yet. "We also have an inquiry, an inquiry by Marshal Allingham," Hobbs pulled out a document from his coat pocket, "Well, here, you take a look at it."

The Scotsman did and squeezed the paper, wringing it in his hands, like a wet wash rag as Hobbs continued. "Those are your copies and as you can see, some fairly interesting correspondence between you and a Mr. Norbert Sckogg, a well-known assassin and gunfighter from Wisconsin."

"Yes, and what of it? The son of a bitch is dead, I hear. Killed by your Allingham down in Canyon Diablo some years ago."

"I think you know what of it, Mr. Hall. But that's not our primary intent for this visit. We'll be collecting statements regarding the death of your son," he turned his attention to the sheriff, "with the full cooperation of you, the local law in these parts." He looked at Thad, "but I want to make it clear — perfectly clear — that the Mexican is our business, and now that we know he's alive, our problem. We'll find him and get this cleared up, determine if charges are warranted."

"Warranted?" The Scotsman became furious. "Me boy has been butchered, stock stolen, money stolen, and three of them raped women on this ranch. The whole lot . . ."

"That's a lie!" Pierce had finally had enough. He'd never in his life dared to challenge his father, but it was all too much. He stood up and stared the bloated old man down. "They did none of those things. Donny tried to cheat them, and he was drunk as hell. He ran his mouth and attacked the Mexican with a knife and got killed for his trouble." He turned to Singh and Hobbs. "Marshals, I saw it all and I'll testify. That Mexican done nothin' wrong, neither he, nor any of his men done nothin'

wrong. They didn't rape no one, they didn't steal nothin' and Donny tried to knife him. Donny even give this to me." He pointed at the gash on his face and then over at Thad. "Thad give me all the others, the broke nose, the black eye, 'cause I stopped him shootin' the Mexican when he was floatin' down the river."

The Scotsman cut him off. "Shut up, you half breed son of a bitch." He pointed his shaking finger at his son and shouted. "Get the hell out. You're finished here. You're not my son, I've finished with ye. I've finished, you are to leave here at once and ye'ere never to return."

"Thaddy, me boy." The Scotsman sat, drunk, with the story of Sckogg balled up in his right fist.

"Yes, father?"

"You're me good boy. You go. Go and find that Mexican. Bring me his head." He looked around as if to check for spies. He whispered in an evil tone. "Forget about the sheriff. He's gutless. Go alone, Thaddie, me boy. Go alone and follow the river. They'll be downriver and you'll catch him before he reaches Mexico. If you don't catch him there, go," he handed him a slip of paper, "here." He tapped the page with a fat index finger, "Here is where the Mexican lives. Go to his ranch and kill him."

"Yes, Father, yes." Thad fairly vibrated with excitement. He'd do his father proud. He'd come back with the Mexican's head!

CHAPTER X:
THE SCHOOL MARM

Mary Rogers was a big woman who carried her girth with much grace and a level of femininity that only elevated her desirability. She also had a splendidly large bosom, which made heads turn wherever she walked. She was from Delaware and had been in Arizona for just over a year, arriving on her twenty-second birthday. She was the best school teacher in the county. Everyone loved her, everyone enjoyed her company and every child paid attention to the pretty redhead.

She'd heard about the terrible murders of the redheaded prostitutes and even made a little joke about keeping her locks covered and hidden away. She'd never, in her wildest nightmares suspect that she'd be in such a predicament. All the victims were prostitutes and apparently captured in dark and ugly places, places pleasant Mary Rogers would never remotely consider to venture.

It was incomprehensible to think such could happen to her.

But now she was awakening from a chloroform haze and just realizing that he was abusing her once again. She looked about wildly and pulled at the ropes binding her hands and feet to the narrow bed.

She could smell him; smell his sweat and breath and, despite his good dress and grooming, was not at all a pleasant man. This added to the horror and discomfort of his terrible treatment of her.

"Oh, good." He leaned back and looked her in the eye. "You're awake. Speak to me, Momma. Speak to me."

"What . . . what shall I say?" She felt the panic welling up inside her. There was nothing she could do so she decided to beg. "Please, please let me go, mister. Please don't hurt me. I, I'll keep quiet. I'll not tell anyone anything. I swear."

"Stop!" He looked at her with a savagery she'd not seen in another human being in all her life. She waited. She wanted to cry.

"Not that, not that!" He was manic, frenzied. "Talk! Tell me a story. Tell me a nursery rhyme."

Her mind raced. She'd read and told them hundreds of times to the children in her class. She could not think of one. She stuttered and stammered and he hit her soundly across the cheek.

"Out with it, Momma. Out with it!" He pulled his hand back to strike her again and she began.

"Four and twenty blackbirds . . ."

He became calm, and she realized her voice was soothing him. Her voice was what he sought. Soon he moved down her body, pressing his face to her bared breasts. "Talk, Momma, talk some more."

She did and he fell asleep lying on top of her. Suddenly she could not breathe and moved her torso a little to the left. This eased her breathing. His head was just below her mouth and she tried to breathe without smelling him. She became very cold and she wanted to cry but she dared not make a noise for fear of waking him. Soon she, too, fell into a light slumber.

When she awoke she was dressed in a frilly night gown and shackled to a stone wall in a deep root cellar or cave. There was another bed here, identical to the one she'd been in earlier. The place smelled of dirt and was dry. She looked around but didn't see him. Then she heard him somewhere overhead. There were floorboards above her so she realized she must be in a dwelling and not in a cave.

She had to urinate and found a chamber pot and used it. This was painful as he'd savagely abused her many times. She was otherwise unscathed. Not even her face was damaged from the slap she'd received earlier. She began to pray.

In a little while he returned and looked her over. He smoked a cigarette but did not speak to her. He handed her a plate of beans and a cup of water. She decided to talk a little to see what effect it would have on him.

"May I go now?"

He brightened. The voice was soothing to him. "No, Momma. No. You'll stay here." He reached over and kissed her gently on the temple as he caressed her auburn hair. "You are perfect, Momma. You're perfect here," he reached down and touched her breasts, "and here," he reached down further to her sex, "and here." He kissed her again, gently, on the forehead. "But your voice is the most magnificent of all the wondrous things."

He watched her eat and she ate well, despite her churning stomach, her insides shaking constantly. She was hungry and even thirstier.

When she was finished, he took the plate and cup from her and placed it on a little table by the bed. He unshackled her and for a moment she thought about running but was simply too weak and scared. She did nothing and felt especially ashamed of herself for that. She should fight him or run or hit him with her fists or try to stab him with the knife he'd given her for eating her meal, but she did nothing and it broke her heart and spirit. She did nothing for fear of provoking him. At least, for now, she was alive, which was better than the prostitutes she'd heard about.

He motioned for her to get onto the new bed and she slowly complied. At least it was clean, with unsoiled sheets. She suddenly felt ill. She thought she would vomit, afraid he would rape her again. But he didn't.

"Now, lay back, Momma." He refastened the bindings and took a cursory inventory of her body. She felt cold again. His touch was like a cold wind or a winter splash of rain. She felt as if a wraith had touched her on her most intimate parts. She was sadder and more frightened than she'd ever been in her life.

He held the chloroform rag to her face and she fought him. "Now, now, Momma, don't fight. Don't fight. It's better you sleep while I'm gone. Sleep, Momma, sleep. Rest that lovely voice. Rest that lovely body. I'll be back."

"Pregnant at last! Pregnant at last!" Halsted fairly danced about the room. He was giddy and overjoyed at the prospect of being a grandfather. Then he suddenly felt ill at the thought that the baby might favor Allingham. He dismissed it. Rebecca was a beauty and she'd favored her mother. It would be the same. It would simply *have* to be the same.

"And it's good luck to have a doctor so close at hand." Halsted patted the physician on the back.

Dr. Webster smiled and looked at the end of his cigar. He'd become a regular fixture at the Halsted home. Rebecca was not so certain about having him serve as her obstetrician. Halsted sensed it and tried to remove the tension. The physician chimed in.

"Oh, I'm not so certain that's the most appropriate path, Mr. Halsted."

"No." Rebecca spoke up. "All due respect to you, doctor, but a midwife will serve us just as well. There is no need for a physician. I'm young and fit and have no need for a doctor."

"Nonsense!" Halsted was used to his

daughter's forceful and independent mind, but this was too much. He'd been waiting for a long time for this, and wanted to ensure the safety of both mother and child. "You shall have the best care possible. The doctor here is at the top of his profession, he . . ."

"He's fine, Father, and I thank both of you, but I've made up my mind. And besides," Rebecca blushed a little. "I'm not comfortable with such an intimate relationship with a man I've known on a personal level. The two are quite different: a personal and medical interaction. I, well, feel more comfortable with our local midwife."

"Then there's nothing more to discuss." The doctor smiled and offered a toast. "To Mrs. Allingham and the new child." He looked at Halsted reassuringly. "Women have had babies for thousands of years without the aid of a physician, Mr. Halsted, and I'll be standing by, just in case I'm needed. But I am certain Mrs. Allingham is in good hands."

Allingham rushed in and looked at his blushing wife. He looked at her belly, which was as flat as ever. He could not get his pregnant wife off his mind. He knew he was interrupting something pleasant. He didn't want to do so but felt he must.

"A young school teacher is missing."

Rebecca could see it in his eyes. Not just missing, but taken by the murderer. They all suddenly knew it. The doctor tried, in a dreadfully inept way, to make the best of it.

"Perhaps there's nothing to it." His face betrayed him, and everyone knew it was a ridiculous thought. He continued. "Perhaps she's traveling, or has run off with a lover. Maybe she's basking in the California sun as we speak."

Allingham suddenly wanted to punch the pleasant fool of a doctor in his sappy smile. He felt a rush of intense anger and, for a moment, actually hated the man and wanted to kill him. How dare he make such an idiotic statement! How dare he make light of this horrific situation? How dare he come up with some preposterous scenario? It was insulting to the poor victim and to everyone in the room. They all knew it was the monster again, and pretending or holding out a hope that it was not, was a stupid and worthless endeavor.

Allingham knew for certain that the doctor had no business in the affair now. He was worse than a rank amateur. Even the most clueless sheriff in all the Arizona land was more in touch with what was happening. He wanted to grab him up by the scruff of his neck and eject him into the street. He wanted to beat him until he was unrecognizable. He decided instead to ignore him. He looked at Rebecca's pretty hair. "Maybe you should go back East for your confinement, Rebecca. Maybe you should . . . not be here right now."

CHAPTER XI:
RIVER RATS

Ramon la Garza was awake, but he did not let on as such so that he could take everything in and determine what his saviors were all about. The woman was quite handsome but apparently a whore or at least a very loose woman. She wore a shear outfit which was almost always wet and which made the material nearly transparent.

She was a tall woman of Germanic or Nordic stock as she had beautiful golden hair and piercing blue eyes. She was well proportioned, as well, with an ample bosom and tiny waist. However, she was not young, likely thirty at least, perhaps older, and she'd evidently lived a hard life.

The man was tall as well, but lanky and ruddy in complexion. He had long black hair that had not been cut in a long time. He had no hair on his face but, instead, the skin was covered by pockmarks, giving it an appearance not unlike the surface of the moon. He had brownish-yellow teeth stuck haphazardly in bloody red gums. His breath was about what one would expect from such. He wore brightly colored orange trousers with a blue check pattern and a cotton work shirt the color of straw. He had a scarf, but not around his neck. Instead, it was stuck in the back pocket of his trousers, half in and half out, so he looked a little like a whitetail deer with a scarlet colored tail.

He wore no vest but had a gun belt with a six shooter on his right hip. He had a big knife on the left side. He wore black boots from the army but these were likely surplus as he was obviously no Indian fighter and was too young to have fought in the great rebellion.

He hopped about like an organ grinder monkey, never still for a moment. He handled the boat well. He talked a lot to the woman and once in a while he'd grope her and she'd playfully swat him away but there was something between them, Ramon could tell, at least as well as something that could be between a whore and a man. Perhaps, probably, likely, he was her pimp and not her husband or lover. He was most definitely not a brother or cousin or platonic friend.

The boat was one of the kind that was

especially designed for this type of river travel. It had a shallow draft and the bow was covered a good one-third way back. Amidships there was a kind of raised cabin and this was fitted to be watertight in the event the craft would be turned over in the rapids or swamped. On the deck of this cabin was where Ramon slept for almost an entire day.

He sat up slowly and the woman gave him a warm smile and bent over until her breasts nearly spilled out and Ramon had a difficult time averting his eyes. The man was smaller than Ramon but well heeled, and Ramon was too weak to fight. He did not want to die now over ogling a whore's breasts.

"How you doin' handsome?"

He suddenly had a thought and answered in Spanish. "Hola, señorita."

She looked back at her lover and smiled. "Awe, he's adorable, and he speaks only Mexican."

"Spanish, ding-bat."

"Yeah, yeah, whatever you say. Sounds like Chinks talkin' to me."

"No it don't." The man eyed Ramon carefully, taking his measure. Neither he nor the whore had been this far south before; neither spoke any Spanish. It would be interesting, and likely difficult to get the

Mexican to do much of any kind of work, but the thin man would give it a good try.

He looked up ahead as he adjusted the oar in his hands. "All right, get ready, there's white water up ahead."

Ramon turned to look in the direction the man had indicated, remembering that he was not supposed to understand the words. This would be tricky, and he wondered if it would not be wiser to just speak to them in English and get it over with now.

The woman jumped into action and Ramon dropped down and stood on the deck of the boat and held on as he watched the couple negotiate the rapids. They were pretty good but still green, and Ramon knew this because anyone with any sense would have pulled to shore and walked the rapids down to survey them before just riding over them. It was going to be a long ride back to Mexico.

But the woman was nice to watch as she was agile and pretty good at paddling and pushing off of boulders and, as it is always nice to see a beautiful woman nearly naked doing anything, Ramon was satisfied with the view. He took his ride on the rapids in stride, careful not to be too obvious in his ogling. She had pretty bare feet and he mostly stood still looking forward, then down at the deck and the barelegged beauty out of the corner of his eye.

They rode downstream fairly swiftly and uneventfully the rest of the afternoon and Ramon was encouraged by this as they were moving faster than a cantering horse and going dead south by his reckoning of the sun. He felt through his shirt and realized his compass was gone. He looked over and saw it resting securely in the woman's cleavage. It appeared to be still functional after his long fall.

They stopped much too early, however, and Ramon was a little disappointed in this, as they could have gone another three or four hours until losing daylight. He surmised that the two were in no great hurry to get wherever they were going. And this now vexed him.

The man jumped overboard and hauled the boat ashore. The woman began handing Ramon camping gear and at one point touched his hand, holding it and looking him in the eye. She looked back at the thin man collecting firewood and decided to give Ramon a wet kiss on the mouth. It was a pretty good kiss and Ramon now wondered what lay in store for him on the remainder of this journey.

She smiled a little wickedly. "Hmm, pretty good kisser. Better if you try, sweetie, a lot better if you try."

When the camp was set up, the woman handed Ramon a belt with a sheath knife attached. There was also a holster for a six shooter, but she did not give him a gun. He was glad for the knife and later found a stone and sharpened the blade as his father had taught him from the time he could remember. Now he'd be on nearly even footing with the thin man in the event things got ugly. Ramon thought, in light of the recent kiss by the wild whore, that perhaps they would.

They had a good meal and shared it willingly with Ramon. The thin man looked him over as Ramon cleaned the dishes and stacked firewood as he thought that being useful would be more helpful than not.

"Goddamn, he's better than havin' a nigger."

"Stop that." The pretty whore smiled devilishly at Ramon and then back at the thin man.

"Don't you speak any American at all mister?"

Ramon caught himself and did not look up. He kept working at his tasks.

"Hey, you!"

He finally looked up and gave a little imp-ish grin, the way the farm workers used to do when trying to avoid confrontation.

"You speak any American at all?"

Ramon nodded his head gravely, "No sé," and shrugged his shoulders, remembering again the way the peons used to do and how it amused his father so much on the haci-enda.

"English, you ding-bat, not American. American is a place, not a language."

"No sé." The woman looked up vacantly. "What do you suppose that means?"

"Well, it has no in it, don't it? Probably means he don't know, ding-bat. Jesus, woman, you're dumber than a box a rocks."

"Go to hell, Jimmie."

"You go to hell yourself." He pulled out a bottle and drank deeply, handing it to her then kissing her passionately in front of Ramon. He began groping her breasts and she responded in a way a man groping a woman's breasts would hope. Ramon got up and went looking for firewood.

He waited out there, beyond the glow of the campfire and Ramon was now certain that the trip would definitely be interesting.

At midnight he felt hands on his thighs and then further up and he hoped it was not the thin man. To his great relief it wasn't. The woman was on top of him before he could do or say anything and she was very good at what she did for a living. It was mechanical and not as good as what he'd had in his time with the love of his life in Spain, but that was long over and Spain was a long way off and Ramon had not been in such a situation in a long time. He'd not ever run with whores, and was not used to such a casual treatment of the act, but he was tired, not certain what lay in store for him ahead, and just too played out to do anything more than enjoy the ride.

Ramon had heard from the peons all about women of the baser sort; heard stories about the whores who really appeared to like their craft and this one seemed to be one of them. She was quite loud and Ramon enjoyed watching her enjoy herself so much at his expense but still had the presence of mind to keep his new knife nearby.

Luckily, the thin man did not awaken as he'd gotten himself quite drunk before passing out. This made him useless to the whore and Ramon figured that was why he was being treated in such a companionable way.

She finally slaked her passion enough for the moment and kissed him hard on the mouth, better this time than earlier. "You're damned good Mexican boy. Damned good."

"Gracias." He worried again that he'd gone too far by responding to her compliment. She patted him on the cheek and rolled off, evidently too dim to suspect anything.

He watched her wash up in the river, using it as a giant bidet, and this was more provocative to him than the act itself. She was a beauty, and in the dark, with only the moonlight to illuminate her, and more importantly, to shadow the years of hard living and neglect, she was stunning.

When she was finished she began to wade back to her pimp and then suddenly seemed to change her mind and, instead of going to bed, stripped naked and dove into the river and swam and lay on her back and floated, her breasts like two magnificent mountains jutting out from the depths of the river washing over her. Ramon fell into a deep sleep.

They pushed off far too late for Ramon's liking, wasting yet another two good hours of daylight. At this rate, it would take him two years to get home. He wondered what they were doing, as they were certainly traveling. This was not their life. They were not making a living of traveling down the

Colorado River. But he could not make out their purpose, as Ramon was a hardworking and resourceful man, unaccustomed to the ways of bums, miscreants, and ne'er do wells.

He was always planning, working, worrying over the future, what he had to do, what he had to accomplish. He did not know much about having fun. It was incomprehensible to him that people just lived. Lived from moment to moment, and this is what the skinny man and whore were doing right now. They were living, with little care for enterprise or their future. They had enough to eat, good traps, and a way to take their ease in the world, and that was much more than they had the right to expect. It was a very foreign concept to Ramon and he thought about it a lot.

He thought about his father, who used to rail on about the wastrels, the young sons of the wealthy hacendados who did not come up hungry or ambitious. He'd complain that they had no drive and were simply bent on spending the fortunes of their fathers, and then he'd press Ramon on the shoulder and say to anyone who would listen to him brag about his boy, "My son, he is not this way, my son is going to be a great man."

■ ■ ■ ■

The thin man seemed different this day and he motioned for Ramon to take the oar and stand next to him, as the pretty whore lounged on the cabin roof and showed them various parts of her body until she got tired of that and slept.

As they paddled to keep the boat headed the right way, the thin man began talking, babbling really, staring the entire time at the whore. He spoke nonsense mostly, but Ramon could make out various comments; rants and diatribes about Ramon in fairly unfriendly terms. The man seemed to be working himself up into quite an agitated state and eventually began mumbling continuously about Mexicans and white women and how he thought Ramon might end up lynched at the next copse of trees they found ahead.

Ramon didn't like this and watched the man turn mad before his eyes. This made no sense to him as the man seemed very much in control of his faculties only the day before. He looked at the whore and she seemed to be in a deep sleep, oblivious to this change in her companion's behavior. He wondered if she were not acting as he had just the day before, pretending to be asleep. Perhaps they were in on this together. Perhaps they planned to kill him. Ramon became fairly scared.

The rapids ahead would ultimately decide Ramon's fate for him. He looked at the man who grinned maniacally and then nodded at the rough water ahead.

"How you like that, Mexican?"

Ramon tried to take control, paddle to shore and out of danger, but the current and the thin man worked against him. Before he could prepare, they were in the worst of it, battling for their lives, Ramon too worried about the vessel being dashed apart to listen to the ravings of the addled man. His mania seeming to grow with the water's increasing energy, until both man and water were raging most certainly out of control.

At a particularly rough spot the woman awoke and took up a position between them. It was hot and she'd been sweating and Ramon could smell her and could feel the energy of the river beneath his feet and the ravings of the man pounding in his ears. At one point Ramon turned instinctively and saw the blade of the pimp's oar, directly on a collision course with his skull. He ducked and the thin man lunged forward, his energy not absorbed by the impact of Ramon's head. He toppled over the stern of the boat. The frothy water gobbled him up. He disappeared.

The woman squealed with delight. She laughed and watched the water as Ramon pushed off of rock after rock. They soon found themselves spinning in a whirlpool below the last drop-off. The water was deep and the thin man would have to be in there somewhere. The pretty woman dove over and was impressive in her swimming prowess. She dove again and again, like some manic dolphin, hunting for its friends, eventually losing her dress. She finally returned to the surface exhausted, too tired to get back into the boat and too heavy for Ramon to pull on board.

He threw her a line and then, using the oars, managed to maneuver the boat out of the whirlpool and to the western shore, pretty whore in tow.

They both lay on the little beach for a long time. The thin man didn't appear; didn't pop out of the whirlpool or walk down the little beach or cry out for help from the rocks on the other side. He was gone and Ramon remembered the woman laughing incongruously at the thin man's plight and then, just as incongruously, diving into the mad water again and again to save him. She was indeed vexing.

He looked her over as she now sat on the sandy beach, contented and just as casual as if they were watching a mid-day regatta. She cared nothing about modesty and even gave Ramon a little satisfied smile, as if getting rid of Jimmie was on a long list of accomplishments that she could finally cross off.

Ramon got up and looked into the boat's little cabin and found a dress and a blanket and covered the shivering woman up, almost as if she were a child too ignorant to take care of herself. She reclined on her back and let the sun beat down on her face. She looked like an angel when she wasn't speaking and when her eyes were closed — and when she was on her back so that gravity could help trick the ravages of time and hard living. She looked very much like a sleeping angel and she was more beautiful to Ramon now than at any time he'd known her.

"What the hell was that?"

She sat up abruptly and grinned. "You son of a bitch, you do talk American."

"English. Yes, and better than you."

"Oh, don't start that shit. I just got rid of one *know it all* bastard. Don't need another one to take his place." She stood up and was dizzy from all the exertion and cold and sat back down. She put on the dress retrieved by Ramon and covered herself in the blanket.

"Get us some tobacco, sweetheart."

He did and rolled her a smoke and lit it and smoked one himself. She grinned again. "You're a lucky bastard."

"How so?"

"Jimmie was crazy as all hell. Hated when a man just looked at me, and, oh boy, you got away with it. Well, really got away with a lot more than just lookin'." She gave him a devilish wink. "And you ducked just right. You're a quick bastard, ain't you?"

"I guess." Ramon looked on at the thin man's watery grave. He wondered how long the whirlpool would keep his corpse pressed to the bottom.

"Do you have a grappling hook?"

"For what?"

"Don't you want to fish him out?"

"No, to hell with him." She spit into the pool. "Let the water have him. Better grave than I'd have ever expected for him." She grinned again. "You know what, handsome?"

"What?"

She shucked the blanket and pulled him

126

onto her body. "This has put me in a mood." She kissed him passionately and Ramon stood up, disgusted by her casual reaction to the death of her lover. He walked away from her, preparing to make camp.

He slept fitfully that night, and the woman was likely more responsible for that than anything else. He could hear her breathing in her sleep, just inches from his head. He could smell her. She smelled good — of a woman in her natural state, the smell of a woman uncluttered and unmasked by hair treatments or perfumes or soaps or oils; just good, like a woman who was alive and fertile and full of sex and desire. He loved that smell, and she fairly reeked of it.

He eventually drifted into a restless sleep, but not for long, as the fire flared up for some reason and awoke him to Jimmie sitting, soaking wet, dripping river water, by the fire. He looked strange, as his skin was pure white, bloodless, and Ramon surmised that he must be dead.

Jimmie looked at him out of the corner of his eye and then passed a bottle to Donny, the Scotsman's son whom Ramon had killed with Adulio's daga. He was pale as well, but dry from head to midsection. Oddly enough, however, when he took a deep drink of the whiskey, a great rushing sound could be heard, and Ramon looked down in horror at the whiskey freely pouring out of Donny's gaping gut wound, mixed with blood and effluent, onto his boots and then into the hissing fire.

Donny seemed to notice it at the same time, and looked at it, then at Ramon. "Goddamn, never gonna get drunk this way." He pointed accusingly at the wound with his index finger. "Look what ye did to me, greaser."

"Greaser! Hah! That's a good one." Jimmie slapped Donny on the back and laughed as if they were two long lost pals.

Donny glared at him and pulled away. "Don't touch me, ya filthy river rat!"

"Go to hell, saddle bum."

They looked as if they might kill each other, had they not already been dead. Then, just as quickly, they seemed to lose interest, turning their attention back to Ramon.

They all three said nothing for a long time. Ramon felt so tired, too tired to keep sitting up and looking at them, yet compelled to do so, as they were hideously fascinating, horrific and ugly and fascinating. But, he just wanted to sleep some more and his two visitors were putting him off significantly. He looked at the sleeping whore and could not understand why all this banter did not wake her up.

Donny pointed at her, as if Ramon's interest in her had brought her to Donny's attention. "He don't fool around, do he? Bedded down together right off. Took up housekeepin' with her right off." He gave an ugly grin and looked at Jimmie derisively, doing his best to aggravate and humiliate his dead companion. "Bet he's bedded her already. Bet sure enough he's had a ride."

"Oh, he didn't even wait for me to cash in for that. Rutted with her right away. Night before I drownded. Bastard didn't even ask permission, didn't even *pay me* for the privilege!"

"Goddamned greaser." Donny drank again, this time holding his slit gut closed ineffectively as bilious bloody fluid leaked between his fingers. He looked down in disgust. "Stinks like shit! Goddamned greaser, this country was good until they started comin' along, takin', takin', takin' our work, takin' our women, takin' our money. Goddamned greasers."

Jimmie smiled, but was undeterred. "Oh, he can have the miserable bitch. He can have her. Best punishment I can think of fer a man is to have *her.*" He grinned as Ramon tried to keep his eyes open. "Oh, yeah, Mexican. You wait an' see, you wait until you've had a belly full of the bitch." He drank again. "You'll be lookin' for a stout rope to hang yerself after that."

Chapter XII:
Marshal Rosario

Hobbs pressed himself tightly against his woman's back and brushed a lock of hair from her forehead when he felt her stir. "Good morning, my darling Señora Hobbs."

She pulled his hand to her breast and wiggled her body against his. "When did you get to bed? You stayed up so late and I could not keep my eyes open any longer."

"Three." Hobbs yawned his answer and breathed in the scent of Rosario's hair. "Those boys, Hall and Old Pop, they were pretty wound up and I couldn't leave them until they settled down." He laughed a little into her hair. "Old Singh wouldn't stop. We rode straight on through. Old fellow couldn't wait to get back to Rebecca."

She turned onto her back and began pulling the big sack of a nightgown free of her body. Hobbs was pleased and worked on his own undergarments.

131

He remembered something that he forgot to ask her the evening before. "Were you the one who wired us the news of Rebecca?"

"Sí, I knew Hira would not forgive me if I did not. He's been waiting for this baby as much as Señor Halsted, maybe even more."

She pulled herself onto him and kissed him gently on the mouth.

"I'm going to miss you on this preposterous ride to Mexico, my darling. I'm going to miss you, certain enough." He felt her and was happy.

"I do not know this thing, Hobbsie. I must have gone to bed before you hatched this plan. Where must you go in Mexico?" She held her hand over his mouth so as to command him to concentrate, wait until the business at hand was conducted. He could answer after she was finished with him.

In a little while they lay exhausted as such carrying does that to people of their age and they slept for another two hours. When they awoke, he thought of the question posed to him by his wife.

"We didn't get far before the young fellow Pierce and his top hand caught us. The lad said his brother'd gone off to find this Mexican just as soon as we left the Scotsman's ranch. Old bastard put his boy up to it, no doubt." He looked at his hands. "I think there's no choice, darling. Singh should stay with Rebecca. More for his own sanity, but also for the well-being of Rebecca. At least for as long as this murdering son of a bitch of redheads is lurking about. And the captain needs to focus on catching the black-heart as well. So, that leaves me. I think it is my obligation. My job's to follow it up." He felt his heart flip flop and waited for it to calm down. He cleared the tickle deep in his throat. "That poor fellow, that Pierce Hall, seems a nice sort. He seems on the level, but his brother is just bad. We need to stop him running that poor Mexican and his people to ruin, or worse. Oh, Rosario, they're a terrible bunch, just terrible." He smiled at the thought of Allingham's trump card. "The evidence linking the Scotsman to Sckogg was just the ticket. Took the wind right out of his sails, and it certainly made that sheriff up there go white as a sheet."

"Sí. I understand. How could this Pierce muchacho have such a rotten family?"

"Don't know. Seems he's the black sheep, but not because he's bad, actually the opposite. He's good. Had a different mother, an Indio, they say. Some little liaison the Scotsman had and he kept the boy around after the mother died, but treats him like hell. He's the best one of the bunch and gets treated the worst. Terrible, terrible the names they called him."

"Darling, how are we to find this Mexican boy? He fell into the river and that's all we know. It seems it would be easier to find a needle in a haystack."

"I know." It was a vexing problem. He looked at her and smiled weakly. "I think the more important job is to keep an eye on the bad son, Thad. We've got to track him down before he tracks the Mexican fellow down. The captain says we can arrest him for assault and conspiracy since he failed to heed our warning. I should have just arrested and taken in him when we had the chance." He looked at Rosario with bloodshot eyes. "I'm not much of a lawman, darling, but I know he'd have not gone without a fight. Singh would have likely had to kill the whole bunch, father and son and sheriff as well." He reached to the bedside table and poured a big whiskey. He drank it with shaky hands.

Rosario comforted him. "No, you did the right thing. Sometimes, you just cannot make men do the right thing, and pushing too far, well, you are right, Hira would have had to kill them all." She shrugged and poured a drink for herself. "It would not have been the right thing, for either you or dear Hira."

"So, now we get to go running all over hell's half acre and bring him in, dead or alive." He grinned and felt silly saying that, as he was not a law dog. He was a secretary to the captain, and a good manager and administrator, but he was not a policeman.

Rosario got out of bed and moved around the room naked and Hobbs watched and enjoyed her. She was working again and he knew he'd sleep no more today. She was packing and this got his attention.

"What are you doing, my love?"

"We will be gone a long time, Hobbsie. We will need to pack well for this journey."

"We?" He grinned and knew there was no point in questioning her about it. She'd made up her mind and Rosario did not change it, once her mind was made up.

"Of course. I can be as good a deputy to you as I was to Francis, the sweet boy," she blessed herself and kissed her fingers, "when we went to get Red Shirt. And you will need a translator down there, if we end up in Mexico. Neither you, nor the boy, nor the one they call Old Pop can speak the language very well."

He smiled at her and hoped she'd not get

cold. As long as she wasn't cold, Rosario would not dress, and watching his wife work naked was one of his favorite things to do in the world. The trip now did not seem nearly so terrible to him. It would be an adventure with his lovely Mexicana wife by his side. He suddenly felt energized; his heart even behaved itself a little as he began helping her pack.

CHAPTER XIII:
FALSE HOPES

Rebecca stood by as Allingham looked the dry goods store over as if he was visiting it for the first time. The storekeeper gave a pensive nod to them both. He knew why they were there. It made him feel sick again.

"Anything I can do, folks, anything at all, just tell me."

Allingham addressed him without looking up. He was examining everything: floor, walls, goods, recreating the school teacher's last actions before being abducted.

"What did she buy?"

"Oh, some soap, a couple of bits of thread for her needlepoint, some tea, flour, cereal, and hairpins." He stroked his chin. "Well, here, here's the order. She didn't want to carry it and the boy was to deliver it to her room, once he was back from his morning rounds."

Allingham looked everything over then handed it to Rebecca. "And she was alone?"

"Oh, yes, yes, as always. The young lady was always alone."

"How'd she leave?"

"Through that door there." The clerk quickly followed up as he knew well enough that Allingham was not a man of much patience. The marshal did not want to hear the obvious. The clerk touched his arm gently and walked Allingham outside. He pointed off to the left. "Miss Rogers always took off to the left, then down the alley to the street where her boarding house was located. Never walked after dark. She was a careful girl, a careful girl." His eyes welled up. "She was a real lovely girl. I'm . . . I'm," he looked at Rebecca who grabbed him by the hand. "I wouldn't have let her go on alone had I known. I'd a fought to the death to save her." He nodded his head solemnly. "No one's ever had problems here, folks. Everyone's always been safe walking here, even down the alleys. She was such a wonderful, wonderful girl."

"Still is, still is. We have to keep thinking of her as living, remember that. We have to think of her as still being alive." Rebecca patted the merchant's cheek and turned to catch up to Allingham, whom she found around the corner, sitting on the ground, cross-legged, elbows on knees, head resting in the palms of his hands. She plopped down beside him and waited.

Suddenly he was looking at her with frustration in his eyes.

"What is it, darling?" She leaned forward, face knit into a frown.

"I can't find him! Damn it, I can't find him!" He clenched his fists in anger. "There's nothing, and time's running out, and I haven't found a damned thing to help."

She hugged him. "Darling, you're the best at such things; you're our hope, my hero. You believe that, and it's going to be difficult, you know that. Becoming desperate is not going to help." She pulled his face to hers by his chin. "Look at me."

He did and she brushed a thumb across his cheek. "Now think, darling, focus. Sit down here and look and think and I'll be quiet and sit with you. Think, observe. Think."

He took a deep breath and closed his eyes. He imagined the time of day. The girl walked into the shop, had a list, perhaps, spoke to the merchant, paid, turned and said good bye. She turned up the alley and something happened. Something happened to let the bad man abduct her in broad daylight at a respectable place in town.

A breeze blew dust in his eyes and he blinked and watched the wind move things toward the southeast corner to the building beside him. He observed the ground. Wagon ruts were there, many, which was normal, as many wagons moved through the alley on a regular basis. Hoof prints, old footprints from a muddy day. Nothing recent. He began crawling on his hands and knees, following the wind.

Up under a loose clapboard on the far edge of the building; nothing there. Down below, a barrel had been discarded with a little pile of nail embedded wood; below that, a bit of fabric, stuck amongst the debris.

Allingham picked it up gently and opened it, laying it flat. He felt it and sniffed at it carefully.

"Look at this." He turned and walked it back to her.

Rebecca reached out for it and Allingham pulled it away, out of her grasp. "I don't know what it's had on it, Rebecca. Don't touch it." She nodded in comprehension.

He held it up again. "Likely chloroform. And look, face powder. We'll see if it is the kind she bought at the dry goods store." He looked at the corner of the material and could just make out the letter "M" sewn delicately by a fine hand.

"It's as if he's leaving us clues, Rebecca." He put the handkerchief in his pocket and dropped to the ground. Lying close to the dirty street, he cast his eyes in every direction.

Next, he found a ladder in a back yard and propped it against the building. He climbed to the roof and observed the street below.

"Stand over there, Rebecca." She complied. He squinted and it revealed the entire terrible incident. "She was walking about where you are standing. She stopped and turned to see a wagon approach. He quickly grabbed her from behind, administering the chloroform. Just as quickly, he pulled her into the back of his conveyance, likely a light delivery wagon with an open cargo area in back. He probably had a tarp to cover her. He threw her in it, covered her, and made his escape. He could do all of this in less than a minute."

"Could he have dropped the handkerchief then, in his haste, by accident?"

"I don't know. Not likely. He's too thorough in all his other actions." Allingham spoke down to her from the rooftop. He looked for more clues as he regarded her question. "I think he planted it for us to find. The initial likely means nothing. Look at the workmanship."

He held it up as if Rebecca could see it from such a great distance. "Germanic." He looked off and thought and absentmindedly spoke, "But we'll go to the shops and see if there is anything to it. They might remember selling it to someone."

"So you don't think it's the man's German wife or mother or sister who made it for him?"

"No."

"Why not?"

"It's premade, mass produced, the kind you might order in a catalog. It's too mechanical." He felt a little silly saying it, but it was true, "It's not made with love. It's something mass produced, not some handmade object, Rebecca. Well, you know what I mean. It was handmade, but by a person who did not know the recipient. Back in New York there were thousands of women embroidering handkerchiefs and things, or making brushes and assembling garters after their day was done, in their homes at night. This is likely from such a shop, likely nothing more than that."

He deftly descended the ladder and Rebecca thought how agile her big husband still was, even though he was getting on close to his forty fifth year. She took his hand and looked him in the eye. Gone was the despondency. When Allingham was working, it made him less prone to sullenness and Rebecca was pleased at that.

"Where to, now, darling?"

"The school teacher's room."

It was in order, the box of items delivered from the dry goods store still sitting, unpacked, on a table by the window. The landlady had let the boy in to deliver them, and called the sheriff next morning, as the school teacher would never fail to come home without warning anyone ahead of time. The old housekeeper stood in the doorway, afraid of what she might hear or find out. Allingham closed the door between them as Rebecca called out, "Thank you, Mrs. Hudson. If we need anything else we'll come get you."

"Hmm."

Rebecca watched him. "Hmm, what?"

"Someone's been in here since then."

"Really?" She looked about, wondering what led him to such a conclusion. Everything seemed in order, well ordered, to her.

"Needlepoint."

"Really?"

"Yes. The girl was fond of needlepoint. She had a habit of making a sampler for every one of her students. She worked on it constantly."

"Oh?"

Allingham was pleased. He never blamed Rebecca for missing a clue. This was not an easy one.

"Look, Rebecca, she has a whole corner of her room dedicated to needlepoint."

"Yes?"

"Well, look at what's missing."

"Her current project?"

"Exactly." He rummaged through the box of delivered items. "And, as I suspected, the thread that she ordered from the shop is not here. Oh, she's a clever girl. She's clever and she's alive. She convinced the murderer to come to her room to fetch her work." He smiled for the first time in days.

"Oh, darling, that *is* good."

"Yes, he must have her hostage somewhere. He must and she's endeared herself to him, hopefully. She's asked for her needlepoint work to keep her occupied." He stroked his chin and was looking for more clues when the handle of the door turned slowly. He pulled his six shooter and pushed Rebecca behind him.

Chapter XIV:
Hilola

Ramon moped around the rest of the day. The girl did her best to make him talk, engage, but he would not. He was growing disgusted with her by the minute as she seemed completely unconcerned regarding the death of her partner and lover and constantly paraded around in her sheer outfit, legs bare up to mid-thigh. She was appealing and repulsive at the same time, and Ramon wondered how he was to function around this Teutonic Amazon for the remainder of their little odyssey south.

She finally sat down beside him as he cooked trout he'd pulled from the river.

"What's your name?"

"Ramon." He looked her over and admired the fine downy golden hair covering her bronzed thighs.

"And yours?"

"Lola."

"That's not a name."

"Sure it is." She shrugged. "My name."

"No, it is a nickname. What's your real name?"

"Promise not to laugh."

"No."

"Then I won't tell you." She folded her arms and pouted unconvincingly.

"Go on, tell me." He looked her over again and went back to the trout. "I probably won't laugh."

"Promise not to." She looked and sounded like a child saying that.

"What if it's funny? I'll *have* to laugh then."

"Hilola." She looked out of the corner of her eye, through a thick lock of golden hair and he suddenly wanted to bed her right then and there.

"Well, that's not funny at all. It's very pretty. Unusual, but pretty." He looked up at her, "Hee-lol-la. Is that right?"

She nodded her head in the affirmative and was pleased, as most men butchered her name, and that's mostly why she went by Lola. "I've never even heard of such a name."

She bent her leg at the knee and examined the ball of her foot, exposing herself for Ramon and all the world to see. He looked away and back at the trout in the frying pan.

"What kind of name is that?"

She lost interest in her foot and looked at Ramon and shrugged. "How the hell should I know? My Pa named me after some stupid fortune teller. She read his palm or his cards or some such bullshit and said he'd hit it big. The day I was born he found a five hundred dollar chunk of gold. When he came home and learned that I was born he said he hit it big for sure, and named me after the gypsy."

"What happened then?"

"Don't know. Ma said someone cut his throat for the rock of gold. I never knew him. Never even saw him." She stretched her back, more as an exhibition than to work the kinks out. "Never even seen a picture of him."

They ate. The sun was down now and the air cooled quickly. Ramon decided to take an inventory of the boat's contents. He grabbed it by the bow and pulled it well up onto the beach. He looked at Hilola doubt-fully. "What have you got in here, rocks? No wonder it rides so poorly."

"Nothing." She jumped up and stood in his way, blocking his access to the inside of the little cabin. She kissed him hard on the mouth and maneuvered his hand over her breast. "Let's go to bed. I'm tired and cold." She smiled wickedly at him and was just as quickly disappointed as he pushed her aside.

In a little while he had all the contents out on the beach. It was a well-provisioned vessel with food, water, whiskey, three rifles, two six shooters and a shotgun. There were plenty of cartridges and shotgun shells. There were carpentry tools for repair and a good sized keg of tar for caulking. It was obviously outfitted by someone other than Jimmie. He was simply too dense to put this all together and Ramon was fairly certain it was most likely stolen. He looked the empty boat over and picked up the bow with both hands.

"Still heavy as all hell."

He pulled a lantern out and lit it, looking inside carefully. He felt Hilola behind him and turned to find her pointing a shotgun at his head. She didn't have the presence of mind to pull back the hammers and Ramon didn't let on that such was required to send him to the great beyond.

"What's this?"

"Gold, Ramon!" She grinned a little and nodded. "Go ahead, pull on that one plank there."

He did and revealed a compartment gleaming with many bars of gold, each easily weighing ten pounds. He whistled through his teeth.

"Where did you steal that?"

"Didn't steal it."

"Well, then your pimp sure did."

She poked Ramon in the ribs with the gun. "Do not call me that!"

"What?"

"Whore. *Not* a whore."

Ramon grinned. "Well, if you're not a whore, then I don't know what one is." He extended his hand and she handed over the shotgun without an argument. It was preposterous to shoot the only person who could help her out of this wilderness. They both knew that.

Ramon went back to assessing the treasure. "This is from that robbery I read about, up in Utah. Mormon gold, isn't it? You two aren't smart enough to make that happen. What did you do, rob the robbers?"

She ignored him and sauntered back to the fire, flopping down and resting her head in her hands. She enjoyed watching Ramon. He was a beautiful man, better than any she'd seen in a long time. He had a nice voice with a pleasant accent and spoke well without swearing. He didn't insult her the way the others had; he was a gentleman. She thought she could love Ramon. He was smart, a gentleman and a good lover. He was not weak like every other man she'd ever known.

"Not a whore and don't say it again."

"Okay, whatever you say. What are you then?"

"Promise!"

"Promise what?"

"You won't call me that again."

"Okay, I promise." He laughed and decided to tease her a little. "What are you, then?"

"I'm an entertanoar." She straightened her back proudly as she made the declaration.

"A what?"

She thought hard about it, knew that wasn't quite right and tried to remember the correct word. It wouldn't come to her so she repeated the same word, with the accent on a different syllable this time and an extra consonant for good measure. "An entra, entratrainoar."

"An entertainer?" Ramon laughed politely. She was an entertainer certain enough.

"No, no, a person that's in, in business. I'm a business lady." She poked herself in the breast with a thumb, defiantly.

"Oh, an entrepreneur." He stood up dramatically and, pretending to pull a hat from his head, made a deep bow. "A thousand pardons, my lady Hilola. I did not know."

She was pleased and smirked a little as she pulled her knees to her chin. Ramon grabbed a blanket from inside the tent and carefully covered everything below her waist. It seemed everything she did, every movement she made, was designed to keep him distracted.

He laughed out loud. What a predicament. What a crazy predicament to have more money than he'd ever need in his life. Money enough to put him in good graces with el Presidente Díaz, and set his mother up in a fine Spanish villa for the rest of her days, all sitting, just a few feet away, and a delusional whore the only thing separating him from the booty.

"What's so funny?"

She sat back and watched Ramon's curly raven locks shimmer in the moonlight. If he'd shave that silly droopy Mexican moustache from his lip, he'd be perfect. She thought she might do that one night for him as he slept.

"Oh, just thinking." He lay down beside her and wanted her and was disgusted with himself for wanting her. He did not run with the whores, and it only made him miss his love all the more desperately back in Spain.

As if she could read his mind, she asked about it. "Why don't you have a wife?"

"Who says I don't?"

"I do." She looked him over and found tobacco and twisted a cigarette and put it in his mouth. She lit it for him from a twig burning in the fire, nearly dropping a glowing cinder in his eye. She was a klutz as well as a ding bat. She waited for him to finish beating the ember out against his damp shirt, eyeing her menacingly.

"Hilola?"

"Yes?"

"You are the most confounding and scandalous woman I've ever known."

She giggled. "Thank you."

She pulled out a jug and sipped it and got Ramon drunk and they talked into the night. She was ignorant and crass but he enjoyed her simplicity more than he'd enjoyed the company of anyone in a long time. It was as if they were acting out some ridiculous play.

She looked him over with glazed eyes. "So, tell me of this woman who broke your heart."

"She's from Spain. I've been living in Spain for more than six years. I actually grew up there. Until Presidente Díaz had my father executed. Then I came home.

She stopped him. "Oh, Ramon, I'm sorry for that. Did you love your pa?"

He wanted to cry at the memory of his father. He nodded and continued with his story. "She is there in Spain and I wanted to marry her but her father will not let a mestizo marry his pure Castilian daughter." He spit into the fire at the thought and took another drink. He looked at Lola and could not focus. He blinked hard and she laughed at his drunkenness.

"Ramon, you are funny. What's a mesezto?" She hiccupped.

"Mestizo."

"Tha's what I said."

"Mixed race, part Mexican Indian and part Spanish. I am not a *pure blood.*" He spit again. "You know what? That son of a bitch her father is a quarter Arab blood. No one ever complains of that, though. Hypocrites, all bastard hypocrites." He drank again.

"Is she beautiful?" Lola sidled up to Ramon and placed a hand high up on his thigh. She felt the thick muscles contract through the fabric of his trousers at the touch. She kissed him on the temple. He didn't buck her this time.

"Sí, she is the most beautiful creature I've

ever known," he gazed into Lola's pretty blue eyes. "Well, almost." He gave up resisting her and reached over to kiss her on the mouth.

He suddenly fell back and began to snore. Lola would not have any relief tonight. She looked around at all the gear strewn on the beach. She found Jimmie's razor and went to work.

Ramon was up early. He picked up one of the Winchesters he'd found in the boat's cabin. It was a good one, just like he'd used to hunt with his father. There were sheep in this part of the country and Ramon liked sheep and goat meat better than beef. He'd see what luck he would have.

He wandered through a few canyons and found some old dwellings, not unlike the ruins on his father's hacienda back home in Mexico. He rested awhile and felt the strangeness of his bare lip with the thumb and forefinger of his right hand. It had taken him four years to cultivate that moustache and he should have been angry at the crazy blonde, but he was not. He thought a lot about her, knew the whole thing was preposterous. It was sex with her he liked so much, of course. He was certain of that. There really wasn't much else; she was crass and ignorant. She wasn't stupid, but so vulgar he wondered what it would be like to spend much time with her. He was afraid he was going to find out as, by his best reckoning, it would take the better part of two seasons — or even more — to get to the Mexican border. He'd be shed of her then.

Still, it wasn't so bad. He was well provisioned, and actually enjoyed the woman's company. If only he could keep her sex off his mind. She was the first woman to have such an effect on him. Back in Spain he was in love, and obsessed with his love, but he did not want to make love to her every single waking moment, but this is how he felt about Hilola. He could not keep his eyes off her, and worse yet, could not keep his mind on anything but bedding her.

He resolved to enjoy it a little and take his time getting back home. At the next settlement, he'd get a wire to the men and let them know he was alive and well and making his way back to them. That would put them at ease, and perhaps make him feel less strange about his journey south with Hilola.

Adulio and Paulo would round up more horses and they didn't need him for that. He was the one to negotiate for the sale, but the real work of the vaqueros was handled by the tough old men. He could certainly keep up with them, even after living the soft life back in Europe, but they never really needed him for that kind of work.

He wandered further into a slot canyon and found a deep crevice. The gold would be well hidden here, and he was confident he could make a map so that the government men could find it. There'd likely be a good reward.

In another hour he settled on a diminutive ewe that stood, not knowing what to do about him, all alone on a narrow ledge. The creature fell a good forty feet closer to his camp and it would be easy to carry out. He passed on some magnificent rams, good curl to the horns and he thought again of his father and missed him terribly. His father loved to hunt and would always save the best trophies for Ramon. One great ram he saw would be the one his father would point out to him, then with a gentle touch to the shoulder tell him, *'Take that one, my son.'* And when the animal was down, his father would backslap him and shake him by the hand. He missed his father.

As expected, Hilola had done nothing while he was gone. She was a terrible camp mate.

She was lazy and inept at just about any-thing but swimming and looking beautiful and doing the things that women did to drive men mad.

There did not seem to be much else that Hilola could do. Ramon shrugged and thought that if a woman could do nothing else, swimming beautifully and fornicating wildly was not such a terrible repertoire. He dropped the sheep at her feet and set about methodically breaking it down.

"Oh, goody. I'm about sick of dried pork and fish."

He liked her company. She sat and watched him work and liked it. He was proud of his skill as a hunter and woods-man and proud that he knew how to skin and dress an animal. He was showing off a little and while he had her attention, decided to break the news to her.

"I found a good spot to hide the gold."

"What?" She looked up from the work he was doing, into his eyes, as if he'd suddenly started speaking to her in his native tongue.

"The gold. We'll leave it in a slot canyon over there." He pointed with his bloody knife. "We'll give the authorities a map as to its whereabouts." He casually walked over to the map that had survived his fall into the river. He opened it carefully and pointed to the spot he was certain was their present location. He looked up at her and waited for the battle to ensue.

"Like hell we will!" She stood up and looked at him as if he'd lost his senses. "Are you completely nuts?"

"No. Only partially."

"I, I was going to give you hal . . . ten percent of that gold for helping me get it out."

"Out where, Hilola? Where are you going to get rid of it? It has marks all over it. What are you going to do, build a fire and melt it down? Turn it into coins? You're never going to get rid of it. You're going to get yourself hanged."

"No, no. Jimmie told me, there's a place down in your country. In Mexico. By the sea."

"What sea?"

"The gulf of Cortez or something. There's a fence down there. He'll buy it and give us money for it."

Ramon laughed. "I know this joker by the Gulf of California. He buys trinkets and junk from the bandits. He's barely got a pot to piss in, Hilola. My God, what an idiotic idea!"

"What's so idiotic about it?"

"You don't take gold to a poor country to

sell it, stupid. Mexico is a poor country. That fence hasn't got money to pay you for all that gold."

"It's not all that much." She began to pout.

"Really? Really? Not that much! How much, my dear entrepreneur, Hilola, do you suppose it is?"

"Oh, a thousand dollars or so."

Ramon laughed; maybe she was really more stupid than ignorant. He smiled and shook his head. "You are way out of your element, Hilola. Way out."

They worked into the evening, or at least Ramon worked while Hilola did little more than prattle on endlessly while smoking cigarettes and watching him lug bar after bar of gold back into the depths of the canyon.

It was a good hiding place, rocky, with a stone floor and stone path all the way up from the shore. He made his way as far back as he could go, and then even further by squeezing through an opening not much wider than his hand. Hilola had to pass the bars through to him, one at a time. No one would ever be able to follow their tracks.

Once he was finished, Ramon surveyed the hiding spot and was satisfied. He returned to the boat, grabbed a pack and began climbing the sheer face of the cliff, forcing Hilola to follow him to the very top, overlooking the river below.

They were so high up the boat looked no larger than a matchbox below. He could see a pair of mountains, due east, and took the compass from around Hilola's neck and checked his reckoning. He laid out his map and found the spot where he was certain they were located. He looked behind him and saw the sun setting on a low stretch of mountains there. He made a mark on the map and looked it over, satisfied. He looked about again, checking and rechecking. When he was convinced he had it all right, he sat down for a smoke. Hilola watched him with great interest.

He smiled at her. "What date is it?" Hilola shrugged. She wasn't certain even what month it was. Ramon counted back to the day he'd killed Donny and made a notation of the current date on the map. He made a fire and wrote by the light of it, as it was dark enough now to see the moon clearly. He looked up and saw the stars above him and started making notes along the edge of the map. He flipped it over and recreated the constellations above his head. He noted the time of day, by his best estimation, as well.

"What's all that?"

"The moon and the stars, the location of it all on this date at this time. Anyone good at navigation should be able to find this spot based on the moon and the stars on this date, and they can adjust for the time when they come looking for it. But that shouldn't be necessary. The points I've marked out are from each direction. All they have to do is line everything up." He looked down at the map, satisfied. "And tomorrow, we'll make a cipher mark on the rock. Something that might be mistaken for an Indian petroglyph, but one a search party will recognize easily enough." He looked up again and then at Hilola who had a funny, almost reverent look on her face.

She thought that Ramon might very well be the smartest human being she'd ever known. It was giving her some ideas again, as men of power and men of great intelligence seemed to do something very primal to Hilola. She watched Ramon unpack and wondered what he was up to now.

He nodded. "Come on, help me set up."

"What?"

"Camp." He nodded. "Too dangerous to climb back down there in the dark, we'd end up breaking our necks. We'll sleep up here tonight." He dug around and pulled out a bottle. "And besides, we've got everything we need in here." He tossed it to her and she took a deep drink.

And Ramon was right. He'd brought a sleeping bag, dried beef and plenty of spirits and soon had a cozy fire built up. It was large, like a bonfire. The stars were out in their full splendor now and Hilola was able to sit back and pull on the bottle and have a smoke and admire the smart Mexican checking over his notes on the map.

He looked especially handsome to her when he was concentrating. The firelight danced on his knitted brow and Hilola wanted him to stop looking at the map. She had other ideas and thought she might want to hide the bottle for now. She wanted to do more than lie down and listen to him snore under the stars. He looked up and saw her watching him and gave a little knowing grin. He folded the map and put it in his pack.

"How do you know all this?"

Ramon shrugged. He liked the fact that he was impressing her, yet did his best to appear nonchalant. "The Jesuits, I guess."

"What are Jesuits?"

"Priests, in Spain, well, all over really.

They're the great educators of the church."

"You a Catholic?"

He straightened his back a little. "Well, yes, of course."

"Huh." Hilola drank and handed him the bottle. "Jimmie said all you Catholics can't be trusted. You serve the Puntive."

"Pontiff." He looked at her with one eye half closed. All the work had made him tired and more easily drunk." He laughed at Hilola's interrogation. "Do you know who the Pontiff is?"

"No."

"The Pope."

"What's that?"

"It's a he. He's the leader of the church."

Hilola was starting to lose interest. She never gave much of anything Jimmie said a lot of thought. She shrugged.

Ramon decided to press her a little. "So, you don't like Catholics?"

She shrugged. "I don't know. Don't know any 'cept you." She grinned and ran her fingers through his curls. "I like you all right. You're a smart son of a bitch, Ramon. Smart as hell."

"Thank you."

They soon lay back on the sleeping bag and stared up at the stars. "That's Polaris, the bright one. And can you see the stars that look like a cup, with a handle? That's the saucepan."

"What's the other real bright one?"

"That's the moon."

"No, not that one, *ass*. I know what the moon is." She laughed and liked it when Ramon teased her. She rested her head on his chest and he could smell her hair. She wasn't trying anything with him now, and it felt good; felt good for the human contact without a lot of drama and performing and expectation. It was good to have Hilola so close and not doing anything but enjoying the night. She pointed again. "That one."

"Oh, that's Vega."

"They're beautiful, ain't they, Ramon?" She pressed herself against him and held his hand. "I been on this earth for a long time, ain't never noticed till now, how beautiful they are."

Chapter XV: Desperate Times

Old Pop jumped off the bed he'd slept better in than he'd slept in years. He bowed deeply to the pretty Mexicana and Hobbs spoke up quickly. Though not a jealous man he wanted to make it clear to both of them, the old one in particular, that his pretty Rosario was off limits completely. "This here's my wife, Señora Hobbs. Rosario, this here's Old Pop, and that fine young man is Pierce."

"Good morning, gentlemen. I hope you slept well."

"Oh, like babies, ma'am. You have a lovely home." Old Pop knew Rosario to be the housekeeper, but his compliment was not lost on her. It *was* her home.

She looked at Pierce doubtfully and gently touched him under the chin; she moved his face about in the sunlight streaming through the bedroom window. "Such a fine face to be treated so roughly. I have something to fix that." She quickly left the room and the men stood awkwardly until Pierce spoke up.

"We thank you for your hospitality, Mr. Hobbs, but I reckon it's time we got on. My brother'll be halfway to Mexico by now, and he's like a dog with a bone when he gets something in his head. I'm fearful he'll find Señor la Garza and I aim to be there when he does. I aim to stop all this bad business conducted by my family." He looked at Old Pop. "Enough is enough."

Old Pop cleared his throat. "You're not your brother's keeper, lad."

Hobbs nodded. "And you're not a lawman either, young man. We've got a warrant for your brother. We'll ride with you and catch him up." He nodded reassuringly.

"You mean you and the gentleman, the Indian man?"

"No, no. Mr. Singh has an expectant mother to worry over." He grinned. "No, my wife and I'll be going with you."

"The lady? The lady we just met?"

And at that, Rosario walked in. She beckoned the lad to the side of the bed and began dressing his battered face.

Pierce watched her work and liked the look in her eye. She was a determined woman, and she was tough. He realized he no longer thought it was a stupid idea for her to accompany them. Fact was, she'd likely be protecting him along the way.

She finished and got a mirror and showed him what she'd done. At least now the tails of Old Pop's thread were not hanging down, and the unguent Rosario applied seemed to have an immediate effect. He felt better already.

"I'll be thankin' you, ma'am."

"Da nada."

Allingham nodded at Rebecca's purse as he pointed his revolver at head height. He pulled his wife behind him as she drew her own weapon. He cocked the piece just inches from the man's right eye.

"Oh, dear Jesus!" The doctor turned pale and held up his hands. "Don't . . . don't shoot me. Don't shoot me, please!"

They sighed in relief as the hapless Webster entered the room. He looked terrible, as if he'd had the fright of his life, and Rebecca kindly reached over to loosen his collar as he sat on the school teacher's bed.

"What the devil are you doing here, doctor?" Allingham was annoyed with the bungling man who seemed always to be under foot these days. He was a damned nuisance and Allingham was fed up with his meddling and his nonsense.

"I'm sorry, marshal. I've a patient in this

boarding house and was told you and Mrs. Allingham were here. When I saw the door shut, I thought it would be all right to enter. I didn't mean to scare either of you." He breathed deeply and the color was coming back into his face. "I guess we're all a bit jumpy." He looked around the room and suddenly began to cry.

"Doctor, what's the matter?" Rebecca patted his hand.

"I'm sorry. I'm sorry. I've seen a great deal of carnage in my time, Mrs. Allingham, what with the war and even in my practice, and now that I see this young beauty's room, well, it, it just breaks my heart."

Allingham cut him off. He looked Rebecca in the eye and made her understand with the barest of gestures. He spoke in his most authoritative tone to the physician.

"Doctor, I understand your interest and I appreciate your inclination to help, but I must insist that you stop."

The physician looked up as he wiped his eyes with his handkerchief. He did not fully comprehend. "Stop?"

"Yes, stop. Stop following us around, stop helping. We don't need your help. We don't want your help. You're welcome to visit our home and Mr. Halsted and Mr. Singh, but you are not welcome to meddle again in this investigation."

Allingham turned and left the room, giving Rebecca the time she'd need to make it clear to the man. Allingham could rely on her for that. They were a good team and he knew he'd have her unwavering support in this matter.

The doctor looked into Rebecca's pretty eyes, questioningly.

"It's true, doctor. My husband has things well in hand, and this is simply too much strain on us all. Please, come home with us, dine with us tonight, but please, please don't talk any further of the investigation. My husband has his methods and needs complete concentration." She reached out her hand so as to help him to his feet. "And cooperation." She smiled the smile that no one, man, woman or beast, could resist. No one could ever resist Rebecca Allingham.

"This one's lost her feet."

The pale sheriff held the door for Allingham as he walked in on the horrific scene. Another redheaded beauty. She was a whore, and younger yet than the others. As Allingham had suspected, and predicted, the violence had been elevated as the poor woman had no eyes. These soaked in a glass of spirits on a table next to the bed.

Everything else matched the other murders. The murderer was the same, as far as Allingham could surmise.

The sheriff was correct. Both feet were gone, sawn away with a precision instrument, just above the ankle. From the amount of blood, it was evident to Allingham that she'd been alive when the amputations had occurred. Allingham was furious, not with the murderer, but with himself, as he was no closer to solving this horrific string of crimes.

He looked up at the sheriff and felt sorry for the man. The sheriff was distraught, as he was out of his element. He was a county sheriff and elected to collect taxes and perform other such bureaucratic tasks and assignments. Dealing with a monster was not a normal part of this appointment. Allingham would not be terse with this man. However, he needed to think and be in the room alone with the corpse for a while.

"Sheriff, please go on out for a bit." He nodded and felt odd. It felt like someone had taken his voice and spoken those words. He'd not been as compassionate before, except with his wife and, of course, his people: Mr. Singh, Rosario, Hobbs, even with his father-in-law, but it felt queer to be so kind to this stranger and fellow lawman.

The sheriff cast his eyes over the victim and then looked at Allingham as if to say, "*No,* I will *not* allow you to be alone with such evil." The sheriff felt as if they were now brothers in a way that men become brothers after living through horror and degradation. He wanted to tell Allingham he'd not leave his brother in such a horrific place by himself but, instead, did as he was told and walked out.

Allingham was finally alone and stood for several moments staring at the pathetic victim. He looked at each wall of the room, then at the ceiling, the floor, the bed, the bed covers, the table, the plate . . . every item. He imagined the killer handling these things. He closed his eyes and took his measure. He could see him. He knew his height and his shoe size, how he dressed, his chipped tooth, his strong hands and clean shaven chin. He knew so much about him and yet not nearly enough to catch him.

He suddenly lost all of the thoughts as his wife's pregnant belly came into his mind and he remembered that he was more than sixty miles away from her. He wanted to jump on his horse's back and ride until he was home and not let her leave his sight again. He breathed deeply; the corpse was decomposing and the stench of death and decay made him ill and he wanted to vomit.

He walked out and left the sheriff on the porch smoking a cigar. He said nothing to the sheriff as there was nothing to say. Allingham was speechless and literally without a clue. He rode back to Flagstaff.

Chapter XVI:
Desperate Ride

They got under way. The river was swift for a better part of the day. No rapids were encountered and they had time to enjoy the scenery and pleasant weather. They had the rare time to live in the moment as there was no real work to do other than move the oars periodically to keep the boat moving downstream efficiently.

Ramon enjoyed the boat now. It rode well in the water without the gold ballast weighing so heavily in the bow. He caught Hilola watching him work every now and again. Ramon liked when pretty women paid attention to him. He was a handsome man and women had admired him from the time that he was a child. He was the kind of man, had he been less scrupulous and moral, who would have been titled a heartbreaker, a Casanova even, but Ramon was well bred and imbued with a morality that was of another time; a time of knights when chivalry was held in higher regard than how many women a man could bed in a lifetime.

The Jesuits used to teach them all about Saint Ignatius of Loyola, the founder of their order, who was wild and reckless as a young man. Ramon thought it might be fun to live such a life, but he was not cut out for it, and the few near dalliances he had with the fast and loose life ended up as failures. He was just not cut out to be a wastrel and a fool. That is how he ended up courting the Spanish beauty while studying in Spain. Ramon was old beyond his years, and he knew, always, that he wanted to have a wife and a family. From the first moment he laid eyes on her, he wanted to marry the young Castilian beauty. He thought of her now and missed her. She'd broken his heart and he still had difficulty purging her from his mind.

But it had to be. Spain was a lifetime away, a whole other world away, and he didn't hold out much hope to visit it again. He guided the boat and gazed upon Hilola's long and lovely legs. They were, if he was honest with himself, more appealing than the ones he'd known. Hilola was more appealing, really, than any woman he'd ever known.

His reverie was broken by Hilola who

pointed to a copse of cottonwoods shading an expansive beach on the western side of the river. She suggested a break for lunch and Ramon obliged.

He worked quickly to get a fire going and soon had some of the sheep stewing. Hilola, uncharacteristically, did a little foraging and found a nice garden, apparently planted by Indians, with an abundance of squash and some beans. She picked some of these and brought them to the campsite, carrying them in the skirt of her dress, worn and threadbare. She deposited them on a big rock, next to Ramon's campfire.

"Where on earth did you find these?" He was pleased.

"Over there." She pointed. "A garden."

Ramon grinned and looked about. It seemed very much a land not touched by human beings and, yet, here was a garden. He welcomed the fresh vegetables and added them to the pan, creating a thick stew.

They ate in silence for a while and afterward Hilola stood up and stretched, backlit by the sunlight. Ramon had difficulty swallowing. His heart was in his throat and Hilola saw it and grinned devilishly. "Let's swim."

She pulled off her dress and quickly dove in, teasing him by flaunting her womanly charms and just as quickly hiding them from his view by sinking into the swiftly moving water. "Come on!" She playfully splashed him and got everything around the fire wet. It hissed and steamed. She had generally made a mess of everything.

Ramon stood up, red faced and furious. "Stop it, *idiot!*"

"Don't call me a idiot, ya half-breed Mexican ass."

"Whore."

"Mesesto."

"Mestizo! He glared at her as he wiped the water from his face. "You're so damned dumb you can't even insult a person properly. Mes-ti-zo. Mes-ti-zo. How many times must I tell you, you stupid bitch."

He turned and dug through the boat's cabin and found a couple of trade knives. He walked in the direction of the garden and remained gone several minutes.

Hilola sat by the fire and dried off and dressed as she waited for him to return.

"Where'd you go?"

"To pay the Indians."

She laughed and looked at him as if he were stupid. "You chump. The deer probably eat more than we took. Those savages would never miss it."

"Don't call them that. *Savages!*" He

looked her over. "Who's calling who a savage?"

He packed up and got on board. He looked her in the eye. "Come on, we're leaving."

"I'm not ready to leave yet." She threw another bit of wood on the fire which Ramon had thoroughly extinguished, and looked back at him defiantly.

"I don't have time for this nonsense, Hilola. Come on, we're wasting daylight."

"Who the hell died and left you king of this company? Sure weren't Jimmie." She laughed out loud at the thought of Jimmie in his watery grave. "He'd have a fit if he could. Which he can't 'cause he's *dead.*" She threw her head back and screamed at the sky. "Dead! D-E-D, *dead*!"

Ramon stood, glaring for a long moment. He was furious with her. He considered manhandling her and pulling her back on board so they could move on, but he thought better of it. She was wild and unpredictable, this one. He wondered who'd come out ahead in a fight.

He got out of the boat and sat some distance away. They looked like a pair of siblings who'd just had a big falling out, Hilola facing upstream, arms crossed over her chest and Ramon, staring south, smoking furiously on a cigarette.

He'd have to wait for her to stop showing him who was boss. He settled down to smoke. He grew tired of sitting and got out a rod and fished for a while but it wasn't a good spot for trout. He kept pulling in the dreaded squawfish, which he threw back.

He leaned back on an elbow and eventually fell asleep. In a little while he felt Hilola's delicate touch as she ran her fingers through his thick curls from behind him. She was so close he could smell her. She smelled good; of sweat and river water and just Hilola. It was nice but he quickly pulled himself away. She was like an enchantress and he didn't want to fall under her spell. He didn't want her manipulating him.

"Come on, Ramon, you big baby. Let's not fight." She pushed him on the shoulder and Ramon was impressed with her strength. He was glad he didn't try to physically control her.

She pouted some more and turned to face him, standing between him and the river. When he wouldn't look up she squatted down and smiled. "Don't ya like me, Ramon?" She looked down at her open dress front and admired her own ample bosom. He was confounding. She could easily seduce any man she'd ever known and she knew Ramon liked women. That was abundantly clear from his performance the night she'd visited his bed.

"You're, you're just . . . , it's not the proper thing to do, Hilola." He reached over and gently buttoned her dress to the neck.

"Oh, that's a good one." She stood up and stretched again, arching her back like a queen cat in heat. It seemed Hilola liked to stretch a lot. "You said you were with your love in Spain, didn't you?"

He looked up, a little confused as Hilola did not seem the type for dialectics. "Yes."

"And you never married her?"

"No, I never married her. Her father would not have it."

"Then yer nothin' but a hypnotist." She knew that wasn't the right word, but it was close.

"A hypocrite?"

"Yeah, that's it, a hypocrite." She waded into the water up to her knees, turning her back to him. She began splashing water toward Ramon's fishing line. She looked like a child playing on a Sunday afternoon and Ramon's heart was breaking. She was a lot smarter than she looked.

They finally did get back on the river and Ramon thought more of Indians. He'd

179

heard of the ones around here. They were peaceful for the most part. There were a few stories of adventurers and prospectors losing their lives, but that often was the fault of the intruders, not the Indians. He had a lot of things on the boat to trade, and he was not afraid of the Indians in the least. They'd likely know the rudiments of his language, so he could communicate with them. They'd probably have a good command of English, as they'd been trading for long enough with the steamships for firewood. He'd communicate one way or the other, do some trading and maybe even bring some nice trinkets back for his mother. She so loved Indian things.

He thought of Hilola, now napping in the sun on the cabin deck, legs splayed in a most unorthodox attitude. He shook his head and wondered at her upbringing. She was completely uncouth. And she had the audacity to call the Indians savage.

He suddenly worried about her. The Indians were not likely to have ever seen such a beauty: tall, fair, and bosomy, with the pretty golden hair. Would they abuse her? Probably not. They might want to buy her from Ramon and that would be awkward at the least. He didn't want to kill Indians over the wild girl, but he knew he would. He was too much a knight to not, if things were to get out of hand.

But maybe they'd just admire and revere her. They might think her a goddess, or perhaps an embodiment of the Virgin. That would be ironic, Hilola mistaken for the Virgin Mary — or any kind of virgin, for that matter.

Certainly the Indians had been exposed to Christianity over the years. The Spanish priests had moved all over the land in search of souls to save; even more importantly, gold to mine. The priests would have, without a doubt, shown the Indians images of the Virgin.

Ramon laughed to himself at that thought. The Virgin was always depicted as fair, often with golden hair just like Hilola's, and lily white skin. He knew from his study and reading of history and philosophy with the Jesuits, that the Virgin was likely as dark as his own Mexican people, since she was an Israelite Jew.

But the ones making the statues, and the ones making the rules, were the European whites, and they were obliged to make the images of God and Jesus and the Virgin, and all the saints, as white as they. It always tickled him to think of that.

He was suddenly relieved. This could

likely work to his advantage, though the Indians held onto their own faith, despite the padres' best efforts, they'd incorporated certain things that they liked, and the Virgin was always a little seductive. There was sex there; any good religion had sex. That was a given.

Hilola awoke to the sound of voices. She looked up at Ramon whom she'd caught absentmindedly glimpsing her nether region. He ignored her and looked at the east bank. Up high, there were Indian children playing and they called out and waved and the couple waved back.

The Indians suddenly started gesticulating wildly and Hilola was amused. She began mimicking them until she saw the look on Ramon's face, which had lost all color.

"Jesus, Mary and holy Saint Joseph, look ahead!"

Chapter XVII:
An Unlikely Posse

The unlikely posse made it to the first river rat town and Hobbs could not help but be reminded of Canyon Diablo. The same scum occupied the settlement and, as they rode along, men in various states of decay sauntered up to them and sized them up. Hobbs had put badges on all of them, even Rosario who sat with her ten gauge across her lap. She kept her free hand resting across the hammers. It was an adequate deterrent and old Hobbsie was proud. He did not ever have to worry about his wife.

They checked with the local law who was also the local saloon keeper and ferry attendant. He was a sallow man who spent most of his time drunk, but he was a moral man and fair minded and obliged the marshals in their inquiry.

He'd not seen the Mexican but knew about him, as he'd met Thad. He spit tobacco juice when they brought up his name. Pierce was pleased as Thad was off-putting to most everyone he met. Thad was also a lot bigger in his own mind than most people thought of him, and he'd not intimidated the lawman in the least.

Pierce opened a flask and took a drink and handed it to the lawman. He'd learned this strategy from Old Pop who taught him that doing such would often put men at ease. Men who liked to drink would often loosen their tongues after a gulp or two of decent whiskey, and Pierce had good whiskey, as he'd stolen all of his father's supply for this journey south. He even had some of his father's special scotch, but whiskey would work adequately on this lawman.

"That man's my brother."

"Oh." The lawman wiped his mouth with a dirty sleeve and looked at Pierce for the meaning of such a statement. He did not know if it was meant as a warning or threat.

Pierce continued. "But he's a murderous bastard and we need to stop him."

The lawman smiled. "Well, he left out of here two days ago. Didn't dally here," he looked about at the terrible place. "Not much to keep a fellar occupied, as you can see."

It was getting late and they had to stop for

the night. The lawman also had a boarding house. At first, Hobbs thought it the best place to stay and they took a couple of rooms until Rosario held up a brown stained mattress and picked off a louse. "We will camp in the desert, my love." They dutifully followed her out into the desert, close to the eastern shore of the river.

She got a good campfire going as the men prepared their beds and settled the horses for the night. Desert living was not foreign or particularly bothersome to any of them, except Hobbs, who was used to beds. Hobbs, by his own admission, was not a man who took comfort lightly. He loved comfort and hated rough living. He hated lying in the rain, hated the cold and hard ground and only smiled a little when Rosario handed him a plate of steaming stew and opened a bottle of beer for him. The good scotch would be dessert.

He also saw the bed she'd made for him while he foraged for firewood. It was set up for two and this made things easier on his mind. The other men did not have women to sleep with and he felt like a king. He so loved his wife. His heart fluttered again and he coughed. He felt the tickle in his throat from the blood backing up into his lungs. He took a deep breath and recovered as best he could.

It turned out to be pleasant; the river was not far off and they could smell it. Hobbs thought that maybe they'd get some fish on this journey and that pleased him, as well. Old Pop and Pierce held up a hand as Rosario prepared to clean up. They were good men and wanted it understood that Rosario was their guest on this journey, not a servant or a cook. She was a deputy US Marshal and she'd be treated as such. She shrugged and smiled and sat down beside Hobbsie and rested her head on his chest. This was more a holiday for her than work. She began humming a little tune and watched the men clean up.

Old Pop finally sat down and pulled out a harmonica and began mimicking the tune Rosario was humming. She sang a few stanzas for him and he soon had it down well. They had a regular little concert until Hobbs's snoring began to drown them out. They all laughed at their unlikely leader and settled down for the night.

They slept well and Rosario got a good three hours before she lay fully awake as Hobbsie snored in her ear. She watched the stars and prayed a little and thought of all the things that had happened to her in the past couple of years. She prayed for Rebecca and her baby, for Allingham, Mr. Halsted and Mr. Singh. She thought of Rebecca's two fathers and was happy for them as they would both be grandfathers soon.

She prayed that Allingham would use his great powers to catch the horrible murderer. She knew he would, it would just be a matter of time, and then she cried a little as she realized that the longer it took him to complete the puzzle, the more poor women would die. She also prayed a special prayer for Allingham; she could see the strain on him. He was really a kind man, despite his tough outer shell and she knew that every murder was another tear at his heart. She wondered if he would ever fully recover from this terrible thing. It was as if he was just as much a victim as the poor women and this made her feel sad and love him all the more.

She prayed for the Mexican and hoped he was safe and maybe even back home at his hacienda. She thought about that. Eventually, she'd be back home in Mexico and she was excited about that, as, despite Hobbs's offers many times to take her home, she resisted, afraid of what she might find when she got there. She preferred to remember the good things about it. She'd heard that el Presidente Díaz had not made things easy for the poor. He'd made great strides in modernizing the country, railroad tracks abounded, and the telegraph had linked all the towns together. Many good things were happening for the businesses and the rich people of the country. But the poor, as always, since before the time of the conquistadors, had been left behind. It was the way of the Mexican peon. They were always given short shrift and it would likely never change.

So Rosario had mixed feelings about returning to Mexico. She'd just have to wait and see and pray. Hopefully it would come out right. She prayed some more and when she was finished got up for a pee and found Pierce fussing over Alanza, the Mexican's prized mare.

"Good evening, ma'am." He whispered close to her ear, hoping not to disturb the sleeping men. "I hope I didn't wake you up."

"No." She smiled and it made her like the young Pierce all the more. He'd taken special care of the Mexican's horse and was even so hopeful for a good outcome that he'd brought the animal along, so that man and beast could be reunited as soon as possible.

"She's a beautiful animal, ain't she,

ma'am?" He curried her blonde mane with a brush and the horse snorted, half asleep.

"She is, my boy, but you should let her sleep. We should both try for a little more sleep."

He smiled. "Just can't, ma'am." He lit a cigarette and offered her one but she refused.

They walked a ways toward the river and watched the moon play off the rushing current. Pierce was pleased with how quickly it was flowing. He hoped it was taking Ramon la Garza home.

As always, Rosario slept best just before it was time to rise, and this day was no different, except that Hobbsie was crouched over her in his underwear, six shooter in hand. He handed her the ten gauge and held a finger to his lips.

"Something's stirring in the brush, darling." He crab-walked to Old Pop and Pierce and gave them the same warning. It was dark now, darker than when they'd gone to bed as clouds covered the moon. They could hear plenty and Hobbs figured it was at least four men after the horses. More than likely they were drunk as they stumbled much and had difficulty being quiet. They were a hapless bunch of horse thieves and now that Hobbs had everyone awake and armed, he decided to try a strategy to scare them away.

He fired over the head of the nearest man and they fired wildly back. It had the opposite effect and soon they were pinned down without a clear target to shoot.

Hobbs looked left and right. His men were well hidden behind rocks. Rosario was nowhere to be found. He called out to the bad men. "You men, we are US Marshals and if you don't want to hang, either give up or walk away."

"Give us your horses and we'll go away."

"No." Hobbs felt better. He felt like Allingham, giving such a terse reply.

"Then face the consequences of your actions, old man."

"Who are you calling old man, bastard?"

"You."

Hobbs waited. He was angry and not frightened. His heart fluttered, but it was treating him well enough. He could think and he had enough energy to fight. He looked to his men. It was getting light enough to see them fairly well. He called out again. "If you boys don't give up or move out in the next minute, I'm going to put my best man on you and he don't take prisoners. He'll shoot you all in the guts with his scattergun. And I ain't bluffing."

"Go to hell."

A shot flew past Hobbsie's cheek and he ducked down. "Sons of bitches."

He pointed his rifle and waited for a clear shot. A second later, two blasts of the ten gauge erupted. Two men cried out in pain as the buckshot found its mark. Pistol firing could be heard and he knew Rosario was using her six shooter, preferring it to reloading the shotgun. Bad men were popping up like dandelions in a field, and Hobbs and Old Pop took careful aim. In short order, four men lay dying or dead.

When no more bad men offered resistance, Rosario made it back to their little camp, dropping fresh shells into her scattergun as she walked. She looked Hobbs over carefully, then Old Pop, and finally Pierce, who'd stood frozen the entire time, unable to either run or fight. It was all over in less than a minute.

Hobbs kissed his wife on the forehead. "Thanks, darling."

"Da nada."

Old Pop and Pierce looked on, jaws agape, as Hobbs put on his best poker face. He was so proud of his Rosario that he thought he'd burst. He checked the prisoners instead. The two with the shotgun wounds would not survive.

CHAPTER XVIII:
THE QUACKSALVER

Rebecca's morning sickness had come on with a vengeance and Mr. Singh did his best to help her. "I wish I could get you some mango, Kaur. Mango is good for such things. He made the room dark and soothing and burned spearmint oil and offered his herbal tea. He was a good nurse and soon Rebecca was well enough to see her father and the ubiquitous visitor. The doctor wanted desperately to help.

"Mrs. Allingham," he smiled uneasily and produced a bottle from his coat pocket. "May I recommend a remedy that has always worked for my patients?" He uncorked the top and found a teaspoon on the serving tray. He prepared to pour the tarry substance when Mr. Singh deftly snatched both bottle and spoon from his grasp. The Sikh smelled it doubtfully and put it in the pocket of his suit coat. He did not offer an explanation and the doctor did not demand one. Instead, he pursed his lips knowingly and backed out of the room. "I, I'll leave you to it, then." He nodded respectfully and left.

Halsted thought about smoking and realized that Mr. Singh was prepared to eject him as well. He looked at Rebecca who smiled knowingly at her hapless father. Her Sikh warrior never let her down. "Come. Sit, Father. Sit, Bapu." She patted the sofa on either side of her. She swallowed hard and waited for the wave of nausea to pass.

Her two fathers had been disagreeing about the doctor and Rebecca needed to make peace, despite her present infirmity. She knew both men too well. It had to end now.

"Father, you are very fond of this doctor."

"Oh," he looked at Singh and looked away. "I think he's a pleasant chap, that's all. It's nice to discuss things with a learned man. He's all right, I guess."

"And you, Bapu, you are not so enthusiastic?"

Singh shrugged and walked over to the waste can. He threw the bottle of patent medicine away with a resolute thud and wiped his fingers clean of the sticky residue.

Rebecca pushed him. She knew her Indian father did not like to speak ill of others, and he did not like to argue with Halsted over such trivial things, but letting the disagreement fester was not a viable option. "Please, Bapu. This is your home as much as it is anyone's. If the doctor somehow doesn't please you, tell us."

Mr. Singh sat for a long moment. He straightened his turban absent-mindedly. "I, I don't know what it is, Kaur. But something is not quite right."

Halsted leaned forward and took a drink of his whiskey. He'd been so irritated lately. He did not want to be so with Mr. Singh and certainly not with his daughter. He became serious and looked his friend in the eye. "Hira, I am sorry. I never intended to let the man overwhelm our household. I know he's a bit pedantic and always under foot but, well, he's a physician, and you know how the men of that trade can act."

Mr. Singh smiled. "I am not certain, how do you say, I cannot put my finger on it, but there is something not right about the man."

"Do you suppose he's a fraud?"

"Not necessarily a fraud, but perhaps a quacksalver." Singh grimaced. "No, not even so much that, perhaps. But the man is not as intelligent as he'd like us to believe him to be."

Rebecca smiled. She'd felt the same way. There was just something about him. She'd felt it as well. Allingham especially felt it and made no reservations about it.

"Then perhaps we should cool this relationship off?"

"Oh, no, Father." She knew he'd been entertained by the man. "Let him come around. He's harmless enough." She smiled at Mr. Singh and then looked at the trash can with the patent medicine. "And Bapu will make certain he does not try any hokum on me or my baby." She rubbed the beginning of her swelling belly. "Let him come around. I feel a little pity for him. He is a hopelessly lonely and sad man, I think."

Halsted finished his drink. "Indeed."

The school teacher held him in her arms and tried her best not to fall apart. The rape was not as horrible now. She'd accepted the role of mother to the deranged man. She decided to be bold and spoke up.

"Did you mail the sampler for me?"

"Yes, Momma, just as you requested." He buried his head more deeply into her breasts. She looked down and observed him sucking his thumb. He would revert to an infantile state soon and she needed to speak while she could still engage him.

"I've got another one, for another child, and it must be mailed tomorrow. Will you do that for me?"

He removed his thumb from his mouth. He was nearly incoherent now, lost in the fantasy he'd created. "Yes, Momma."

She was a little emboldened by her progress. "Why don't you go on and sleep in your crib and untie me. I've got to use the privy and want to wash up a bit."

He stood up and suddenly became an adult again. She was appealing as a woman now and was no longer his mother. He raped her again.

Chapter XIX:
Two Squawfish and a Broken Mirror

They shot down the rapids and could see Indians lining the banks high above them. The Indians weren't certain what to do. It was as if they were witnessing an unfolding horror that none could stop or control. It was too horrifying to watch, yet too mesmerizing to look away. The crazy white people would certainly be dashed to pieces.

Hilola jumped to the starboard side, next to Ramon, and did her best to fend them off of the boulders while the Mexican used his oar as a rudder with little effect. It was a wild ride and could have possibly been fun, had the chance of death been less.

Some people, when faced with danger, can conjure up nothing but the emotion of terror, others have the clarity of mind that allows real logical thought during the life threatening act. Ramon was of the latter persuasion and was now wondering if this is how his life would end. He looked over at

Hilola and could see the resolution in her eyes. She was captivating, beautiful, as the muscles and sinews of every part of her body tensed and flexed in reaction to the insane descent down a part of the river that not even fish would likely dare to go.

He suddenly laughed out loud. Instead of fear, the overwhelming emotion at that moment was lust, and if he'd not had an audience of Indians above, and if he'd not had to man the oar and do his best to stay upright on the craft's deck, he'd have thrown her onto the roof of the cabin and had her right then and there.

She turned to look at him, to see what preposterous thing could have possibly solicited such a guffaw from her traveling companion and could see the lust in his eyes. She laughed aloud and reached over, nearly devouring his mouth.

But the heightened sexual awareness was not to last. Now the river deceived them and fell away for a good thirty feet into a great whirlpool many times larger than what had eventually become Jimmie's watery grave. Ramon and Hilola spilled over the bow and into the angry water, the boat hurtling toward them like some giant coffin; the gods or fates, or Indian spirits intent on finishing them off here and now.

Ramon popped up first and saw the boat drift harmlessly to the western shore, intact and unscathed. He called out for Hilola. She was nowhere to be seen. He dove three times, sweeping the bottom desperately with his hands. He felt nothing, surfaced, and repeated his quest again and again. He swam to the shore, climbed the highest boulder and peered into the whirlpool, hoping for a glimpse of her.

She was there, on the bottom, her blonde hair and white dress glowing through the blue-green depths as tons of water swirled endlessly around and around, pinning her to the rocky bottom. He dove again, fighting with all his might and felt her hair. He reached further, under her head and pulled her out of the force of the vortex, up to the surface and air.

She was dead, or at least no longer breathing, and he shook her and screamed into her face. He turned her on her side and beat her soundly on the back. She sputtered and vomited great gouts of water. She was alive. He waited for the convulsive gagging and coughing and wheezing to stop. He waited for her body to register that it could get the precious oxygen it needed to keep heart and brain alive.

She fell on her back and looked up at the

sky, at the cottonwood branches overhead, and realized what had happened. She knew that she'd been to the very brink of existence, nearly going to the great beyond. She slowly sat up and now, fully conscious, smiled and looked about a little wildly, confused, feeling as if she'd been asleep for a day or more and suddenly, unexpectedly, been jolted from her slumber.

She pulled herself into a ball, knees to breasts, then, just as quickly, grabbed for Ramon needing his warmth and physical contact. She needed him to cover her up, like a great human blanket. "Hold me, Ramon, hold me. I'm so very cold."

They slept until nearly nightfall and when Ramon awoke the boat was back in the middle of the whirlpool, spinning lazily like a child's top. He waded out, chest deep, and grabbed the bowline when it twirled past him like the second hand of a slow moving watch. He pulled the boat to shore and got out several blankets. Spreading one out on the sandy shore, he carefully and lovingly undressed Hilola. He picked up the sleeping beauty and placed her gently in the middle of the blanket and then covered her with the others. He then started a fire.

They were alone again; the Indians far

upstream, likely convinced that the adventurers were no more. They were now in a long canyon with shear sides more than a hundred feet high. The walls were smooth and straight and not even Indians could negotiate them. He watched her slowly awaken.

She smiled and opened the blankets for him. He crawled next to her.

"Why are you crying, Ramon?" She pressed herself against him and quickly helped him off with his clothes.

He was not certain himself. He breathed deeply and tried his best to speak without a quivering voice. "I thought for certain I lost you." He kissed her forehead and pressed it against his cheek. "You, you were gone, Hilola. You were dead." He fought back the tears. "I thought I lost you!" He kissed her passionately on the mouth.

She kissed him back. "Now, that's more like it." She threw back one of the blankets and formed a little tent over them with the lightest one. They made the most passionate love either had ever known and Hilola wept, too, now, but not from fear or sadness, but from joy and lust and exhaustion. She lay back and pulled him to her breast. She breathed deeply and enjoyed the scent of his musky, river-washed hair.

"Remind me to get drownded more often, sweetie. I should get drownded ever dog-gone day."

They might just as well have gone through a wedding rather than a near drowning. Ramon waited on her, doted on her and could not get enough of his new prize. He really had loved her all along. And Hilola felt the same. They just seemed to fit and now they could not do enough for each other.

He went on another hunt and killed a doe. He could not find any more sheep. He brought it back to their camp. Hilola had done her best to make the area nice and proudly displayed a big squawfish that she'd caught all on her own. She was prouder of it than anything she'd done thus far. Ramon did not have the heart to tell her the fish would taste like scum covered rocks.

He prepared it and they ate. Hilola got a funny look on her face and blurted out, as she spit a mouthful of bony meat onto her plate, "This fish is awful." She looked at her plate with disdain and threw the whole of its contents into the river.

She looked at Ramon with a quizzical expression. "What the hell?"

"I'm sorry, Hilola," he suppressed a laugh,

"but you were so excited about getting us a meal. That fish you caught, squawfish, it's the most horrible tasting fish in the river. Up until now, you've been eating trout."

He worried how she'd take it and was relieved when she laughed out loud. "Squawfish? That's a funny name. Should be shitfish." She thumped him on the shoulder with her fist and laughed again. She looked him in the eye and knew he was being kind to her, kinder than any man had ever been in her life. She dropped her dress at her feet and pulled him onto their blanket bed. "Not very hungry now, anyways."

They floated down a large expanse of the river for two days. The current was slow and Ramon wasn't much inclined to row. The truth was he was smitten with Hilola and did not want to rush the journey just now. They made love many times a day and often just lay out on the deck in the sun, enjoying each other's company. They explored each other's bodies and partook of carnal offerings.

At one point he caught her gazing at him and smiled uneasily at so much attention.

"What?"

"Oh, just thinking." Hilola was suddenly a little self-conscious, the first time she'd felt that way in her entire life. "I just," she laughed. "Don't know why I'm trippin' over my words." She kissed him and they made love yet again.

They dozed and awakened together and Ramon remembered the conversation before it had been interrupted so wonderfully.

"What were you going to say, Hilola?"

"I was going to say," she shuddered a little at the thought and her face flushed, her neck now red, but not from sunburn. "I've never." She sat up resting an elbow on the deck. "I've never felt this way with a man in all my born days." She kissed him again.

"Like what?" He loved her simplicity. She was older than him by more years than either would like to admit, but she was almost childlike in her ignorance of so many things. He knew what she meant but was having fun watching her articulate her feelings, emotions, thoughts that were both new and foreign and wondrous to her.

"That feeling, like a fit, like the shakes you see on a drunkard. Like that. Never felt it in all my days."

"That's an orgasm." He felt a little strange speaking so freely about such things, but with Hilola, it felt right. He'd have no more uttered the word *orgasm* to his Spanish lover than he would to his mother or his priest. But with Hilola, it just felt natural and right.

"A what?"

"An orgasm. It's God's way of getting us to go through with it."

"With what?"

"Carrying on the species." He liked to talk philosophy with Hilola. She was a blank slate. "You've not had a baby, have you?"

"Oh, God no." She blushed at the thought.

"Well, you know what it's like, though, don't you?"

"Oh, hell, yes. Terrible painful."

"So, the orgasm, it's God's way of tricking us into having babies, producing children to carry on. God's trick to get us to do it. If it wasn't fun, we'd probably be extinct long ago."

She smiled and was glad she'd learned of orgasms, at least the kind Ramon could give her. "Well, I swear, and, Ramon, I ain't tryin' to build you up here. I've had fun with it in the past, but what you do to me, my goodness, well. I just don't know. You're a real man, Ramon, a real, real man." She kissed him again. "I ain't lyin'."

"I love you, Hilola."

She turned and suddenly sat up and pulled her knees to her chin. It was as if

Ramon had thrown a bucket of ice water on his lover's head. She looked off at the shore. He realized she was crying. "Hilola, tell me, tell me what's wrong, sweetheart. What did I say?"

She looked him in the eye. "Don't you play with me, Ramon." She wiped the tears from each eye with the palms of her hands. "Don't say love unless you mean it. Don't say love and then drop me onced we get down to Mexico. Don't do that, Ramon, just don't do it."

He pulled her into his arms and kissed her again. "I don't play that way."

But after the third day he was bored, not with Hilola, but by the slow progress they were making. "We are traveling slower than a baby can crawl."

He held her in his arms as they floated along. "What we need is a sail."

She sat up and thought about it. A sail would be nice, not that she much minded the slow progress. She worried that this dream would end and Ramon would not be with her for the rest of her days. She could think of nothing else, only being with the Mexican. But a sail would be good and it would please him. It would most definitely please her Ramon.

They'd passed a few Indian settlements in the past days. One settlement in particular, in a valley, had large tents of army canvas, apparently traded for whatever it was the white man found worth trading with the Indians.

"I bet one of them tents would make a sail. And the poles for the tent, that could be the, the, what do you call that thing, Ramon, the thing on a boat where you hang the sail?"

"Mast."

"Yeah, mast, that's right, mast. Bet we could get all that from the Indians."

The next day Hilola became the ambassador of their little expedition. She worked out a trade while Ramon was off hunting. Soon, two Indians were working away on the boat, fitting it out.

Ramon eventually returned from the hunt and watched the men at work. They were pleasant and respectful of Hilola and he watched as they smiled and waved to her and said goodbye when everything was finished. He offered his latest kill for compensation but they waved him off. They had not received, or even seemed to expect, payment and Ramon found this to be very curious, indeed. He watched Hilola proudly look the handiwork over and just as quickly lose her smile.

"What's wrong?" She looked as if someone had kicked her in the gut. Ramon looked about the same.

"Oh, I think you know what." He picked up his Winchester and walked away, looking back over his shoulder. "Still a lot of daylight left. I'm going hunting again." He marched off.

She fell asleep waiting for him and awoke the next day to Ramon diligently working on repacking the boat. He would not talk to her or even make love to her even when she paraded around nude and tried her best to get him to smile or interact in any way. She shrugged it off and soon they were sailing. It was grand. They were moving along at a minimum of a horse's canter and Hilola was simultaneously proud and put off by Ramon's indifference to the success of the vessel's conversion to a sailing yacht.

She'd finally had enough. "All right, you big baby, what's going on?"

He sat, staring blankly at the river ahead, steering the vessel as he observed and avoided shoals and rocks. "I already told you, I think you know what's wrong."

"This is stupid." She stood in front of him

to make him look her in the eye. "Tell me what's wrong!"

"You don't think I know that getting the sail and the mast and getting those Indians to do all that work had not come at a price?"

"No. I know you know it came at a price." She looked him in the eye and began to laugh; she laughed more loudly the more she thought of it. "Oh, I see." She lost the smile and suddenly became angry. "I see. The whore traded her body for all that." She pointed accusingly at the canvas in front of them. She twisted a cigarette and smoked and blew smoke at the shore and turned to look him in the eye.

"Take it back."

"Take what back?"

"Callin' me a whore."

"I didn't call you a whore."

"You did. You thought it. You thought I'd do that with someone besides you and I want you to say you're sorry for that."

"I won't."

"Then we're through."

He shrugged and worked on the sail that had caused so much tension and unhappiness between them. He half muttered to himself. "If you do such things, then what am I to think?"

"What things?" She stood, feeling a bit

smug. She'd make a good lawyer, he thought.

"You know what things. Hilola, it's bad enough it happened, don't make me say it. Don't make me say what you did."

She was furious now, furious at his superiority and his low thinking of her. "You know what I paid for all this?"

"Ah, yes, ah . . . no! But I'm not a child. I have an imagination." He was blushing now.

"I'll tell you so's you won't have to work up your dirty 'magination. Three trade knives, a broken axe, and two squawfish, and, oh, yeah, a piece of broken mirror." She turned away as he reached for her. He was devastated and humiliated by his own corrupt thoughts.

She pushed him away. "Don't touch me! Don't touch me and don't look at me. I think I might hate you." She sounded very silly and childish saying that but she meant it and now they got as far away from each other as a fourteen foot boat would allow; Hilola at the bow and Ramon astern.

He felt it as the realization washed over him, felt an ache in his heart. There was a bitter metallic tang on his tongue. It was the feelings of a man who'd done something terrible and stupid and mean. He felt like shooting himself.

CHAPTER XX:
GENTLE PIERCE

Old Pop rode with Rosario and watched Pierce be miserable. He admired the Mexicana as she was a lady and simultaneously tough as an iron rod. He wanted to talk and she sensed it. She smiled her encouragement.

"Pierce is a good boy, good heart and fearless, but he's no killer, ma'am."

She nodded and was impressed with the old man's devotion to the lad. She smiled again. "He is lucky to have you for a father."

He blushed and cleared his throat, as that was likely the kindest thing anyone had ever said to him. "Oh, I'd be proud to call him mine. But he ain't."

"Yes he is." Rosario rode and did not look at him, but instead talked at the back of her husband's head, as Hobbsie was leading them down the trail. "Being the fruit of one's loins is only a small, and the least importante part of fatherhood. It is not the thirty seconds it takes to make a baby that counts, it is the twenty years or so after that which makes the man, and Pierce, he is a good man, and you are the reason, Señor. I can tell that without knowing anything else about either one of you. You are the reason he is a good man, the reason why he is chasing his brother to save a Mexican that he does not even know, the reason why he is taking good care of that mare. You are the reason why one day, when that old Scotsman is gone, and this mean brother is gone, that your ranch will be put a right." She smiled and looked at him warmly. "You are the reason, Señor."

They arrived at a lively spot on a slow and wide part of the river and this had a real town with decent businesses and even women and children. The place was pretty clean and there were plans, to everyone's delight, for a railroad line to come through. It would settle things for sure for the people and the town if that were to happen. It seemed railroad lines always brought prosperity, or at least the promise of it. Everyone, with the exception of the steamboat operators, liked when the railroad came around.

Rosario followed Hobbsie into the town's

general store which served as post and telegraph office as well. A thin man sat behind the flimsy bars set up between host and patron at a kind of ticket counter, as one could procure riverboat passage from this place, too. He looked very much like a prisoner, locked away in his little cubicle. He nodded a respectful greeting to Rosario and waited for the marshal to speak as he eyed Hobbsie's badge. He suddenly had a thought, grinned brightly and pointed to it. "Shouldn't that be a Magen David?"

Hobbsie snapped back with a savagery Rosario had never known in her husband. *"What's it to you?"* The trip was beginning to wear on old Hobbsie's nerves.

The diminutive man threw his hands up in surrender and quickly pulled his own star out, hidden behind a cravat and hanging from a chain around his neck, revealing to Hobbsie the fellowship. Hobbs nodded just discernibly and began to relax. He'd not seen the man's yarmulke, hidden by an ample crop of bushy silver hair.

"It is nice to see another Jew for a change. Shalom Aleichem."

"Aleichem Shalom."

"How can I help you, marshal?" He looked around to see if a gentile was not with him. Jews were not generally lawmen in these

214

parts, or in any parts, really, for that matter.

"We're looking for two men. One is named Thad Hall, a very rude character and assassin, and his intended victim, a Mexican who'll be perhaps traveling down the river, named Ramon la Garza.

The clerk nodded and opened a little narrow door and beckoned them to come back to his office. He slapped a dusty chair seat with a rag and offered it to Rosario. Once they were seated comfortably around a table cluttered with many papers and forms, he poured wine and nodded again to Rosario. "Kosher." He clicked her glass and then Hobbsie's. "Your health."

She sipped it and smiled. "It is good, Señor. Thank you."

He smiled at Rosario and then spoke to them both. "Yes, it was quite exciting, but there's one more player than you mentioned. There is a beautiful German girl, oy, such a lovely." He winked at Rosario. The clerk liked Rosario very much.

Hobbs looked at his wife and nodded. Pierce would be pleased to know that la Garza was all right. Hobbs was warming up to the clerk and warming up to the wine, though he'd not let on to the man that he was not much of a Jew himself. He'd not followed his faith most of his life, whereas this man was most certainly devout. "Please, go on, Mister?"

"Blume." He reached out to shake Hobbsie's, then Rosario's hand. "Leo Blume." He held up his hand. "Let me start from the beginning." He topped off their glasses again.

"First came this Mexican and the German beauty, they'd been traveling the river in a well provisioned boat. The Mexican sent a wire to his home in Mexico." He smiled again at Rosario, proud of his post as telegraph operator. "I sent it for him. They got some supplies and moved on." He gave them a look to make certain he was making sense to them, and continued.

"So, then along comes this Thad Hall, the one you mentioned, and you are most certainly correct, a horrible fellow. Beat a young Chinese boy nearly to death, for no reason at all. Then he lay with a prostitute and you should have seen the marks he put on her." He looked at Rosario, embarrassed, "Beggin' your pardon, ma'am."

Hobbs scowled and coughed a little as his heart was fluttering again, giving him the deep tickle that had been vexing him more and more these days. He nodded to Blume. "Yes, we know him well; he's the one we're after."

"Yes, well, he was brimming with money and throwing plenty around and bragging about how he's going to gut this Mexican the way the man had done to his brother."

"So, Thad Hall, he went by land or water?"

"Oh, land. Once he learned all he could, which was nothing from me, by the way, he took off along the river. There are settlements pretty regular all the way down to the Gulf of California. I guess his intent's to intercept them along the way."

Chapter XXI: A Clue

"This one's got no hands, marshal." The sheriff was twitchier than ever. Allingham wondered if he'd not become a drunkard and derelict from all of this. He walked past him and entered the building located just on the outside of town.

"Who found her?"

"Railroad man. This place was put in by the railroad, surveyor's shack, but it's not been put to use for several years. They're planning some more work here, and the railroad worker was coming to see what was needed to get the place in order again."

It was a small single-room building with windows on all sides. It had a stove in a corner and the murderer had used it. The victim lay on the floor, as there was no bed. Her hands were, indeed, gone; amputated, obviously, by the same means used to take the feet of the previous victim.

The sheriff stood in the doorway and

watched Allingham work. Allingham called him in closer. The hapless man would have to do, as Rebecca was still too ill to assist. "What do you make of that?" He pointed to two punctures, each in the anterior part of the victim's forearms.

The sheriff shrugged and Allingham continued. "Do you smell that?" He looked the man over, prodding him to help. "Chemicals. Undertaker chemicals. He put the preservative in her arms before amputating the hands." Allingham almost exhibited a smile. "We're dealing with an undertaker. An undertaker!"

"Why'd he start doing that?"

Allingham considered it. "He's no doubt collecting these body parts. Maybe they aren't keeping in this heat. Maybe he's learning as he goes along. But he's definitely preserving them, definitely practicing the mortuary arts."

"And that's good?" The sheriff could not make a connection. Could only think that in some perverse way, Allingham was suggesting that this made it less horrible that such a person was the perpetrator of such an horrific deed.

"Yes, it's good." He looked at the sheriff as if he were observing a colossal oaf. "It narrows the field significantly. Significantly!"

Allingham turned his attention from his companion, stood back and scrutinized the room. The stove had been used. The murderer had spent some time here. He opened the stove's ashbin door and slid it out. He walked out into the sunlight and dumped the contents onto the ground. He sifted through it with his fingers. "Oh, this is good. This is so good."

He unfolded the charred remains of a cigarette paper book. The color was familiar. He could just make out the name. "These are P. Lorillard papers, from a small company in New York." He looked at the sheriff. "Have you ever seen them sold here?"

"Never." The sheriff was hopeful and watched Allingham move back into the room. He looked about, dropped to the floor and looked from ground level.

"Oh ho, it's Christmas!" He reached under the stove and removed cigarette butts, apparently meant to be thrown in the open lid of the stove. He put them in his hand and moved back out into the sunlight. "What's different with these than any butts you've seen, sheriff?"

The sheriff looked on, pensively, trying hard not to anger or disappoint the marshal.

"The way . . . , the way he's crushed them out?"

"Exactly! What we have here is a signature, my friend. We have a signature, because the murderer smokes his cigarettes down to the same length every time. He then extinguishes them, crushing them at precisely the same point, every time." Allingham held up two cigarette butts, mirror images of each other, just to prove his point.

"How'd we miss this on the others?"

Allingham snapped back. "I didn't!" He suddenly caught himself. "I mean, this is the first time he's smoked, or at least left butts."

"Not really." The sheriff looked at the floor sheepishly. "The first time, the site you didn't get to see, he smoked a lot. He left a lot of butts around. I just never thought to do anything with 'em, marshal. I'm sorry."

Allingham wanted to tell him that it was a serious blunder. He wanted to give the man hell, but it would have done no good. It would have likely put shame and a guilt on the man that he'd never overcome. He, instead, did something he'd been trying to do ever since Rebecca had come into his life; he acted with a modicum of compassion.

Allingham shrugged. "No matter."

■ ■ ■ ■

Rebecca read with interest the letter addressed to Allingham's old colleague in New York:

Sgt. Gorski:
This letter follows my wire to you. Add to investigation any strange activities by undertakers in New York and regions as far north as Boston, as far south as Pennsylvania.

Investigate P. Lorillard Tobacco Company, sales outside of NY, particularly Arizona territory.

Investigate any mutilations of red-headed women, or others, or animals.

Investigate any undertakers who've had complaints issued about them, moved, acted suspiciously.

Investigate any men at large wanted by police who fit description wired.

Investigate embalming fluid manufacturers and sales to Arizona territory.

Respond with all haste, any information, via wire to address provided.
                                    Allingham.

She looked at her husband and considered

the fact that he was more hopeful now. "So, you know more about him?"

"A little. I'm pretty certain he's an undertaker, or someone trained in the mortuary sciences. He's using the techniques of that craft. I'm pretty certain he's from New York. And we now know he's got a signature."

"The cigarettes?"

"Yes. I'm not saying no one else crushes a cigarette in such a way, but our man, he is very peculiar and methodical in how he does it." He pulled out a cigarette and demonstrated. "He smokes it down to here." Allingham tore the cigarette at the correct point. "Then he pushes down like so." Allingham demonstrated. "And what you end up with," he held the butt in front of Rebecca's face, "is this, a stub in the shape of the letter L." He smiled uneasily. "So, all we need to find is such a man with a chipped tooth, long fingernail, and shaven chin, who stinks of embalming fluid."

Rebecca laughed, knowing it was her husband's uncharacteristic attempt at a joke.

CHAPTER XXII:
RECONCILIATION

La Garza finally got her to speak, at least in the most rudimentary terms, and they agreed to camp amongst a beautiful copse of cottonwood trees next to a sandy beach. Hilola worked quietly and did not notice Ramon slip away.

He was gone many hours and finally returned just before sundown. He said nothing but, instead, walked up to Hilola who stood by the fire finishing her meal of trout and tortillas. She would not look him in the eye until he dropped to one knee and grasped her gently by her right hand.

"I am a fool and an ass and a young arrogant boy, Hilola. I want to be a man, and I know I can be, with your love." He stood up and led her along a path to an opening in the center of a little group of trees.

He'd picked flowers and had them ready for her. He had placed blankets near the fire to make a comfortable bed. A silk fire lantern made from one of Jimmie's scarves was anchored by its string near the blankets, a small candle burning in the center heating the air, causing it to be airborne where it hovered as if by magic, just about waist high.

He pointed to a letter, tethered to the whole affair.

She was pleased. She'd already forgiven him. He had moped as if his guts had been kicked out and she knew that he was as sorry. But at the same time, she felt she needed to torture him just a bit longer; long enough to make him beg. This was the best begging she could hope for.

"The Chinese write love poems and send them, with these fire lanterns, into the sky. This is my love poem to you." He held it for her to read.

Hilola blushed and looked at the paper blankly and Ramon understood. He'd not humiliate her.

"May I read it to you, Hilola? Please?"

She smiled with teary eyes and looked away, overwhelmed. She was a little embarrassed by all this romance. No man she'd ever known exhibited even the slightest notion of how to woo a woman. "Sure." She shrugged her shoulders self-consciously.

He did and then tried to launch his little lantern until she held his hand steady, clenching the string in his fist. She removed the note and folded it carefully, placing it down her dress front, over her left breast, just over her heart. "You can let it loose now, Ramon."

They watched it, hand in hand, as it rose higher and higher, then dipped down with a wind current and drifted off to the west, into the desert and out of sight. Hilola looked at Ramon and then at all his preparations. "This is kinda nice." She eyed the bed and pointed at it. "What's ya got in mind for that?"

He kissed her. "To lay with you, if you'll have me."

They loved and slept and loved some more until it was nearly daylight. The wind picked up and thunder rumbled and the rain began to fall in drops the size of quarters. Soon they were drenched and lightning was illuminating the sky and the cottonwoods all around them.

They ran for the boat and together turned it upside down. They crawled underneath and watched the day dawn. They were safe and dry and Ramon peered up at the rain pelting down in front of them. He looked up at their makeshift roof and admired it. "This is a dandy boat." He grinned a little slyly at Hilola. "How'd you manage to get it?"

She turned her back on him and he knew he'd said something dreadfully wrong. "Hilola, what is it?"

She turned to face him, crying and distraught. "Men died 'cause of this boat, Ramon. Two men. Jimmie kilt 'em."

"Oh." Ramon suddenly felt guilty at the thought of using the dead men's traps. "I see."

She turned and looked him in the eye frantically. "I, I didn't know he was goin' to kill 'em Ramon, I swear. I ain't a killer, Ramon." She began speaking, rushing the words, as if they were coming by a force of their own. It was a kind of cathartic purging of the worst experience of her life. "I was supposed to just tease 'em a little. Two old men, prospectors or somethin'. I don't know what they was doin' out there in the middle a nowhere, but we had a wagon and it was full a gold and we needed to cross the river. And these men, they was campin' and Jimmie told me to keep 'em occupied. Ya know?

"You know how, Ramon, and I did, and he was just supposed to get up behind 'em and make 'em give us the boat. God, he shot 'em both in the back a the head! Oh, God,

227

Ramon, oh God."

"Shh, shh, Hilola, calm yourself." He held her and she rocked in his arms. He'd never seen her so distraught. "Jimmie scared you, didn't he, Hilola?"

She looked about wildly, as if talking about him might conjure him up. "I know he, he, wasn't very big, an' all, Ramon, but, but . . ." She couldn't finish.

"I know, Hilola. Sometimes, monsters don't have to be big. Sometimes, the little monsters are the worst of all." He held her. "I'm mighty sorry for all this, Hilola, mighty sorry you got mixed up with that man. I'm mighty sorry you saw those men killed. It shouldn't have happened to you. It shouldn't have."

"I dream about 'em all the time, Ramon. All the time. They was nice old men. They was a pair of soldiers from the great war. One was a Yankee and the other a Reb. They told me . . . told me they survived all sorts a horrible things, and they were like brothers. And, and . . . Oh God, I can see their faces when I close my eyes."

"I know, I know." He thought about his own nightmares, the images of his father shot down by a firing squad and he hadn't even witnessed it. He had only been told about it. He could not imagine what Hilola was going through.

He patted her gently. "Now it's done, and we'll make it right. When we get back to our hacienda, we'll find out who the men were and we'll make it right with their families. We'll, we can even make them a grave in our family cemetery." He pushed back her tear-soaked locks and kissed her gently on the forehead.

She grabbed him around the neck and hugged him and wetted his cheek with her tears. "Oh, Ramon, y're the best. The nicest fellow I ever known. Y're better'n I should get. Better'n I deserve."

He smiled as he knew the answer to his question, yet asked it nonetheless. He needed to cheer her and get her mind off the memory of the two slain men. "Then I am forgiven?"

She pushed her head into his chest and felt him breathing into her ear. "Gosh, yeah."

He was encouraged as she started to settle down. At least she wasn't crying anymore.

"Marry me, Hilola? Marry me, please?"

She sat up and looked into his eyes just as a flash of lightning turned everything blue. She could see by his expression that he meant it. She also saw a very young man, a boy really, and it made her even sadder. She wanted to cry again. The dream was too good to be real. In Hilola's life there were always many great, even fantastic, dreams but they'd never become reality. Not one had ever panned out, and here was another one, and this is why she wanted to cry.

He sensed it. "What is it, Hilola? Don't you love me?"

"Ramon," she was not an articulate woman, but she knew what was right and what was realistic and what was preposterous. This whole idea was both unrealistic and preposterous.

"I can't read, Ramon." She put a hand to his lips before he could protest or argue. "I'm thirty one years old and you are, what, twenty?"

"Twenty-one in three months."

"I been, I been with lots a men, Ramon." She looked him in the eye, a little defiantly. "I'm not a whore, Ramon, not a whore. But a woman like me, well, it ain't easy makin' it through life out here. In these wild lands, without a man, without means, and, well," she looked as though she might not be able to finish what she had to say. "I, I've been with a lot a men. Jimmie wasn't even the worst."

She looked at him again. The light was dawning and she could see him well. He had a look that was confident, a look that made it clear to her that he was not in the least deterred. She wasn't remotely getting through to him. She thought about what else to say. "I, I ain't smart, Ramon. You're a smart man, an educated man, and I ain't." She pulled his declaration from her breast. "I can't even read this."

"You are ignorant, Hilola, not stupid." He held up a hand when he saw the beginning of a hurt look on her face. Hilola did not understand the difference between the two terms. He needed to make her understand it wasn't an insult to be considered ignorant. "Ignorance is a lack of knowledge, Hilola, nothing more. I'm ignorant of many things."

She grinned uneasily. She could not imagine Ramon being without knowledge of anything. He seemed to know everything, which was astonishing to her, as she'd only ever known stupid men, and Ramon was so young. It had seemed to her that he'd already packed a lifetime of knowledge into his young brain.

"Yes, ignorance. It's not a bad thing, Hilola. It just needs to be overcome. Ignorance goes away with learning. You can fix ignorance, but you can't fix stupid." He kissed her again. "And you are by no means stupid." She laughed and that emboldened him. "Marry me, right now. Right here, right now."

"That's silly." She blushed and shrugged her shoulders again. "There ain't no justice a the peace, or riverboat captain or minister around." She looked about as if to make certain one had not materialized, somehow conjured up by Ramon for the occasion.

"No, but there's God and there's you and there's me." He held her hand in his. "When we get to a place that has one of them, we'll make it official. But as far as I'm concerned, if you say yes now, we're married."

"But I'm so *old,* Ramon. I'm old, and you can't fix that. Can't fix that with anything."

"You're not old to me, Hilola. You're my love. You . . ." He kissed her gently on the cheek. "I thought I was in love in Spain, but now, now that I've met you, I know I didn't have the first idea about love. So please, Hilola, please make me happy. Please say yes. If you do, I'll make certain that you are loved and worshipped and cared for, for the rest of your days. I swear it, Hilola. I swear it."

She opened the love note and looked it over again. She thought on it. She'd seen the words, could even make some of them out. Was it all that simple? She felt the flutter deep down inside. Perhaps it could happen. Perhaps. Maybe this was a good one; a good man who loved her for who she was, not for her sex, or her beauty or her body, but for Hilola.

She looked him in the eye and tears ran down her cheeks. She smiled and sniffed hard to stop her nose from running and tried to gain control.

"Okay, darling, okay. But first, read this to me again, read it to me one more time."

Chapter XXIII:
The Esmeralda

Rosario watched the Esmeralda tear up a sandbar and marveled at its power. They were the last of a dying breed, these paddle-wheelers, at least on this river. The railroad made them obsolete on the Colorado. They used to run the length of the river, from the Gulf of California all the way up to the Mormons, but now they merely acted as feeders to the east-west routes of the railroad. The stern-wheelers were king when it came to navigating the river.

They had a shallow draft, were powerful, and easily worked against the downstream currents. When they encountered a sandbar too shallow to navigate over, the pilots simply turned the craft around and attacked the obstruction with the powerful wheel, throwing up a shower of brown water to clear the way as they backed and chewed through the silt encumbrance.

"She's something all right," Leo Blume

stood beside the Mexicana, pleased to be the one to act as guide and show her such a sight. "And once she docks, madam . . . I'm telling you, you'll have one of the best meals south of San Francisco."

And Leo Blume was right. They dined and were great celebrities. Blume knew the captain well, a German from a town in Bavaria not far from Blume's ancestral home. They were great friends and often commiserated over the impending death of the stern wheelers.

The captain was a good man and very kind. He insisted that Rosario sit next to him at the table. They could all relax a little, now, as they knew that Ramon la Garza was alive and at least in good enough health to travel on the river; and that Thad Hall was pretty far behind him.

The stalwart German would hear a train whistle off in the distance and grimace. "Oh, those damnable contraptions, all that rocking and click-clacking. No one can ride in comfort in such a terrible thing." He smiled widely at Rosario. "Have you ever been a guest on one of our ships, madam?"

"No, I have not, Señor." She looked around the dining room and admired the opulent décor. Despite the decline in business, the captain kept his craft in top shape.

He was proud of it, and this was evident by the way he worried over it so.

Even Hobbs was relaxing a little. She smiled at him as he sat and ate and enjoyed the excellent meal and fine place setting for a change. Hobbs liked comfort. Rosario nodded to Pierce and Old Pop who looked out of place.

Despite the fact that the old Scotsman was very wealthy, he never wasted time on such frivolity, and neither top hand nor son had much experience with such things. She caught Pierce watching her eat, aping her actions. He was a good, albeit ignorant, boy.

"Are you reassured by the news, Pierce?" Rosario hoped to get at least the modicum of a smile out of the lad.

"Yes, ma'am. I only wish," he thought of a question and looked past Rosario and to their host. "Captain, how is it traveling down the river, from here on?"

The German smiled. "The river is very low, Mr. Hall. The water has been low for a year now, which makes for two problems. One is that the rapids are worse, as there is not so much water running over the rocks, which we can typically just float over. And two, the sandbars. But if your man, the man you are after, has made it past this settlement, he'll be fine. Progressing slowly, but fine."

Pierce looked at Old Pop. It made him uneasy, as he thought that his brother would certainly catch up to the Mexican. He leaned close to his old mentor and whispered so as not to be overheard by the rest, particularly Rosario. "I don't think we really ought to be sittin' here, Old Pop. We're wastin' time in all this."

At this, Old Pop had a thought. "Eh, Captain, where do you go next?"

"Oh, on down to the very end, to Mexico. Once they're finished unloading, and then reloading, we'll be off. We should make good time from here, south. We only stop briefly along the way, to drop off mail and pick up and discharge passengers."

They rested at Blume's boarding house that night, and Old Pop made the proposition to Hobbs. Hobbs and Rosario would travel by boat, and he and Pierce would travel by horse, hitting all the settlements on the way to Mexico. This way they could try to intercept the Mexican and his female companion on the way.

It made good sense, but Rosario was not so certain. She worried over what would happen if the two caught up to Thad. It would no doubt not turn out well, and someone would die. She was not certain if it would be the one who needed killing.

She lay in bed with Hobbs that night and shared her concerns. Hobbs held her and thought about it. He himself was happy with the plan. Though he was concerned for young Pierce and his companion, the reality of all this was slowly coming to weigh on him. He was no lawman. He was old and tired, all the time. He, like Allingham, was coming to hate more and more, having to deal with bad men.

They were both tired of it. They wanted shed of it. Rebecca's money had made his life easier just as much as it had Allingham's. He was no leech, and earned his keep as housekeeper and secretary to them all. The Halsted and Singh fortune provided him a warm, safe and comfortable way to live out the winter of his life.

As he rested in one of Blume's comfortable beds, the idea of traveling south to Mexico in a comfortable stateroom was much more appealing to him than living rough in the desert and in little no-name settlements along the river. In fact, the more time he spent along the river, the more the memories of the hellhole, Canyon Diablo, preyed on his mind. He thought of Francis nearly every day. Losing the lad was one of the hardest things he'd had to bear in his long and tumultuous life.

Pierce was probably more responsible for those memories than anything else, as there was something disturbingly similar about the two men. True, Francis was much less sullen. He had been happier, always cheerful, and fearless; and very capable of the kind of barbarity necessary to keep the animals at bay.

Pierce was not an aggressive man but he was, in other ways, a lot like the young deputy from Pennsylvania. Pierce was a good and moral young man. He was handsome and caring, and that was what made Hobbs think of Francis. He was glad it was dark, as he found himself crying and didn't want Rosario to see him in such a state.

He wiped his eyes with the back of his hands and tried hard to stop the quivering in his voice. He sat up on the edge of the bed and cleared his throat, as was his habit. Rosario rubbed his back. Nothing could fool her.

He began to speak, to give a good argument that would sound like something other than a defense of his desire to take his ease. Rosario interrupted him.

"You are sad, my love."

He blew his nose hard; wiped it and then his cheeks with his handkerchief. "Just a little overwhelmed. Thinking of Francis again."

"This is all a bad business, and we are old. We should be preparing for a baby and, instead, we are chasing a bad man and you are remembering the old days and all our friends." She pulled him back into bed and held him as she would a child.

"I feel selfish as, I have to admit, traveling rough has been preying on my mind." He held her, almost desperately, "And putting you in danger, making it necessary for you to use your scattergun. Well, I just don't know. I just don't."

He sat up again and belched and felt sick to his stomach. His heart was fluttering like a butterfly's wings. He had trouble breathing and coughed to settle the tickle deep down. Rosario got up and found her peppermints. She gave him one and it helped a little.

"Rosario, this law work, like soldiering, is for the young, not for two old birds like us."

"You are right, my love." She found a washcloth and wetted it and wiped his forehead. She put him back to bed and fussed over him and settled him down.

"Tomorrow, we will go on the steamboat as planned. It is a good plan and it is what we will do."

He fell asleep in her arms and awoke to the stern-wheeler's whistle, blowing off in the distance. Rosario prayed into his chest and felt him stir. She looked up and smiled.

"Sleep a little?"

"Yes, a little."

"Why don't you pray, my love?"

He didn't know the answer. Then thought about it. "I, well, I've, I don't know, Rosario."

"You need to pray and you need to remember Francis more, not less. I know you believe in God. Your God, your Jewish God, no?"

"Yes." His headache was coming back, and the tickle was bad deep down in his chest, he felt his heart doing flip-flops again. He shifted his weight to hold her more comfortably. "I'm not much of a Jew, Rosario."

"But you believe?"

"Yes. I guess so." He thought about it. "I, something Mr. Singh said, has got me thinking. You know, the man is without fear of any kind?"

"Sí, I know this thing. Hira is one with his God. He fears nothing in this world."

241

"Well, he said that his turban, his hair, his beard, the fact that he stands out, even in his own land, is an important part of his faith. And, well, I, you know, we Jews, the good ones, the devout ones, we're the same. You saw Blume, you know he stands out like a sore thumb, especially here. And I, well, I turned from that path long ago. Rosario, I feel a regular damned coward for it."

"Tell me why you did this thing, my love. I do not believe it is because you are a coward, just as I do not believe that you want to forget Francis."

"We Jews." He sat up and looked Rosario in the eye. "Do you remember Blume's comment, when he saw us at first? Do you remember when he looked beyond us, looking for a gentile? Do you know why?"

She shrugged.

"It's because Jews don't do these things. Jews aren't lawmen, not deputy US Marshals. Not because we don't want to do them, or that we are not good at doing them, it is because we are not permitted to do them. It is why we have been the moneylenders, and business owners and, always, always on our own. We are on our own. We must make our own way in the world, because no one will have us otherwise, Rosario. And I turned away from that, turned away and tried to hide out in the West. I abandoned my faith and my family. And I was doing well enough, and then you came into my life; you and Allingham and Singh. And lovely Rebecca and her father. You all came into my life and took me in, accepted me for what I was, and now I feel ashamed. I feel like a coward."

He looked at her sadly. "Mr. Blume could do it. He did it, endured it; and I could not. And now I'm sad and sorry and tired. I don't want to go after this Thad Hall or have to deal with any of this. I, I'm just tired, Rosario. Just tired."

She sat up and got out of bed and began packing up their things. She left the room and came back and had something of Blume's and began combing Hobbs's hair and fussing over him. When she was finished, she pulled out a hand mirror from her carpet bag and showed him his reflection.

"This is one of Leo's. When we get back home, we will get you your own."

Chapter XXIV:
Samplers

Rebecca Allingham sat staring at the samplers through a magnifying glass belonging to Mr. Singh. She felt good as the morning sickness had passed and there had been no murders recently. She looked at Mr. Singh and smiled and went back to her examination of the missing school teacher's work.

"Come here, Bapu. Sit with me."

He complied and looked at what had so much of her attention. Mr. Singh was not as encouraged as Rebecca. He feared that it would be just a matter of time before they found the poor young woman dead, but Rebecca held out hope. The samplers seemed to give her renewed encouragement and that at least this horrible part of the story would turn out well.

"She *is* a clever girl," she looked at each letter of the alphabet carefully. Both samplers were identical versions of the alphabet, as the teacher had a habit of making one for every student under her care and, at first glance, could not be told apart. "There must be a clue here somewhere."

Singh shrugged. "Perhaps she is just trying to keep the communication going. Trying to get the murderer to reveal himself and trying to keep herself alive to the rest of the world."

Singh suddenly pulled one of the pieces closer. "Rebecca, look here." He pointed to a letter. "She's changed the lower right corner stitch, here."

"I saw that. But, no, you are right. Look, not all the letters, just some. She held out the fabric at arm's length while Singh put on his reading glasses.

Rebecca became animated. "Here, and here, and here, and here." She got up and pulled some writing paper and a pencil from the desk. She sat down as Singh began calling letters out.

In short order, Rebecca had the following written out: E-I-L-M-V. They worked on the second piece of fabric, which revealed: C-E-F-I-O. She looked up at Singh. "It *is* a cipher."

They were interrupted by Allingham and, shortly thereafter, Rebecca's father and Dr. Webster followed.

The doctor called out to her in his usual

cheerful tone. "And how is the patient to-day?"

"Fine, doctor."

Allingham interrupted. "I just got a message from the sheriff. We've had another one, down in Phoenix. Not a prostitute this time." He looked through the morning's mail and tucked a large envelope from Stosh Gorski under his arm.

"I'm off to the train." He touched her gently on the arm and looked over what she and Singh had been working on. He gave Rebecca a look that she soon understood. He did not want the doctor privy to the clues or the samplers sent by the school teacher. The man was a nuisance and more a distraction than help.

"I can accompany you if you like, marshal." The annoying doctor peered over Rebecca's shoulder, holding his hat in both hands, looking much like an overgrown rodent. Allingham ignored him and marched off to the train station.

He was met by the sheriff who stood, forlornly at the railway platform. The man did not want to go through another examination of the corpse with Allingham, whom he found to be morbidly overly thorough. He settled into a regular funk these days whenever he was confronted with any business related to the murders. He sighed in relief when Allingham ordered him to stay put.

"I'd rather you follow up on a few things for me, sheriff." Allingham gave him a list of tasks and hurried off. The sheriff nodded as he wiped his sweaty brow.

CHAPTER XXV:
HOPIS

The lovers sailed south for a full day without seeing another human being. They were in the regular habit now of stopping every time a pretty piece of landscape presented itself, and would swim and love and sleep for hours at a time. Ramon no longer felt compelled to rush back home and waves of guilt would periodically wash over him at the thought of leaving his men to do all the work on the hacienda while he played with his Amazonian princess.

She caught him in a particularly pensive mood and kissed him out of his musings. "What's got you thinking so hard, lover?"

"Oh." He sat up and brushed the seat of his trousers clean. "Just wondering how the boys are getting on at home." He looked up at the sky, as if to gauge the time of year and then turned his attention to Hilola. He kissed her again and smiled. "I think you might be a witch."

She smiled. "How's that?"

"Because you have cast a spell on me and I don't want to do anything but be with you."

She grinned and was happier than she'd been in her life. "I'm glad you said that."

She fairly knocked him to the ground and kissed him. "So, do you think they'll like me all right at the ranch?" He could see the fear in her eyes. She was still not convinced she'd be anything more than an embarrassment to him.

"Oh, trust me. These men are men — the best of men — and they love women. We treat our women well on the ranch. And you, my Hilola, are going to break their hearts."

She was becoming distracted and whispered into his ear, "It's not the men I worry about."

"Oh, the women will like you just fine. They are pretty down there, and you will maybe give them a reason to spend some extra time in their beds satisfying their men, but other than that, you'll be fine."

"And the most important one of them, your mother?"

Ramon lied, "Oh, she'll love you all right." His mother would actually despise his woman. He shrugged, "And anyway, there is no man worth his salt who will let his mother influence him regarding which woman he takes for a wife."

They sailed again, through the afternoon, past an encampment of Indians who waved to them and called out in their native tongue. Little ones scampered up onto some high rocks on the bank to look down at them and one, the smallest of the lot, not more than three, suddenly toppled over and fell not thirty feet from the boat. She sank like a rock and suddenly Hilola was overboard, swimming with all her might. She dove again and again, as she'd done for Jimmie, as Ramon had done for her, and after the third dive emerged with the little package, as limp as if she'd been turned to a sack of wet flour.

Ramon met them on the western bank. He secured the boat then waded to help with the drowned child.

Soon the Indians surrounded them and the grandmother of the little one scooped the baby up into her arms. She pounded on the child until the toddler was brought back to life. Everyone cheered and soon Hilola was swept up, as if the group had suddenly formed a kind of strange singular body. Ramon was left dripping wet, by the boat, not certain of what was to happen next.

This group was Hopi. Ramon knew of them from stories since his childhood. These were the pueblo people, great farmers and builders, and this particular tribe had clung to the old ways, despite the incessant movement of whites, the railroad, and stern-wheelers constantly pushing their way through the lands of the Indian peoples.

They were far from home, though, and this surprised Ramon. The Hopis were not typically found so far south.

Ramon changed to dry clothes and was soon visited by two young men who would escort him to their village. It was several days hard walking to the northeast. He was sequestered from Hilola, who was now happily traveling with the women and children who'd run up next to her and lightly pull on her golden hair, giggle, and run away.

He didn't mind much. It was true, he'd lose time getting back home, but he also knew he didn't have much choice in the matter and resolved to just let it happen. The Hopis were kind people, peace loving and gentle and Ramon knew they'd not fight him if he bucked them, but he didn't want to do that. He didn't want to offend them and, by their actions, he could tell they thought a great debt had to be repaid.

Ramon was gracious enough to let them repay it.

They were very different from the Indians he'd known in Mexico. They had an unusual way of wearing their hair in bangs down to their eyebrows, covering their foreheads in a way he'd never seen before in any Indians, whites or Mexicans.

This bunch was on a foray that took them far from their land. Ramon soon realized they were taking him and Hilola back to their Pueblos, out of the territory of the Navajos, Yumas and Cocopahs.

It served as another example for Ramon of the inevitable destruction of such a rich culture. The American and the Mexican movement into the land inevitably kicked things into motion that resulted in Hopis having to wander, Yumas to cut firewood for the stern-wheelers, and Navajos to scratch out an existence on lands that would not sustain a rattler.

They were all business in travel, however, and the Hopis did not stop until it was nearly dark. The women went to work quickly preparing the evening meal, and Hilola played with the children, who busily braided and re-braided her hair. She smiled coyly at Ramon, as these people were the first, other than her lover, to give her such royal treatment. She enjoyed it very much.

They had a good meal and Hilola was finally permitted to leave her new admirers and bed down with Ramon. She snuggled against him and whispered in his ear. "What do they fix to do with us, sweetheart?"

"Oh, eat us."

"What?"

"Sure, eat us sure as shooting."

He grinned a little and Hilola knew he was teasing her. She slapped him on the shoulder and laughed.

"I don't know what they want to do with us, Hilola, but you are a heroine now. You are probably going to be made a princess."

"Aw, that's silly." She blushed and shrugged her shoulders up. "Didn't do nothin', really. They'd a got that little girl, sure enough."

"Well," he yawned and knew Hilola would need his attention before bedding down for the night. He covered her with a blanket and went to work. "They think it's something, that's for certain."

When they finally arrived at their destination, Ramon was treated to the first inhabited pueblos he'd ever encountered. All the others he'd ever seen were ancient ruins and fallen into decay.

There'd be a celebration and Hilola was the guest or rather, goddess, of honor, as a council had immediately been called by the cacique, or chief of this town. Ramon's escorts delivered him to a special house, next door to the chief's abode, which was comprised of a suite of adobe-constructed rooms. He did not see Hilola at this point and did not bother to ask for her. He knew she was in good hands, and did not want to appear rude or anxious in front of his special hosts.

This town was populated by several hundred inhabitants. After a good meal in a neatly appointed apartment, Ramon decided to do some exploring. He climbed up the ladder until he was on the roof of his apartment. He looked down on the irregularly laid out streets. He could see by the sun's orientation, that they ran roughly north and south, and that the kivas all faced east.

He marveled at the technology, as many of the pueblos were as tall as four stories, neatly constructed of stone laid in mortar. Terraces were created by a means of stepping back the second story, and then the third and fourth. Access to all rooms was via the roof, with ladders.

Here and there naked children could be

seen, scurrying about like wild little animals. It was hot this day and Ramon suddenly felt very sleepy. He climbed back down the ladder to the cool dark of his first floor apartment. It felt good there, so cool he needed a blanket. It smelled good: of woven mats and dry earth and wood smoke. He slept for hours until he was awakened by the same two men who'd escorted him to the village from the river.

He was taken to a new building with a large central room and was finally greeted by the cacique and several pretty women, who wore their long hair in dramatic loops or curls on either side of their heads.

Food was placed before him: stew of goat's meat in earthen bowls, and bread not unlike his own native tortillas. Still, Hilola was nowhere to be seen and Ramon could tell that a great celebration was being planned. He surmised it would commence once the meal was finished. This was not concluded until a dessert of dumplings, melons and peaches were laid out and consumed.

He communicated in a kind of Mexican patois that reminded him again of some of the natives on his hacienda. The people were talkative and seemed to enjoy his company. He told the group of his travels with Hilola and they found this very interesting. They asked many questions and were keen to know if Hilola was taken. Ramon indicated in his most articulate manner, that Hilola was, in fact, his wife. The men were satisfied, albeit slightly disappointed.

At full dark, Ramon was directed to another kiva, this one a large subterranean chamber. Access was gained by descending a ladder. In here, Ramon was greeted by ten or twelve shamans. The leader was a large man, significantly taller than Ramon, with a shaved head.

The leader recited several incantations in a tongue Ramon did not understand, and each was, in turn, repeated by the others.

All around them were tablets and statues of various local representations: animals and plants. Rain and corn were the most prevalent subjects of the icons, this ritual would be, as were all the tributes, an appeal for such. Rain and a good harvest were pivotal to the survival of this tribe.

Finally, after much prayer and recitation, the women arrived, Hilola bringing up the rear, the last to descend the ladder. She saw Ramon standing in the corner and smiled coyly at him. He thought back to the memory of his cousins receiving their first Holy Communion. Hilola looked every bit as devout and proud.

Hilola was chosen as one of three to participate in this ceremony. This was a great honor. One woman was quite old, Hilola apparently represented the middle-aged, and a young girl, representing youth, made up the trio. All had a cincture of woven cloth covering their pubic region, otherwise they were nude. Ramon felt that his heart would explode. The idea of Hilola bared for all to see made him feel, not jealous or even embarrassed, but proud. She was stunning, with skin bronzed to nearly the color of her Indian companions, her golden locks tied in the custom of the maidens, with great blonde rings of plaited hair resting on either side of her head. She stood solemnly, without her usual ubiquitous smirk, as she copied the solemnity of her female companions. She was offering the respect due the situation at hand.

They eventually stood in a line, in a corner of the kiva, after much singing and dancing and recitation by the shaman. The bald priest approached each one. Taking in a mouthful of water colored with yellow pigment, he blew a fine mist over the face, neck, shoulders, and breasts of each woman. He then grabbed up more pigments of many colors and, with his fingers, decorated them over the yellow groundwork he'd previously applied by mouth.

For the rest of the night, the three women stayed with the shamans and Ramon, dancing as the men chanted and sang. It was exhausting and exhilarating. The fatigue caused by the constant utterances and dancing put them all in a dreamlike state and only after the sun came up were the two lovers finally reunited in Ramon's apartment.

They were given breakfast to be eaten alone. Finally they stretched out on the grass mat of a bed, and Hilola made love to Ramon, still wearing the wildly painted body decoration and native hairstyle. It was as if they had both transcended their earthly shells and were now living the life of another, otherworldly creature.

Ramon woke her as he gazed at his love, now minus the loincloth. She smiled at the lust in his eyes. "What are you doing?"

She stretched and looked even more appealing to him, lying on their grass mat bed.

"Oh, just admiring my pretty Hopi goddess."

"Hopi goddess, that's silly."

"No it's not. You did a wonderful thing, saving that child and," he looked about, hoping to find an example, but didn't. "You know, they make little dolls of creatures, spirits, and I bet somewhere, at this very moment, someone is making one of you. I'd swear it, Hilola, I'd swear it."

"Well, that's all they get of me." She pulled him onto her body and looked down, disappointed that the paint was now fully dry and beginning to flake off. "You get everything else."

Chapter XXVI:
The Trail of Destruction

They were always at least three days behind Thad, but it was easy to track him, as he left a path of destruction at every place that had significant habitation. He'd made many enemies: saloon rats, gamblers, whores, anyone and everyone who hung around the seedier places. They were treated to Thad's worst.

His list of enemies was growing by the day, and Pierce and Old Pop were confounded that the man had not yet met his match. It seemed it would just be a matter of time before he'd meet the same sticky ending that Donny had. But Thad just kept plugging away.

"What gets me, Old Pop, is that someone's not gone ahead and put a ball through his head or a blade through his liver yet. Hell, I know he's big and all, but we've met some tough hombres along the way. I thought sure Thad would meet his match down along the river by now."

Old Pop nodded and rolled a smoke and handed it to his companion. He rolled another and stuck it in his mouth. "Gotta give the devil his due, Pierce. He's a tough one, your brother, and big as a mountain. He knows how to bully folks, sure enough. Guess some would say it's really his only talent."

"Amen to that."

They, on the other hand, were treated well wherever they went. Old Pop schooled Pierce on the importance of not letting anyone know that he was related to his low-down brother. Old Pop did not mind letting on to folks, perhaps a little deceptively, that they were working in some sort of law capacity. They gained many friends and admirers this way, as folks were happy to aid anyone who might be ultimately responsible for giving the devil, Thad, his due.

They slept rough and Old Pop was missing the Señora's victuals and company. They were close in age and Old Pop had not been with a woman for many years, as the woman he nearly called his wife died a long time ago. He thought a lot about the marshal, Hobbs, and could tell the man didn't look well. It got him to thinking that he might keep an eye in that direction. Perhaps the pretty Mexican lady would become available in the not too distant future.

He regretted that thought. It was wicked and he was not a wicked man. He liked Hobbs and Hobbs had treated him square. Hobbs had taken good care of Pierce and the Mexican boys and Old Pop put that thought out of his mind. He threw some more wood on the fire and hunkered down under his blanket and had just begun to doze when Pierce started talking in his low, just before shut-eye tone.

"You know, Old Pop, I was thinkin'."

"Uhuh?"

"After all this is done, after we get Thad back up to the ranch and get my Pa settled down, there's not goin' to be much for us there."

"Uhuh."

"Maybe we should try our hand down in Mexico. Bet la Garza would give us work."

"Hmm."

"You don't like that idear?"

"Not much."

"Why not?"

Old Pop thought on it. Why didn't he like it?

"Well, one thing, there's not much pay down there, especially for wranglers. It's back-breakin' work as it is. Not much sense gettin' paid a quarter of what you can earn in the states for the same hard damned work."

"Yeah, but it don't cost near as much to live down there neither. Low pay, low output for grub and such. Kind of all works out."

"I don't know." He thought of the real reason. He went ahead and just said it. "That's just as much your ranch up there as Thad's. Really more so. You work harder than anyone else up there and, Pierce, sorry for sayin' a cruel thought, but your Pa, he ain't goin' to live forever."

"Yeah, well, you gotta point. But, Old Pop, men like my father have a way of surprising you. He could live another twenty, thirty years. Hell, his Pa lived to be eighty three. Pa's only sixty five now. My God, you could be pushin' up daisies, and I could be a regular old fart by the time he kicks off. Don't want to spend the rest of my days babysittin' him and making money for the ranch so's Thad can run around like a young buck, pissin' it all away."

He stood up and stretched his back and took a last cup of coffee. He watched the old man's eyes reflect firelight. Whatever he'd do, it would have to be with the old man, there was no question about that.

"Maybe we could start our own operation."

"How?"

"Just go ahead and do it. You got money, don't you?"

"Well, a little."

"Me, too. I got six hundred dollars saved."

"Do tell!" Old Pop was impressed. His whole nest egg was just three quarters of that, and he was nearly three times older than Pierce.

"We could maybe run down and buy horses from them Mexican boys and run them up north somewhere. Maybe Texas. Sell 'em, maybe double or triple our money, then turn that into stock. Hell, land's cheap enough. Hell, we wouldn't even have to stay in Arizona. We could go north, south, go anywhere. California, Old Pop. Anywhere."

It was an exciting idea, the kind of idea enterprising men hatched late at night by the fire, when they were ready to go to bed. The kind of idea that sounded remarkably simple and a sure thing when lying in your sleeping bag with a full belly and a hot fire to keep you warm and dry. The kind of idea that sounded idiotic and preposterous the next morning when the fire was out and your back was stiff and wet and cold.

Old Pop propped himself up on an elbow and looked at the red glow of a heavy branch engulfed in blue flame. He looked at the lad and could see it in his eyes, he wasn't just pipe dreaming. He meant it and the old man wished he was twenty years younger. He wished he was a better man for it, wished he could be a good partner to his favorite lad.

"I don't know, son." He turned and looked up at the thick sea of stars, dotting and illuminating the sky. "I'd not want to take your money, Pierce." He rubbed his temples. "It would have to be split according to the investment."

"No it wouldn't. Fifty-fifty, down the line. What you got to put up, Old Pop?"

He was embarrassed to say. Saving money was never Old Pop's forte. "Three hundred seventy eight dollars and sixty three cents."

"So, let's say, my six and your three, that's nine hundred. We could probably get la Garza to sell us his horses, if we take delivery at his ranch, for say, seventy a piece. Those are some dandy horses, and I hear the Navajos are getting two hundred for a decent saddle pony. Hell, Old Pop, we could net out, what is it? A hundred thirty each."

Old Pop was getting a little excited. Any kind of scheming made him happy, made him dream a little. He pulled out a pencil and paper from his vest pocket. "So, let's say we hold out a hundred for grub and expenses, we got eight hundred, divided by seventy, that's, let's see, that's eleven horses with thirty dollars left over."

"Hell, you and me, we can handle a remuda of eleven horses, that's nothin'. So, eleven times a hundred and thirty, that's . . . Hell, that's fourteen hundred dollars."

"Fourteen thirty. Dang, son, almost a years' pay."

"Yeah, and for what? A couple months' worth a work. And we'd be livin' rough, beans and game. Horses could just eat grass the whole way. Old Pop, what ya say?"

Old Pop thought of Pierce in bandit country. The boy would be useless in a gun battle. He had another thought. "Your Pa, that sour old bastard, he did it, Pierce. He made something for himself, and you're ten times smarter than him."

Pierce's face dropped. The realization of it hit him like a hammer blow. "Yeah, and he's ten times meaner."

"Yeah, well, mean don't make a business man."

Pierce looked at the old man a little dubiously. "You sure about that, Old Pop? Pa used to rant and rave how he was fightin' every day to keep his money. Always goin' on about how rotten the banks and the lawyers treated him. I don't know, I just," he looked a little desperately at his companion. "I don't know. Don't know that I'm up to fightin' all them smart people."

"Well, I do. Your Pa, he's a regular ass to deal with. Treat people fair and you don't need lawyers. Manage your money and you don't need any danged bank. We don't borrow no money from a bank, no reason for a bank to be in our business. Hell, son, when we was up there with them rich people in Flagstaff, well, I was listenin' in on their conversation. That Indian fellow with that scarf around his head, what's he, some sort a A-rab or somethin'?"

"I don't know what he is."

"Anyways, he was talkin' and that other old fellow, the English fellar, Halsted, they were all talkin' about some business and they even talked about it. The dark one, he says you can be a good business man and a good man. You don't need to make your way by cheatin' and dirty dealin'. And I believe that."

Pierce thought some more. "So, if we get over fourteen hundred, then we go on and get back to la Garza and buy that many more horses from him. That's what? Hell, too many for me to figure out. But let's just round it up, a hundred horses, at seventy profit, that's seven thousand. Jesus, Old Pop, we could have seven thousand dollars in a couple a years. We can buy a lot a cattle for seven thousand."

They both eventually lay back and let the fire die down as it wasn't all that cold on this night and thought on the fantasy cattle company. It would be good grist for some nice dreams.

Chapter XXVII:
The Pretty Secretary

It was more of the same, except that the brutality, as expected, had been magnified exponentially. This one had her ears cut off and, by the evidence, Allingham surmised that they'd been ritualistically collected and not eaten.

The face was not recognizable, as it had been beaten so savagely that it was nothing more than a mass of destroyed materials. He found the candlestick used in this debasement, and could see from the blood, murderer used his right hand to swing the improvised club again and again.

He detected no odor of chemicals this time, and surmised that the embalming was reserved for limbs or perhaps torsos, but ears would not require so much attention for preservation. He crawled around on the floor and found a bit of white substance, rock salt, and figured the ears had been preserved and carried away in a box of rock salt; the dehydration could be reversed later, when the ears where ultimately used for their intended purpose.

He found more cigarette butts crushed in the expected way, but this did not help him at all. It proved only that the same man was responsible for all the deaths and Allingham already knew that.

Allingham looked about the room, now, not so much to investigate, as to take it all in; the life of a young woman of modest means, newly arrived from Chicago to be a secretary at a local law firm. He saw a photograph with three women enjoying a day at a park, at the lake on a beach. Written in pencil across the photograph was *Nell, Hortense, and me.* She was the prettiest one of the three.

He looked at the corpse's pretty red hair, now tangled and clotted with blood. He looked back at the mantel at the picture of a young man in a soldier's uniform. On this was written, *My heroic man.* He didn't know if that was a lover, a brother or a friend. He turned to the dead young woman and nodded to her gravely. "I'm sorry. I'm so, so sorry."

He sat in a chair that had not been spoilt by blood and thought about the gruesome episode. He played it out in his mind. He could see him. Like having a dream, he could see everything, watch it all play out, every detail, every horrific act, but when it came to the face, the name, the identity of the man, he had nothing.

He sat and smoked and held his head in his hands and felt ill. The odor of decay was beginning to intensify and he needed to let the men take the poor thing away from this unholy site. She needed to be put into a proper coffin and shipped back home to Chicago where, hopefully, no one would dare to remove the lid.

The local sheriff was on hand and was even more squeamish than Allingham's assistant back in Flagstaff. The man wanted no part of the case, even though it had been perpetrated in his jurisdiction. In this Allingham was lucky. He did not want, or require, any help from the local man.

He checked into the newly built Hollingsworth Hotel. It smelled good, of new construction, and many people were milling about. They appeared to be happy. There were beautiful women being escorted on the arms of handsome and well-to-do young men. He imagined the young secretary being brought here to dinner by a young lawyer in the firm where she was employed.

He'd work to steal her away from the man in the military uniform. That lovely auburn hair, the shapely figure, the youth, the beauty would drive the young men crazy and they probably all fought to gain her attention. She likely felt like a princess here in Arizona where the men outnumbered the women many times over. She probably would have tried to get Nell and Hortense to move down from Chicago, had she lived long enough. There'd be plenty of good suitors to go around. They would all get married and be happy and pregnant by 1887.

He looked over at the bar and saw many men standing and laughing and drinking. It made him ill. He wasn't angry at the merry makers, just sad and miserable and depressed.

He ordered dinner to be taken in his room and worked on his notes about what little he had found at the site until well after midnight. Then he lay in bed, wide awake, worrying about Rebecca. Around three A.M. he remembered Gorski's package and opened it. The Pole's letter read:

Allingham:
Hope all is well. See enclosed. Strange case last fall, New Jersey. Man who went

by name Doctor Wells, found to have experimented with a group of train crash victims. Found bodies in various states of decay, various states of preservation in his basement. Body parts exchanged, heads sewn onto different bodies, as well as appendages.

Man identified as white, mid-forties, practicing medicine without a license, thought to have been an embalming surgeon during war. Left in middle of night after several complaints to police by patients. Neighbors complained of odd odor coming from basement.

Might this be your man?
                    S. Gorski, Sgt. New York

Chapter XXVIII:
A Dying Breed

They stayed with the Indians for another week. Every time they tried to leave, someone would invite them for another celebration of some kind. The children were especially taken with both of them: Ramon, like Hilola, looked nothing like the people with whom they were accustomed.

Finally their departure could not be delayed any longer and several of the women stood by and cried. Hilola kissed the cacique and the bald priest on their cheeks. She removed the shaman's knife from its sheath and cut off a golden lock from each of her braids. She handed one to the shaman and one to the cacique. They looked at the shining tresses in their hands as if they were holding spun gold.

Hilola talked and talked of her time with the Indians. She'd been enlightened, and Ramon was enjoying it. He felt as if he was watching a child who had learned something profound, something that moved the child from adolescence to adulthood. It made him love her all the more.

She smiled at him watching her prattle on about the Indians. "What?"

"Nothing, just you. Just like to hear you talk."

"Awe, I talk like a idiot."

"Do not." Ramon lost his smile. "Don't say that again." He was quite serious. "Don't ever say that about yourself again, Hilola."

Hilola looked him in the eye and could see that he meant it as a compliment, not an admonishment. She shrugged, "Okay."

He paddled to the middle of the river and got the sail up and they moved along at a good clip in some deep water. He beckoned for her to come back and sit with him as he steered with the oar.

"You know, the Indians believe that the wind is caused by animals, great birds or even mythical creatures, beating their wings. They don't believe that it's just the wind."

"Some people think they're savages, Ramon, but . . . , but I don't." She blushed, "At least don't no more. I think they're grand. I think they're wonderful."

"They have beliefs and stories, same as

us." Ramon shrugged. "Some do say they're childish, but," he leaned over and kissed her on top of the head, "I don't know, we believe that our God got nailed to a cross and was buried and crawled out from a cave. Guess that sounds a little childish, too." He smiled and remembered her painted so provocatively and wanted her again. He thought of something else.

"You know they have a great ceremony where they gather snakes from all over and the shamans dance with the snakes in their mouths."

"In their mouths?" Hilola looked on, cringing. "Don't they get bit?"

"I don't know. But they respect the snakes, even when they do bite. If the snake does bite, they bring the snake and victim together and ask the snake to take back the venom. They believe the creatures have spirits and can communicate. It's all connected, the earth and the people and the animals; all connected."

"It's nice." Hilola reached overboard and wetted her hand and ran it across her forehead. She did the same for Ramon. She thought some more about the Indians. "I used to be scared of any Indian. Didn't know there was different ones. Didn't know a Pima from an Apache. Just scared of 'em all, Ramon, but not no more. I think they're grand."

"Well, they are, the ones we were with. They are the Hopis, and they are some of the best farmers and builders you'd ever want to know. They don't want to kill anyone. Fact is, they're victims of the wild ones, the Apaches, just as much as we are."

"Well, I'm glad we met 'em, Ramon. Maybe one day we can go and see 'em again."

"If they last." He looked at Hilola and then at the river. "This country's changing, Hilola. Changing and the old Indian ways just aren't going to fit in, just like in my country. The Indians there, the Tarahumara and the Yaqui, they are a dying breed." He shrugged, "Guess there's no room for them in this world, the world of the white man, the world of the European."

"But you're part Indian, Ramon."

"Yes." He smiled. "It is the part that makes me a grand lover." He reached down and kissed her neck passionately, until the gooseflesh was raised on her neck and arms. Hilola squealed with delight. "You're given' me the shivers."

He thought a lot about what she said, about one day coming back to visit the Indians. It was good to hear her talk of the future in such a way, as Ramon was not fully convinced that he'd sold her on the idea of living the rest of her life with him. He had a foreboding feeling in his gut that, somehow, none of this was real; none of it would really pan out. It was all a big game and one day he'd awaken from it and find Hilola with her bags packed, telling him she'd had a good time, but that he was a boy and she needed to seek her fortunes elsewhere. It was a feeling that he could not shake, and it wasn't Hilola's fault. She'd given him no indication of such a thing.

And then Ramon thought that perhaps he was just looking for that dark cloud that seemed to roll over him every time he had a woman whom he thought was the one and only. He hated dwelling on the negative all the time, but it just seemed in his nature to always look at the worst case in everything.

Hilola interrupted his thoughts. "Do you think it would be all right if I became a Catholic, Ramon?"

"If you want, certainly. What's your religion now?"

"Oh, I ain't got one, really. Believe in God and Jesus all right, I guess, but we never really did go in for it much. Momma would take us to a church when our backs were up against it, when we didn't really have enough to eat and no prospects for gettin' it. We'd go to a church and listen to the preachin' and we'd get a can or two of peaches, or some vegetables. One time, Momma had to become friendly with the preacher so's we could get some meat." She looked up at Ramon to gauge his reaction but he didn't take his eyes off the horizon. "Wasn't a whore, Ramon. Momma wasn't a whore but, Ramon, sometimes she had to do, to get us through a rough time. She had to do."

"I understand, Hilola. I do, and I don't fault her. I don't know what it's like to go without food or a decent place to live. I don't know that, Hilola, but I don't condemn anyone for carryin' on to save their family. It's, it's just, well, just sad, and it makes me sad to know you've known such things. I'm sorry, Hilola, I'm sorry for that."

She kissed him and held him tightly and whispered in his ear. "I'd like to be a Catholic with you, Ramon. It'll please me, and you, and it'll maybe please your mother. I want to be a Catholic, Ramon."

CHAPTER XXIX:
HOBBSIE

Hobbs found the stateroom bed of the Esmeralda so comfortable that he slept for twenty four hours straight. He awoke and felt the ship moving steadily under him. It had a nice hum, a rhythmic whoosh, whoosh, whoosh as the paddle wheel spun. He lifted his head to survey the little room and realized Rosario was off on some adventure. He stretched and felt the flutter of his heart. It no longer really beat anymore and that was a strange feeling, because Hobbs could remember, always, being conscious of his heartbeat whenever lying comfortably in bed.

It had not beat normally for more than a year now, and he did his best to hide such from Rosario, who was really too smart to ever be kept in the dark about anything. Hobbs soon enough found that out, too, but still they never talked of it. They both knew Hobbs had a dying heart and there was not a thing that could be done about it, and there was even less value in talking about it, so they just never did.

He thought on the fact that Rosario had changed her ways a bit. She mothered him more, and at the same time would never allow him to be treated as an invalid. He knew that was why she condoned and even encouraged him to go on with the law work. She knew that, like Allingham, he tended toward melancholy, and melancholy would kill a heart much more quickly than any kind of law work, except of course when such law work involved gun play. But she also knew that Mr. Singh would keep him safe and once he was out of the picture, she would take up the mantle of being Hobbsie's bodyguard. It was constant good work that kept Hobbs busy and not melancholy.

It was really ideal, as Rosario was a deadly lady, but she was, by her own admission, frumpy and not at all dangerous looking. Looks were never more deceiving, however, as Rosario had seen her share of violence and done her share of killing. That's what Hobbs loved the most about her. His Rosario. He thought about her and was pleased that he was aroused as that seemed another bad outcome of having a dying heart. It was also what was helping him come to grips with his mortality. A man who could no longer please, or at least service, a woman, well, he had outlived his usefulness. Seemed to him, a man who could not do what a man was supposed to do, shouldn't be allowed to go on.

But it still worked more often than it didn't, and it was working now. He wondered where his love was at this very moment. He hoped she'd get back to him soon. He was tired again, and wanted to sleep. If she came in while he was unconscious, he'd miss the opportunity.

The damn whistle blew again and this brought him back to his senses. He still could not figure any pattern or logic to the whistle blowing. It seemed, actually, to be directly related to either Hobbsie's attempt at getting to sleep, his attempt at staying asleep, or as a way to break his concentration when he was working on something. It was a high-pitched kind of a screaming sound, and Hobbs thought at least a hundred times that he'd like to throw a couple of charges of buckshot from Rosario's ten gauge at the damnable thing.

He was thirsty and looked at the bed stand and there was the lemonade, as always. A nice steward named Bob was extra attentive to Hobbs and his wife. He was a kind and silent man, and every time Hobbs woke up there was fresh lemonade on the stand with a clean glass. His chamber pot was empty and spotless. Hobbsie never once heard or saw Bob do this, but it was always done, nonetheless.

That was the thing he'd miss most about being dead. He'd miss the kind things that some people did. There were many of them in his time. There were many bad things and people, but there were many kind ones, too. He thought about Bob the steward and thought that it was kind of the man to treat Hobbs so well, and not just because the captain liked them and loved Rosario's cooking, but because Bob was a good and kind man. Those were the ones whom Hobbs would miss the most.

Hobbs thought of the Irishmen, the brothers Paddy and Mike from the Canyon Diablo adventure. He looked off west to California and thought of what the men were doing there right now. They were in San Diego, not San Francisco, as was the original plan. According to the most recent post, they were doing well, and each had an Irish lass and planned to marry. Rosario swore they'd break their mother's heart and never make it back to Ireland. Hobbs could not disagree with her. Neither would likely ever step foot again on the Emerald Isle.

He also would miss that part; the reunion with them, with so many he'd met and known in his time. There had always been plenty of time, it seemed, until now. He had always planned that one day they'd meet up, they'd have a grand old time and talk of the old days, the old adventures. But now there was no more time. He got himself crying again and his heart fluttered and made him cough and clear his throat and he felt the dizziness again. He always felt so certain that he'd see the two young giants again. He liked them so much and had formed a brotherhood with them, the kind that was formed only in battle and strife. They'd protected each other. They'd become a family in Canyon Diablo and Hobbs knew, in his heart, that he'd never see the Irishmen again.

He rested and dried his eyes and slowly sat up and did not feel so dizzy. He stood and still felt fine. He washed up and had a good shave. He did not want to be scruffy, even if he was ready to check out. He combed his hair carefully and put on Leo Blume's kippah. He dressed in a freshly brushed suit, courtesy of Bob the steward, over a white starched shirt and black cravat.

He sat down and opened the door to his cabin and watched the river go by until the strength came back after the exertion of so much preparation. He was ready to go out into the world again, likely one of the very last times. This made him strangely happy to know and not at all sad.

He heard the passengers nearby, an old gambler talking in his gentle yet loud voice. He heard Rosario laugh. She had the best laugh of anyone he'd ever known. It was really what made him fall in love with her from the start. He smelled food cooking and was hungry. The chef was a convert, and Hobbsie could smell Rosario's influence in the cuisine being served up for the evening meal. He thought of how happy the captain would be as he slowly made his way to the party.

Chapter XXX:
The Counselor
and the Duck

Pierce sat on the hard bench in the gallery next to Old Pop at the Yuma courthouse as the session came to order. His brother's defense attorney stood awkwardly with a rather feisty duck tucked precariously under his right arm.

"What in the *hell* is that duck doing in my courtroom, Mr. Swineford?" The judge did not look up, as he was concentrating on cleaning his spectacles with a neatly pressed handkerchief.

At that, the duck soundly bit the lawyer on the thumb. The attorney dropped the duck, which landed with an audible thud, as the creature had no ability to fly.

"Squeaky!" Cap McCartney jumped from his place at the defendant's table and recovered his duck, which then climbed up onto his left shoulder, perched there and peeped into his ear lovingly. He looked at the prosecutor angrily. "You keep away from my duck!"

Swineford looked on, anxiously. "Your honor, the duck is pivotal to my contention that Mr. McCartney, here, willfully, and violently shot and attempted to murder Mr. Sedgwick." He looked over to the man on his right.

The judge nodded his head slowly in disgust and looked at his watch. "This better not stretch out through the afternoon, Swineford, and that duck better not shit in my court."

"No, no your honor." Swineford suddenly sat down and just as suddenly tipped his head forward, falling into a deep sleep. He was poked awake by the state's witness, a red-faced scaly man named Sedgwick. The narcoleptic attorney continued where he'd left off, as if he'd never lost consciousness.

"Your honor, the state will demonstrate how Mr. Cap McCartney, the man sitting to my left . . ."

"Yes, yes, we all know McCartney. He's the one with the duck resting on his shoulder."

"Yes, ah, that's right, your honor. Where was I? Oh, yes, willfully attacked Mr. Sedgwick who did nothing more than try to shoo the duck away, after being repeatedly chased, harassed, and bitten by said duck.

"That's a danged lie!" McCartney jumped up again, nearly toppling the duck from his shoulder. "Squeaky don't bother no one, less they's in her yard."

"Not true, your honor. The animal is a menace, as we'll soon demonstrate." He walked over and took the duck from McCartney's shoulder, carefully placing it on the floor between himself and the judge. He nodded to the bailiff who now walked past the duck with a casual stride. The duck quacked, then defecated on the floor.

The judge looked at the attorney who did his best to stay awake. "And this proves what? That we have a shitting duck."

"He's supposed to attack. He's, he's . . ."

"Ain't a he, she's a she. She's a girl duck, you big dummy."

Swineford looked back at Cap McCartney, and then pointed accusingly at him. "He's, he's signaling to the duck, your honor!" He looked again at the judge who was slowly turning one shade of red after another, moving to a degree closer to purple.

"Swineford, pick that up!" The judge glared at the duck scat on his polished wood floor. "Get that duck out of here, now!"

The defense attorney stood up. "One moment, your honor, if you please."

"What, what?"

"Before the duck is removed, if you please, we'd like to offer some evidence related to the duck."

"Related to the duck?"

"Actually, *the* duck, the evidence is on the duck's breast your honor."

The judge took a long drink of water. He looked impatiently at his watch. He hoped to end this before the hottest time of the day. "Go on, go on." He shooed at the man as if he were chasing flies.

The defense attorney picked up the duck and spoke soothingly to it. The duck quacked as the man moved some feathers aside. "As you can see, your honor, there are hay fork marks on this duck."

"Yes." The judge nodded and looked with some interest at the duck's damaged breast.

"And, these hay fork wounds correspond to my client's." He nodded and McCartney pulled open his shirtfront. Wounds were visible just below the Adam's apple on his boney pale chest.

"Yes, yes. Make your point, Mr. Kline. And quickly."

"Yes, your honor." He walked over to the evidence table and picked up the exhibit. "This is the hay fork used in the attack. As you'll notice, your honor, the tines on this hay fork have been bent by some heavy use. They are very peculiar in their spread, and different from how they were originally manufactured. This was the exact hay fork used to attack my client and his pet duck. It is the attack perpetrated by that man there." He pointed to the state's witness, "When Mr. Sedgwick trespassed on the defendant's property and attempted to make off with a bale of fresh hay." He pointed, "Using said hay fork."

He shrugged, "The duck was merely doing its job. She attacked the trespasser, which alerted Mr. McCartney, who came out from his dinner to see what was amiss."

"With a twelve gauge shotgun, your honor!" Swineford was pleased with his interjection. He nodded smugly at the defense attorney, and then at McCartney.

"Of course with mah scattergun, ya danged fool. Squeaky don't make a fuss 'lessen there's trouble about. Always investigate trouble with mah gun." He looked at his neighbor. "That danged bushwhacker goes and pokes Squeaky with that fork there, then he has a go at me. Hell, only shot him in the foot. Coulda blowed his danged head off, but I din' wanta, so I didn't."

"Nonsense!" Swineford was ready now.

"That hay fork was yours. It was lying nearby, and who's to say you didn't trip on it, get caught up with it? Who's to say the duck, in its ferocious and vicious attack on my client, didn't get accidentally poked as well?"

"I do." Kline spoke calmly.

The judge was now mildly interested. The ridiculousness of the entire case was making it perversely interesting to him. "How so?"

"Your honor, this hay fork is the property of Mr. Sedgwick."

"And how can you prove that?"

"Mr. York, the owner of the dry goods store by the same name, sold it to him."

Swineford spoke up. "Your honor, this is hearsay and preposterous. How can anyone know one hayfork from the next? And Mr. York has not even been identified as a witness."

"We'd be happy to call him in, your honor, but he'd indicated to me, in a signed affidavit," he held this document up for all to see, "that there is a number stamped on the hay fork. He does this with all of the equipment he sells, both to prove they were his merchandise, and as an accounting tool. He's also supplied me with a copy of the invoice. It names Sedgwick as the purchaser of the implement."

The judge called for the item. "Bring the hay fork to me."

The bailiff complied. The judge looked the men over, as if he were suddenly officiating at an auction. "What's the number?"

"One hundred twenty five."

"The number matches, Mr. Swineford." He held up his hand. "I've heard enough." He looked at Kline, most obviously the sharpest man in the room, excluding the judge. "Why were no charges filed against Mr. Sedgwick, Mr. Kline?"

"My client did not want to bother. He felt that Sedgwick paid enough with a foot peppered with mustard, sir."

"So, he wasn't even shot with lead?"

"No, your honor. Mr. McCartney loads one barrel with mustard seed. He says it's deterrent enough, and if someone still wants to fight after receiving such a load, he has the other barrel loaded with buckshot. Certainly if he had murder on his mind, he would have used that barrel."

Swineford cut in: "You see, your honor, reckless, reckless. How'd he know he wasn't going to shoot the wrong barrel off? My God, the man uses a deadly weapon and tries to put it off as some harmless tool, some harmless deterrent!"

The defendant leaned forward and looked Swineford over dismissively. "You danged fool, sure enough know what barrel to tetch off in my own shootin' iron." He looked at the judge with incredulity in his eyes. "Yer honor, a man would have to be either a greenhorn dude or plain addlepated not to know what barrel was shootin' what. I don't even pull the hammer back on the one shoots lead lessen I need to kill somepin."

Kline grinned widely and nodded to his lawyer opponent. It was as if Swineford was working for *him.* He looked at the judge. "No, my client is not a violent man, your honor, just careful, and just interested in protecting himself and his property." He looked on at his client, now sitting quietly cradling his duck lovingly in his lap. "We have no interest in pursuing charges."

The gavel came down and at this, Squeaky jumped from his master's arms to the table in front of them. She wiggled a bit, squatted, and laid an egg. The judge suddenly burst forth with a hearty guffaw. He pointed with his gavel. "Give that to Mr. Swineford. A more fitting tribute to his lawyerly skills, I cannot imagine. Case dismissed."

Old Pop leaned close to Pierce. He pointed to the hapless lawyer, who now stood alone, holding the stool-coated egg.

"And that's who's defending Thad?"

"Yep."

Old Pop smiled broadly and patted his companion soundly on the back as Pierce looked on doubtfully. "Now, *that's* justice."

Chapter XXXI:
The Mule Tamer's Daughter

Hobbs stood on the observation platform and suddenly realized that he'd been experiencing a new and rather strange phenomenon lately. He was actually a little bit happy; actually enjoying himself. This was indeed a new experience for him, as, for a very long time, and especially over the past several weeks, he'd been downright miserable, anxious and distracted.

Getting over the death of Francis was proving to be impossible for Hobbs. He loved the young man and had never, in all his life been so affected by the death of another person. Even the death of relatives had not affected him in such a way. He missed Francis terribly every day.

But now, on a clear and crisp morning, watching the riverboat pull a barge of livestock across to the California side, taking in the majesty of the beautiful sunrise and the awakening of the wildlife along the river, Hobbs felt a little joy in his fluttery heart. He absentmindedly reached up and felt the kippah on his head and his thoughts turned to his Rosario, off doing something in the galley.

She could not stop working; she'd worked since she could remember and had recently struck up a friendship with the chief cook. They were concocting some delicacy for the captain. Hobbs would never admonish her for such. Rosario did not know the meaning of the term holiday. Even when she was relaxing, she was still working.

He felt silly, at first, wearing the head covering. It was typically worn only by rabbis or the most devout of his faith. And most Jews did not wear such a thing in public, something that would point them out and announce to the world that they were members of a group often vilified, derided and thought of in a contemptible manner. It was preferable to hide one's Jewishness, not advertise it.

He suddenly straightened his back and looked down at his marshal badge and felt proud. Damn, he was a Jew and a lawman and he didn't care if someone didn't like it.

His reverie was interrupted by a little girl who could not have been more than five or six, leaning on the rail next to him. Hobbs could have sworn she was mimicking him, as she stood with one foot resting on the first rung of the rail, just as he had been doing.

"Good morning, mister."

"Good morning to you, young Miss." He nodded and would have tipped his hat, had he been wearing one.

"What's your name, mister?"

"Hobbs."

"What were you thinking about so hard just now, Mr. Hobbs?"

"I beg your pardon?" If she were not so adorable, Hobbs would have considered her impudent.

"You were thinking real hard. You had a funny look on your face and I was just wondering what you were thinking about."

"Oh, just, just thinking. Nothing worth talking about."

"I'm Kate Walsh, eh, Katherine, but everyone calls me Kate." She reached out to shake his hand and Hobbs complied, taking her small hand gently, engulfing it in his huge fist.

He looked about for an adult. A child such as this should not be on her own, and Hobbs suddenly wanted to admonish both the little girl and her guardian.

"Don't you know that it is not wise to

speak to strangers, little girl?"

"Oh, my daddy says it's all right when it's a lawman, or when it's a man of God." She looked him over. "You're both, and besides, my mommy is right over there." She pointed to a pretty, well-dressed woman conducting business with an agent. The woman smiled and waved to the little girl. Her attention had been diverted from the business at hand.

Hobbs felt a sense of relief, and smiled at the precocious child.

"You're a Jew, aren't you?" She did not wait for a reply. She held up a hand and her face turned serious as she remembered what her father had taught her. She straightened her back and gave the greeting she'd been taught. "Shalom," nodding seriously as she said it.

"Shalom, yourself." Hobbs was pleased and gave her a broad smile.

"Those are our mules," she pointed to the barge dragging a good distance behind the churning wheel of their craft. "My mommy and daddy and Uncle Bob breed the best mules this side of the Mississippi."

"I see. They look to be fine beasts."

"And every one tamed and trained, either for hauling or riding, so as to suit the customer's requirements." She sounded like an advertising poster saying that, and it tickled Hobbs to hear it from such a tiny voice.

She looked her stock over as they floated across the river. "I'm going to miss them. I love those mules. Lots a people don't like mules. Say they're stubborn and mean, but they're not, mister. My daddy says that mules are the smartest animals on earth, and he even counts people in that." She grinned. "My daddy says a mule is smarter than the human trying to get them to do things, and once you know that, you can get a mule to do anything, as long as it fits into the mule's ideas of what's right, and not what's wrong. As long as you only ask the mule to do the things he thinks are right to do, you can get them to do anything for you."

"Well, Miss Kate, I am certain of that." Hobbs hid his cynicism. He never did like mules very much.

"We're from Cochise County, Arizona Territory, soon to be a state, God willing. Our ranch is just north of a town named Tombstone. Do you know Tombstone, mister?"

"I've heard of it."

"Where are you from, mister?"

"Flagstaff."

"Oh, I like it there. Mommy takes me

there sometimes. Winters are cold up there."

The child was intriguing; almost unnatural in her maturity and Hobbs found himself drawn to ask her more about herself, which was odd, because Hobbs was not generally good with — or interested in — children of any size.

"What is your business, Miss Kate?"

"Oh, we're delivering these mules. Then we're going on to San Francisco. Have you been to San Francisco, mister? I've never been there. I heard it's grand."

"I've heard that too, Miss Kate, but I regret to say, I haven't been there. I've some relatives there, merchants, but I've not visited them yet."

They watched the captain maneuver the vessel and barge to the dock on the California side. Kate Walsh smiled and extended her hand again.

"Well, it was nice speaking with you, mister. And, thank you."

"Thank me?" Hobbs was confused. "For what?"

"For being a lawman. Daddy says to thank lawmen and soldiers whenever I see them. Thank them for making our land safe. Thanks, mister."

"You're welcome."

■ ■ ■ ■

He watched her work with the mules in her pretty city dress, assisting the cowboys in getting the beasts off the barge. The child barely reached a mule's stifle, yet she could handle them like the most seasoned wrangler. He could hear her little voice speak to each one, as if they were old friends going off on some adventure. She kissed each one low on the neck, just in front of the withers, as her daddy had taught her never to put her face near a mule's head or she might end up taking soup for all her meals.

When the task was completed she rubbed her hands together and looked back at Hobbs, watching her from his observation point.

She smiled and waved. "Shalom, mister! Shalom."

Hobbs choked back tears as Rosario came up beside him; the little one had gotten to his fluttery heart. His wife rubbed his back and looked on at the lady and the child.

"Who was that, darling?"

"Oh, just a little girl. A very special little girl."

That evening they dined with the captain

who seemed to be falling in love with Rosario, as her creations in the galley were giving the chief cook some new ideas. The skipper was not a young man and the quickest way, these days, to the captain's heart was through his stomach. Rosario had introduced him to some new gastronomic delights. This night they dined with several wealthy patrons and a gambler from Missouri.

The gambler was a refined man, intelligent, fair and upstanding, who'd fought for the south, and was an old man back then. He was fairly ancient now, but retained a thick crop of snow white hair, and a mind as sharp as any intelligent man in his prime. He wore a beard and moustaches, but was clean shaven on his cheeks. His whiskers were as white as the hair on his head. He looked a bit like a thin version of a Santa Claus Rosario had seen on an advertising poster down in Phoenix. He was dressed well always, partial to white suits of light wool, except for his vest, which was Chinese silk, bright red with little gold dragons embroidered throughout. His cravat was held to his shirt with a great ruby bejeweled tiepin, which matched the vest in color. He carried no visible weapons, and addressed everyone as sir or ma'am, regardless of their race or station in life. He had a habit of smoothing his moustaches with the index finger of his right hand, first pushing the hairs into place on the left, then pulling them on the right. He did this with a certain flourish, and Rosario was intrigued by the courtly southerner.

She learned that he was in a kind of partnership with the captain. He was a good player, never cheated, and was so skilled in his ability at the games of chance that he'd become famous throughout the region. Everyone, from the thickest bumpkin, to the self-proclaimed expert, wanted a chance to best him. This never happened. He could trounce anyone, every time, as he was a professional and a teetotaler. Rosario was especially impressed with this and emboldened enough by his gentle manner to venture to pry.

"Spirits are fine for some, ma'am, and I am no temperance zealot, but they are poison to a man in my trade." He brushed his moustaches and drank his coffee. "Dull the wits, dull the mind, and then the activities of my profession truly become games of chance."

The captain chimed in. "Mr. Collins is purely scientific in his methods, Señora Hobbs."

Collins raised his cup and toasted the captain. "And spirits make a man mean. Just as not having the calming influence of ladies about makes men into wild animals, the addition of spirits is very destructive and just plain makes men mean."

"Is your profession not dangerous, then, Señor?"

"Oh, it can be, ma'am, it can be. But I'm unarmed." He held his coat open to prove it. "I don't provoke a fight, so that helps. Had a belly full a killing in the war, ma'am, and," he winked at the captain, "I receive plenty of protection from my friends."

"Yes, Mrs. Rosario, we do not tolerate rude behavior on our little ship." The captain gave her a reassuring smile. "And your husband will not be needed to curb lawlessness here. We police our own." He smiled at Hobbs then worried over his ashen complexion, giving him a reassuring pat on the shoulder.

The gambler suddenly looked at Hobbs in a curious manner, took his measure and listened carefully to his accent, which he surmised might be from the south, North Carolina, to be exact. "Marshal Hobbs, you would not happen to be related to the late Judah Benjamin, formerly our great Secretary of War under Jefferson Davis?"

"I am not." Hobbs suddenly felt the kippah, weighing heavily on his head.

"Forgive me. That was a bit indelicate. I just see that you share the same faith with the esteemed gentleman — and your accent. Mr. Benjamin had indicated to me that he'd spent his formative years in North Carolina. I knew the man well."

"No, I've heard of him. I heard he recently died back in Europe — France, I believe."

"Indeed, sir. Indeed." He nodded. "Paris, to be exact. A great loss to humanity. He was a good lawyer and a good politician, if you can believe that such a creature can exist." He laughed at his own joke. "A good patriot for the southern cause."

"Are you very sad that the war was lost by your side, Señor?" Rosario had learned a great deal about the Civil War, since living with the Allingham family. It intrigued her that so many of the gringos killed each other. She was curious and asked veterans from both sides, about their thoughts on the war at every opportunity.

"No, ma'am." He smiled sheepishly. "To tell the truth, I knew we were doomed the day after the attack on Fort Sumter."

"Then why did you fight?" Rosario looked at him, a little confused, as he was an intelligent and articulate man. His response seemed to make no sense to her at all.

"Have you ever seen, at night, ma'am, when a lamp is lit, and a moth flies right into it and gets burned up?"

"Sí."

"That's the way it was for me. The war was just like a great burning lamp, and I the moth. No other explanation than that, ma'am. It was just there, and men are compelled to fly toward the flame." He looked into the eye of each member of the little party. "Especially when all your friends and family are doing the same." He fiddled with a deck of cards. "Ma'am, we were all like a great flock of moths; just rushing, flying, hurtling toward that flame."

He smiled at his own joke again. The captain grinned as he'd known enough warriors from the south. Many seemed to share the gambler's sentiments.

Rosario was going to speak and then lost her concentration as she heard the shout of a young Negro man standing on a platform projecting from the side of the ship, which she later learned was known as *the chains.* She pointed to him and asked the captain, "Why does he keep calling out that author's name?"

"Ah, Mark Twain!" The captain grinned. "Otis is our leadsman. He has the most important job on our ship. He makes certain we don't run aground, Mrs. Rosario."

"But why does he keep calling for the writer?"

"That is an old sounding term, and Mr. Clemens once captained these kinds of boats. Not here, but on the great Mississippi, a long time ago. He took his name from this. Mark Twain is a depth, it means twelve feet."

Rosario smiled at her husband. She leaned close and whispered in his ear, "I'll be go to hell."

CHAPTER XXXII:
THE SLEUTHHOUND'S WIFE

Rebecca lay awake for most of the night. She wondered what her husband was doing down in Phoenix. The school teacher's samplers were on her mind and she decided, once she saw the light under her door and heard Singh's footsteps as he prepared for a day at the office, to get up and work on the cipher a little more.

She'd rather sleep in, because the longer she slept the less time she'd have to wait for Allingham to get home. He was due by dinnertime. She couldn't wait as she seemed to miss him more and more as the baby grew. Not even Mr. Singh or her father could slake the loneliness she felt for her husband. She loved him more than anything in the world and worried over what effect all these murders was having on him. Rebecca knew better than anyone that Allingham was actually frail, his rough exterior a ruse. He was sensitive and caring and all of this was tearing him apart. She knew he felt responsible every time a new corpse was discovered, and this is what she worried over as she got out of bed.

She no longer felt sick and that was a relief. She rubbed her growing belly and this gave her comfort. With the distraction of the murders, and the knowledge that the school teacher was still alive — no doubt locked in some horrific place — Rebecca periodically forgot all about her pregnancy. She revisited it now, as if it were a long lost friendship recently rekindled.

She was an inherently optimistic person, and knew it would just be a matter of time before Allingham solved the case, captured the monster and put an end to all this horror. It would just be a matter of time before Rosario and Hobbs were back. Everything would be as it should and there'd be a new baby to love and bring even greater happiness to the home. She smiled at the memory of her father, the one man who was completely transparent to her, as if she could read his mind. She knew he worried over what influence Allingham's genes would have on her little treasure.

She got up and was alone. Delores, the housekeeper hired while Rosario was off being a deputy marshal, had not yet started her day. Singh was gone and Halsted still slept in his bed. Both fathers resolved to take turns guarding her and this morning it was Halsted's turn, as Singh needed desperately to get some things accomplished at the office. She made tea and toast and sat down at her card table with her notes and the samplers.

By now, she had at least established the letters of the cipher, and as she worked, she soon discovered stitches arranged with the intent to indicate a number, or number order at each of the chosen letters. She smiled at the thought of the clever girl. She felt proud of the young teacher's courage and pluck. And just as quickly, a wave of unhappiness and dread washed over her. For the first time in her life, Rebecca Allingham experienced the emotion of despondency. She wanted to cry and she'd never in her adult life felt this way. She took a deep breath and swallowed hard, pushed back the tears and said a prayer for the young woman. She sat up straighter and spoke quietly at the samplers. "I will find you, my dear. I promise, I'll find you."

She took up the first sampler and examined the first letter with the cipher. It was the letter 'E'. There was a single stitch, a dot formed at one corner. At the very bottom, if one looked at just the right angle, the teacher had employed tweeding, but the threads were so similar in color as to be barely discernible to the naked eye. With Singh's magnifying glass, Rebecca could make out the Roman numeral IX.

Rebecca drew up a grid with twenty six columns and three lines. On this she wrote the alphabet. On the next row she wrote 'word count,' on the next 'position.'

For the letter E she had the following; word count one, position nine. She proceeded through the morning until she had a complete grid written for the entire first sampler.

Letter	A	B	C	D	E	F	G	H	I	J	K	L	M	N	O	P	Q	R	S	T	U	V	W	X	Y	Z
Wrd Cnt					1				2			4	1									1				
Pos					9				2,6			3,4 7,8	1									5				

She created a separate grid, now with only five columns, to correspond with the word count, and included only the letters identified by the special treatment given them by the teacher. It looked like this:

Letter	E	I	L	M	V
Wrd Cnt	1	2	4	1	1
Pos	9	2,6	3,4,7,8	1	5

She laid out a series of dashes, of which there were nine: _ _ _ _ _ _ _ _ _, and began filling in letters to correspond with the location and quantity. And by following the teacher's cipher, she arrived at the word 'M I L L V I L L E'.

Her heart pounded and she quickly repeated the same method for the second sampler. She arrived at the word 'O F F I C E'.

She jumped up, prepared to wake her father, when Delores interrupted her. "Señora, Señor Halsted, he is not well, and the doctor, he is here to visit."

Rebecca was overwhelmed. She needed to do something; needed to see her husband or Mr. Singh or her father. She took a deep breath. "Keep him in the parlor, Delores. I will talk to my father."

She crept quietly into his room and Halsted smiled weakly. He was worn out from coughing all night. "Hello, my dear."

"You're not well, Father." She rested her hand on his forehead and worried over him. "I'll call the doctor."

"No, no. Let Webster look me over, he should be by soon. We have a lunch date."

"He's here now. But, father, I don't know . . . shall we fetch our own?"

"No, no." He yawned. "It's just a bad cold."

"Father, do you recall a place named Millville?"

He was drifting. "Millville? Oh, yes. Abandoned. Remember, my dear, a few years ago, the Mormons tried to develop a town southeast of here? A lumber town with a sawmill. Singh and I put them out of business." He grinned slyly, "Not on purpose, of course. Hira would not have it." He blew his nose and continued. "Nothing but a ghost town now."

She kissed him on the cheek and he fell back to sleep. She crept out of his room and startled the doctor looking over her ciphering work.

"Good morning." Rebecca called out to him a little tersely. "I thought Delores asked you to wait in the parlor, doctor."

He jumped and turned abruptly. "Mrs. Allingham! He ignored her admonishment. "I see you're doing some detective work related to the poor missing girl." He looked at her in a way that was disarming; perhaps they'd all been a little too harsh with him.

"Yes, yes." She suddenly had a thought. She began putting on her hat, adjusting it and securing it with her big hatpin. She called the maid to fetch the carriage. "Dr. Webster, how about a trip to a ghost town?"

He suddenly went white, as he understood her meaning. He looked at her cipher. "To, to this Millville?" He sat down rather too quickly. He looked very old and frail to Rebecca now.

"Are you all right, Doctor? You're paler than my father."

"Oh, I, I, Mrs. Allingham, do you mean to suggest that we go looking for this young lady? Where the murderer might be lurking?" He wiped his sweaty brow and smiled weakly. "I heard stories that the ladies of the West were stalwart, but, really, Mrs. Allingham, I, I don't know."

"Oh, come on, doctor. You're a big man. You've been to war."

"I'm, I never fought, Mrs. Allingham." His fearful eyes darted about. He looked petrified. "Mostly sawed limbs off the poor wounded." He suddenly had a thought. "Perhaps if we, if we could pick up Mr. Singh along the way, I'd not be afraid with Mr. Singh as our protector."

"Oh, of course, Doctor. It was my plan the entire time." She felt guilty scaring the hapless physician. "I guess I should have told you that from the start."

As Allingham rode along, his thoughts corresponded to the rhythm of the train clickety-clacking on the rails. He checked his watch; he'd be home soon. He wondered what Rebecca was doing at that moment. He missed her.

Something was very wrong with his investigation, with the conclusions he'd drawn thus far. It was something that he'd not necessarily missed, but rather a supposition he'd made that was perhaps logical, but faulty in its conclusion. He looked at his watch and then out the window. He was now halfway back to Flagstaff.

He looked out and saw a well-stocked ranch and yanked on the pull cord overhead. In short order, the train stopped and a very angry porter was ready to confront Allingham. That is, until he saw the look on the marshal's face as he towered over the diminutive railroad official. Allingham ignored him as he brushed past and onto the dusty track below.

In a little while he was riding a rented horse a short distance to the quiet community of Oak Creek Canyon. Once there, he found inhabitants who knew the doctor. They directed him to the man's peach orchard, not far off the main road up to Flagstaff.

It was a small affair, really, almost too small to sustain one farmer and his family working the land on their own, and Webster had an abundant staff, including a feisty woman from Nebraska, whose husband had died the year before. She was happy for the work. She was pleased to live in Arizona and dreaded the thought of moving back to her home state. Despite her busybody nature, though, she could tell Allingham little about the house, the physician, or the setup in general. Allingham peered through the windows into the dark interior of the home.

"He don't let no one in there. We all just work the orchard and he puts washin' out for me on the porch. Don't do no cleanin' or cookin' for him, mister."

"Marshal."

The woman was exceedingly irritating.

She was the worst kind of busybody, as she was ignorant of anything Allingham wanted to know. At least the busybodies in Hell's Kitchen were useful. They knew many things and Allingham often relied on them to help solve cases. This one was no help whatsoever.

Allingham tried the door but it was locked. He took a step back and kicked it with great force, splintering the jamb away. The woman looked on in astonishment. She followed him slowly as he entered the dwelling, peering about the place as if she were exploring a crypt. Allingham turned toward her and pointed to the doorway. "Out." She complied without any argument; she wanted no part in burgling the doctor's house.

He looked the place over carefully and found nothing amiss. It was a bachelor's abode, a good thirty years old and built by an early settler who'd managed to bring his little orchard into existence with nothing more than his sweat and labor and love. The house was simply built, austere, but nonetheless served the orchardist well during his time in Arizona.

Webster had it well-appointed with books and art. There were some mementos from a life of collecting by a man with a curious and scientific mind. A thick Oriental rug covered the floor. Allingham found a lamp and lit it. He carried it about as he unshuttered windows front and rear. The place now fully illuminated, he could see clearly. It was nothing more than a cottage with a parlor, one bedroom and a small eating area which served as kitchen. It had a pump in the room for water and a few cupboards. There was one bed and a dresser. There was no washstand in the bedroom, which he found odd.

He looked through the doctor's books and was surprised to find no secretary or writing desk. In fact, there was nothing to suggest a venue for handling any kind of such work or correspondence. This made Allingham very suspicious, as well. He began looking the floor over carefully. In one corner of the room, there was a corner cabinet, apparently built into the wall. It was covered by a glass paned door, which opened from near the ceiling, all the way to the floor.

He opened it and looked inside to find a few baubles, things normally collected by a man over the course of his life. He was suddenly struck by the strong odor of chemicals. He barely discerned a draft emitting from the case as it wafted past him.

He lit a cigarette and held the smoldering

tip close to the edges of the cabinet to verify that, indeed, there was a draft. He looked down at the carpet and noticed something had made a slight trench, formed in an arc. He pulled on the outside frame of the cabinet and it suddenly gave way.

The secret entrance led to a staircase. It descended to a cellar. Allingham understood, by the age of the work, that this was no accident, nor was it something constructed by the doctor recently.

The previous owner had taken precautions against Indians as he was one of the first in the territory to try his hand at making a go of settling the land. He could easily hide from any marauders, undetected, until the danger passed. Allingham suddenly felt a chill wash over him, imagining what it must have been like, living the life of a hermit out here, alone, with hostile people lurking about.

With a shaking hand, he pulled his six shooter and descended the stairs, lamp held high to illuminate his way. The chemical smell was stronger now, and it mixed with the tang of rotting flesh. He turned a corner to a singular room, dimly lit by his flickering lamp light.

There on a table lay the culmination of Webster's gruesome labor; a partially constructed corpse made of the bits and pieces of victims he'd collected over the past several weeks. There was no head.

The memory of Abraham Lincoln suddenly flooded the marshal's mind. Pieces of the corpses had been so thoroughly and repeatedly preserved that the flesh bore a resemblance to porcelain, and this is what reminded Allingham of the president, whom he'd seen on the departed leader's long ride in state back to his home in Illinois.

It had been warm that season, and the president's body lay in state for an unprecedented length of time. It always intrigued Allingham, who'd greatly admired Lincoln, that so many who took every opportunity to deride him and criticize him in life, should be so keen to see him in death. He could have used such devotion and support while living, as he navigated the country through its darkest and most terrible time. Everyone, admirers and detractors alike, seemed to want to see the great man once he was dead, and the embalmers voraciously preserved him again and again, until the president looked like a bright white ceramic reproduction of himself. It was an altogether eerie sight, and Allingham never forgot it.

Allingham found candles and lamps and lit them, allowing more light to reveal the horrific creation of a terribly diseased mind. He covered his mouth with a handkerchief and began taking an inventory of the dreadful scene.

As expected, he found the doctor's study, which sat in a corner of the little dungeon of horrors. On the desk was the missing shaving stand. He pulled open the drawer and found make-up, spirit gum, false whiskers. In another drawer he found a set of dentures and then he discovered another of the villain's secrets. These were the teeth he used when savaging the victims.

Allingham immediately chastised himself for his complacency. He felt a fool, as he had assumed too much. He assumed because the doctor had no chipped tooth, that the doctor was not his man. He found a long fingernail, attached to a silver clip. He placed this over his own pinky finger. It worked perfectly. He felt ill. The man had been playing him.

In all the years of his police work, Allingham had never been the victim of the crime. And now he was. The doctor had specifically singled him out. The man had come to Arizona to seek Allingham out with this gruesome game of cat and mouse.

Allingham became more frantic as he looked through the evidence before him.

Then he found the most horrific revelation of all, a newspaper clipping from the society page of the New York Times. It was a copy of the very photograph that Halsted had sent out — much to Allingham's dismay and despite his protests — of his daughter, with the announcement of their betrothal just two summers before. It had been neatly cut out and next to it written in a clear and crisp hand, 'Momma's head.'

Allingham flopped down in the doctor's chair and breathed deeply. He suddenly was dizzy and could not focus. The pervasiveness of the chemicals and the death-choked air made it difficult for him to catch his breath. He could not decide what to do. He was far away from his wife and now he knew the very man who'd been allowed into their home was hunting her. He breathed deeply and counted to ten. His mind cleared and he bolted for the stairs. He had to get a message to Singh. He had to find the nearest telegraph office.

As he started to race away, he thought he heard a sound and stopped. There was the faintest scraping noise; a sound coming from a little closet off to the side, under the stairs leading to the parlor above. He broke the door open and found the sheriff chained to the floor. The man was nearly dead.

Allingham yanked some tubes free. The doctor was embalming the poor lawman alive. His entire right arm was now useless to him. Allingham unshackled him and pulled him up into a sitting position.

"Howdy, marshal." The sheriff smiled weakly, certain he was going to die. "Sure am mighty glad to see you."

"Can you walk?"

"No, no. Leave me." He held up a hand. "I'm done for. He's been running that stuff into me for more than a day. I'm done for, marshal. Get your wife. She's next, get her. You gotta save her. You gotta save Mrs. Allingham."

Allingham pulled the man up into a standing position. He threw him over his shoulder and carried him up the narrow stairs and through the secret passageway above. He laid the man down on a divan and screamed as loudly as possible for the busybody. She wasn't far away.

"Go fetch a doctor." He had a thought. "Get him some help first, then fetch the doctor."

Slack-jawed and completely befuddled, she gazed stupidly in horror at the sheriff's poisoned arm, "Now, woman, now!"

She jumped as if she'd been pinched, and ran down the path toward the settlement. It would take a day to get a doctor to the injured man.

Allingham looked at the sheriff doubtfully. He'd lose the arm all right, and he wondered if he'd survive. He'd never heard of such a thing, embalming a man alive. He found Webster's liquor cabinet and pulled out a bottle and glass, setting it within easy reach of the invalid.

"Not too much, sheriff, but have a few on Webster. I'll be back. I'll be back." He thought for a moment and looked at the man resolutely, "With his head on a platter for you."

Allingham burst through the door of the post office and found a sallow man taking his lunch. The man did not look up at Allingham from the little cage that held his desk and telegraph equipment hostage. He even showed so much impudence as to hold up his hand like he was directing traffic on a busy New York street. "Closed until I've finished my lunch."

Allingham grabbed the grate with his fists and tore the entire partition to pieces. He stood over the clerk, face red, eyes wild, struggling hard to remain calm.

"What in *the hell* are you doing, mister!"

"A telegram! Now! Flagstaff, Hira Singh. Now!"

"All right, all right, go on, I'm listening." The man pushed his soup out of the way.

"Stay with Rebecca. Kill Dr. Webster on sight."

"Now now, I can't send such a thing, mister. That's, that's just plain illegal."

Allingham pulled his six shooter and pressed it to the man's forehead. "*Now,* or I'll kill you and send it myself!"

Chapter XXXIII:
An Unexpected Visitor

Ramon watched the riverboat churn past them as he finished cooking the evening meal. They were having fish again. He looked at Hilola who now seemed tired and a little dirty as her dress was about as stained by the river water as it could get. It was not much more than rags. He was ready to get home and treat his bride to the things that his family fortune and station could afford. His darling meant the world to him and he felt that she deserved some royal treatment for a change.

She smiled as she noticed he had a funny look on his face. She asked him what it was that had him looking so strange.

"Up ahead is a settlement, Hilola. Tomorrow, we're going there. We are going to get a nice room and some decent clothes. We are going to get cleaned up and I'm wiring the men at the Hacienda for some money. We're going home."

Hilola was relieved. The land this far down the river had not been as picturesque and she was tired of it. She was tired of the rough living and the lazy movement of the river. She was tired of being dirty all the time and trying to keep herself pretty instead of looking old and haggard. She worried more now over her appearance than she'd ever done in her life, as she wanted Ramon to love her. She believed that her physicality was the only thing worthwhile, the only thing she could possibly offer him. She did not understand that Ramon would love her regardless of how she looked, for the rest of her days. He had the kind of love for her that made a man love his woman into her eighth decade, if, God willing, they lasted that long.

She sat down beside him and kissed him on the cheek. "Whatever my man wants."

He grinned and leaned back. "Really?"

"Yep."

"What happened to the independent-minded woman I first met?"

"You did."

"How so?"

"Because you don't try to own me."

"So, then, that means you give yourself up to me, wholly?"

"Yep."

"So, if I tried to possess and control and own you, you'd buck me? I wouldn't get you?"

"Yep." She grinned, because she liked to tell Ramon things that vexed him. It wasn't that she was lying, she meant it, but it sounded especially preposterous when he took it, verbalized it, carried it to its most logical conclusion and then just stated it, articulating it in the way only Ramon could do.

"I love you."

"I love you, too."

They loved and then watched the sun go down and watched the glow of the settlement downstream, on the eastern side. Tomorrow they'd sail to it and begin a new life. They were both as happy as was humanly possible.

Ramon reeled as the blow from the big boot struck him squarely on the side of his head, awakening him from his early morning slumber. He squinted and tried to focus as the man stood over him, six shooter at the ready.

"Hello, pal."

Hilola suddenly appeared behind him. *"Jimmie!"* She ran up and reached out to hug him. He pushed her away, and then knocked her to the ground with a backhand across the mouth. She spit blood and carefully felt her injured jaw.

"Don't *Jimmie* me, bitch." He looked down at her as if she were vermin and she just as quickly crabbed on her knees toward him, groveling at his feet. She wrapped her arms around his thighs, giving him a loving squeeze.

"Come on, lover, you can't be mad at me."

Her ministrations were distracting him. Hilola looked good. She looked younger and prettier than she had the last time he'd seen her. He felt her hands move up his right thigh, eliciting the primordial reaction she expected and was confident she could get out of the scruffy man.

"Oh, now we're lovebirds?"

"Sure we are, Jimmie. Same as ever! Same as we always was! Come on, now, you don't think I'd want this nigger?" She pointed derisively at Ramon, hatred filling her eyes. She suddenly remembered something, "And, the lyin' dirty dog can speak English, Jimmie! He talks English better'n me!"

"Oh, really?" He glared at Ramon who worked hard at regaining his senses.

Ramon looked at Hilola for something, anything; an indication that what she was saying was a cruel joke or ruse. Instead, she unbuttoned the top of her garment with trembling hands and peeled off her dress. She reclined, sheer petticoat revealing all, beckoning Jimmie to come lay with her for a quick and passionate reunion right there and then. For the broken-hearted Ramon, it was the cruelest and most devastating torture anyone could mete out.

"Lover, I thought you was dead, sure as shootin'. I swear it! I dove and dove for you," she nodded at Ramon, "he'll tell ya. I tried to save you, Jimmie, but we couldn't find ya. We even camped at the spot where you went over for two days, hopin' you'd turn up."

She looked at Ramon as if she could kill him right then and there. "I even had to hold a gun on him to make him stay. But I did, lover, I did. I swear I did, and then, he got the best a me. When I was sleepin' he raped me. It made me sick. I, I even threw up." She turned and spit a mouthful of bloody phlegm at Ramon's feet. "He's been rapin' me every day, sometimes more than onced a day. He's like a wild animal, he is, constantly on me, pawing at me, doin' things to me. He even traded me for things from the Indians. The Indians, Jimmie, the filthy Indians, more than a dozen of 'em had their way with me, because of him! And then, and then," her voice quivered in anger at the memory of such injustice, "he got the Indians drunk and kilt 'em all, and then took me back. Oh, he laughed his rotten head off at that. He's a dirty killer, Jimmie, watch him, watch him!"

She once again groveled at his feet, trying to make contact as he broke free. "Let's kill him, Jimmie, we can kill him and take the boat and go on down to Mexico like you said." She was desperate now, almost beside herself in her anxiety to win him over. "Come on, lover, gimme your six shooter. I'll shoot him. I deserve to be the one to kill 'im."

Jimmie ignored her and went to the boat. He started looking for his booty. He hefted the bow and Hilola, who knew Jimmie well, could tell he was working himself into a regular fury.

She continued. "Where you been, lover? How'd you survive?"

He continued to search and was becoming more furious by the moment. He answered her, nonetheless, a little too calmly. "Oh, I'm pretty wiry. I floated downstream and then I ended up in a settlement. And guess what?"

"What, lover, what?" She was at least getting him to talk. When Jimmie was talking, he wasn't hitting, and that was always healthier for Hilola.

"I met some dude from up north, some dude named Thad Hall. He's the one looking for our Mexican here. He's the one got this greaser to jump into the river up yonder, where we found him. I told him what happened and he staked me for a canoe and provisions. We were supposed to ride the river together, track you two down, but I left the sucker high and dry. Told him about the gold and said I'd make him my partner. Stupid dumbass! He staked me two hundred dollars' worth a traps. And now, now." He began tearing at the hidden compartment of the boat. "Son of a bitch, where's my gold?"

Hilola pointed accusingly at Ramon. "*He* took it Jimmie. He hid it and said he'd come back with his greasy friends and get it. He took it, Jimmie. Told me he'd stove my head in if'n I argued. Come on, lover," she reached out with her hand, begging him, "let me have your gun. Let me shoot him."

Jimmie ignored her gestures. "Is that so?" He walked up to Ramon who gathered himself, preparing to spring despite the pistol cocked and pointed at his head. The kick had had a greater effect than he first realized and the energy left his limbs as if he were a vessel of water. He reeled and Jimmie had him by the hair, pulling his head back, clubbing him with the butt end of his six shooter.

But Ramon didn't much care now. He was losing consciousness along with his will to fight and survive. Hilola's words, her actions, her lies, caused a great lethargy to wash over him. He felt as if he were drugged or drunk and he simply didn't care if he lived or died. He felt nothing. The blows from the gun's handle felt far removed, as if Jimmie'd used nothing more than a feather against his face. Jimmie gave him an extra violent shake, as if he sensed it and wanted the man to suffer more.

He shook Ramon again. The rogue was just too dimwitted to understand that nothing he could do now would remotely compare to what Hilola had just done; Ramon was literally dying of a broken heart.

"I'll tell you something, Mexican. I'll tell you somethin' right now. I ain't gonna shoot you." He holstered his gun and pulled his big knife. "I'm gonna filet the skin off you like the Apaches do." He smiled and turned to look at Hilola, who was suddenly behind him, only inches away.

She reached over and grabbed Jimmie around the neck, pulling him backward. She impaled him to the hilt of Ramon's big hunting knife. Jimmie stood stupidly, a quizzical look on his face. For several moments he did nothing but look about. Hilola relaxed her grip and stepped back, pulling the six shooter from its place on the dying man's hip. She pulled back the hammer of the gun and pointed it at his head but there was no need to fire. Jimmie was dead on his feet. He'd give them no more trouble.

He looked down at a good three inches of crimson colored steel protruding just a little left of his breastbone. The tip was dripping blood with every beat of his failing heart.

Hilola moved close to him, close enough to half whisper, half spit the words into his ear: "No one lays a hand on my husband! Especially *you, pig*!"

Jimmie fell forward at Ramon's feet. With one last effort, he turned over, his face to the sky. Blood poured freely from his nose and mouth. He gasped out one final word as he focused on Hilola.

"Bitch." He breathed his last.

Hilola scooped Ramon up in her arms, cuddling him like a newborn babe. She worried over the wounds from Jimmie's six shooter and big army boot. "I'm sorry, lover, I couldn't get a swipe at him sooner. Couldn't do nothin' while he was pointin' that gun." She kissed him on his injured head. "Forgive me?"

"Yeah." He began to lose consciousness but struggled to say something. "Hilola?"

"Yes, lover?"

"You're the most confounding and scandalous woman I've ever known."

She smiled again, kissing him with blood-tinged lips. "Thank you."

Chapter XXXIV:
Of the Moon

Rosario gathered food for Hobbs as he slept in. He'd been doing more and more sleeping in over the past six months, and Rosario knew it was likely to be this way from now on. Hobbsie had led a hard life and his heart, liver, and kidneys were steadily giving up on him.

She watched the sailboat glide by and noticed the pretty blonde woman preparing to tie up at the pier just downstream of the Esmeralda. She handed the basket of food to Bob the steward, always present and ready to do for Hobbs. Leaving the stern-wheeler she approached the two travelers.

"Hola, Señor." She smiled at Ramon and then lost her smile as she looked at his battered face. She then nodded to Hilola, continuing before either could react. "You are Ramon la Garza?"

"Who wants to know, lady?" Hilola jumped onto the pier, towering over Rosario, defiant and obviously suspicious. Not another soul was going to harm her man.

Rosario liked her. She liked her right away and could see she was protecting her lover. She would never fault a woman for that. "I am Rosario Hobbs. My husband and two other men have been tracking you. Another man, Thad Hall, is after you because Mr. la Garza killed his brother."

"Are you some kind of law, señora?" Ramon climbed, with some difficulty, from the boat onto the pier and extended his hand. Rosario took it as the young man bowed respectfully.

"We are. We are deputy US Marshals and my husband is not well." She indicated with her head the stateroom behind her. "He is resting."

Ramon removed his six shooter and handed it over, butt first, to Rosario. "I surrender, señora."

She smiled. He was a good Mexicano boy. She held up her hand and refused it. "No need, my lad. Everything is in hand. We are traveling down to Yuma for the hanging."

"Hanging, Miss?" Hilola was intrigued.

"Sí. The hanging of Thad Hall."

"Señora, do you know where I might send a wire?"

She directed him to the telegraph office,

then ordered them to take passage with them to Yuma that day. She watched the lovers walk off, hand in hand. She hurried back to report to Hobbsie.

"You sit right next to me, young lady." The gambler pinched Hilola delicately on the cheek. "Pretty ladies *always* bring me good luck." He smiled and gave Rosario a squeeze on the hand. "Now I have two of you. Holy smoke, we'll clean house tonight!"

Ramon sat nearby. He was proud of his woman. Now that he'd gotten her cleaned up and dressed properly, he slipped off to see the German boat captain. He brushed past Rosario and gave her a loving pat on the shoulder, nodding respectfully to Hobbs.

Hobbs looked after him and then turned his attention to Rosario. "He's a good lad. I'm glad that Mormon gold has a reward. It'll set these young ones up for a long time."

"Sí, my love. You know the la Garza family has had many bad things happen to them; many bad things. It is about time something good happens to them. The young man is going to be a good hacendado back in Mexico. He is the kind of man our country needs. God be with him."

"Hilola, Hilola." The old gentlemen sang it like a tune. "It is a beautiful name." The gambler threw down another winning hand and pinched his companion on the cheek again. "Do you know what your name means, my dear?"

"Gosh no." Hilola blushed and looked at her hands. She was smitten with the old gambler.

"It is Arabic. It mean *of the moon.*"

Hilola shrugged her shoulders and then looked down at herself in her beautiful dress. Everyone at the table stole glances at her, as she was the loveliest creature they'd seen in a very long time.

The gambler watched the moonbeams play off the river as they sailed south. He looked up at the brightly shining moon in the evening sky and then back to his special guest. "It certainly is a fitting name, my child." He suddenly looked at his watch, folded his present hand, and signaled to his entourage. "Gentlemen, it is time."

They all jumped to attention and looked toward the bow of the riverboat. The captain stood in his dress white uniform. Next to him was Ramon in a new suit. Beside him

340

were Hobbs and Rosario. A diminutive clergyman stood proudly, happy to make it all official. Despite all the rumors to the contrary, a captain who was not a clergyman could not perform marriages.

The gambler extended his hand, "Miss Hilola, may I have the privilege of walking the bride to the place of honor?"

She blushed again and looked about self-consciously. She'd not expected things to happen so quickly, and suddenly realized this was no dream. It was actually happening, thanks to Ramon. She was proud and very happy.

She placed her hand on the old man's proffered arm and beamed at everyone around her. "I, I, you all went through an awful lot of trouble for me."

He patted her arm. "Our pleasure, child, our pleasure."

Rosario thrust the bouquet into her hands and the next thing Hilola knew, she was standing next to her man. He was beautiful and looked even more grown up than ever before. Perhaps the difference in their ages was not so vast. No one seemed to mind and all her fears and concerns fell away. They no longer meant anything.

Nothing really mattered, now, except Ramon. It would be she and Ramon together from now on, and she'd be good to him. She'd love him and make him a good wife. She would be the mother of his babies.

She suddenly began to cry. And then Rosario was next to her, comforting her, making it all more wonderful, as she knew now she was loved. She finally understood that she was so much more than she'd ever been led to believe; she was a worthwhile and decent woman. After all the years and all the bad men, all the scratching to survive, Hilola saw, with crystal clarity, that it wasn't her, it had been them. She was a good, desirable, and worthwhile human being, and things would be different from here on out.

They danced and celebrated through the night, and all the ship's passengers and crew joined in. Hilola looked again and again at the marriage certificate. It was real. Although the captain stood by like a proud parent, the sacred business at hand had been carried out by an official of the territory; even more importantly, an official of God. He was not a priest, but that didn't matter to Ramon. A man of God was a man of God, regardless of the silly rules imposed by man.

■ ■ ■ ■

They watched the moon high in the sky as they loved in a real bed this time, actually, a real bed for the first time. It was the best stateroom on the craft and the significance was not lost on the bride. "This is mighty nice, Ramon."

"Fitting for my love, my Hilola, *of the moon*!" He laughed as she blushed.

"That sounds silly, don't it?"

"No, not a bit."

She was tired. She yawned and fought the sleepiness as she didn't want the night to end. They were both tired, yet too excited to sleep. She finally rested her head on his chest and cried.

He started to comfort her and she stopped him.

"Ain't cryin' 'cause I'm sad, Ramon. Crying 'cause I've never been so happy. Never in all my born days thought my life would turn out this way."

"It is only the beginning, my love."

Thad cried like a baby as Pierce and Old Pop stood in the jail cell with the hapless lawyer Swineford. Pierce tried to make the best of it. "Did you get word to Pa? Can he send help, money, a lawyer?" He glanced doubtfully at Swineford who'd nodded off.

"Pa's dead!"

"What?" Old Pop responded without thinking. The old Scotsman dead? His ears were certainly deceiving him.

"Yes, dead. When he heard I got arrested, he fell over, had a fit and gagged on his own vomit. He's dead, dead, dead."

Pierce kicked the lawyer awake. "How many years do you suppose he'll get?"

Swineford shrugged his shoulders up and yawned. "None."

"What do ya mean, none?"

"This is a hanging offense." He looked seriously at Pierce and for the first time showed a modicum of intelligence in his eyes. "Your brother faces execution for this crime."

Old Pop was compelled to ask. He didn't particularly care one way or the other that Thad had a terrible counselor. "How's it that you're a prosecutor for the state on one hand, and then a defender of Thad, here, on another?"

"I'm working independently on this case."

"And, no offence, Mr. Swineford, but what of Kline? He seemed a bit, how do I say this without soundin', well, mean, a bit more up on his game than you."

Swineford stood up. He stretched from his recent mini nap and was impressive in the fact that he was not the least insulted or deterred.

"Kline only takes cases that he has a good chance of winning." He shrugged and looked at Thad as if he were regarding a corpse. "And this isn't one of them."

Thad broke down and wailed like a little child, so much so that even Old Pop felt a little sorry for him. The ruffian grabbed his brother's hands and cried into them. "I'm sorry, Pierce. Sorry, sorry. I'm sorry I treated you mean, sorry I went after that Mexican, sorry I shot that sheriff. I'm sorry, sorry. Please tell 'em, tell 'em I'm sorry, tell 'em please don't hang me. I don't wanna die. I'm scared, Pierce, I'm scared."

"That's enough of that." The guard motioned for them to leave and they complied.

Pierce had difficulty prying himself away from his distraught brother. Both men finally, mercifully, were able to get away from the broken Thad Hall.

They found themselves in the bright sunlight of a late Yuma morning. Old Pop looked at his companion and was heartened by Pierce's demeanor. He was shaken and sad, but handling it well enough. Old Pop suddenly had a revelation.

"You understand now, Pierce, the ranch is yours. All yours. You can run it right from now on. You can run it the way it ought to be run," he extended his hand and Pierce shook it.

"What's that for, Old Pop?"

"Nothin', just want to shake the hand of a man of property, a wealthy man." He nodded his head up and down. "Feels good."

"Sure does Old Pop. And now I know what it feels like, too."

"Huh?"

"To shake the hand of a man of property." He grinned slyly, "Partner."

"Oh, no, oh no." Old Pop waved him off.

"Oh, yeah, and not another word on it." Pierce looked in the direction of the river boat's whistle. "Come on, Old Pop. Let's get that Alanza horse back to her rightful owner. We gotta get back north. We got a ranch to run."

Chapter XXXV: The Price of Hubris

Rebecca Allingham awoke from her chloroform induced nap, lying naked and bound in the bed previously occupied by the young school teacher, Mary Rogers. She was terrified and humiliated as Webster stood over her, ogling her nude form. She watched the maniacal eyes dart here and there. It was the first time anyone other than her husband had seen her unclothed.

Webster turned his attention to the school teacher, chained to the wall at the foot of the narrow bed. "Speak, Momma, speak."

"What shall I say?" She looked into Rebecca's eyes and Rebecca could see the strain the terrible captivity had had on the poor young teacher. The woman was now numb to her own fear yet, nonetheless, still could feel remorse for Rebecca's plight.

"You are my crowning jewel." He turned and looked hatefully at the school teacher. "Say it!"

Mary Rogers spoke to the floor, humiliated at the thought that she was being used as a device to demean and torment Rebecca Allingham. "You are my crowning jewel."

Webster turned his attention to Rebecca's face, lovingly caressed her cheeks, her jaw, neck, and hair. He ignored the rest of her body. "This mortal head will complete my immortal project." He turned again, "Say it!"

"This mortal head will complete my immortal project."

Rebecca tried to reason with him. "Come on now, Dr. Webster. I think perhaps you might be ill. I think perhaps we should get you the help you need. Come now, untie us and we'll all go get some help for you. We'll find you a good doctor and everything will be fine."

He gazed upon her and suddenly something subtle changed and he looked to be himself. He appeared to be natural and no longer in his demented state. He addressed her appropriately. "Mrs. Allingham, don't patronize me." He reached out and rubbed a hand on her protruding belly. "Once I remove your head, I'll take out that little Allingham fetus and feed it to my dogs." He turned and looked back at the teacher. "Say it!"

"What?"

"You know what! Say it!"

The teacher finally broke down. "I can't, I can't. I won't."

He turned and beat her savagely until the blood flowed from her nose and mouth. "You'll say what I tell you or suffer the consequences."

Rebecca suddenly screamed with all her might. *"Help us, someone, help us!"*

Webster laughed and called out even louder yet, mimicking Rebecca's cries; "Help us! Someone please help us! Hah! No one can hear you, Mrs. Allingham. A fitting tribute to your father's avarice. He put the Mormons out of business in this little town. It's abandoned now because of him, him and your falsely pious Indian servant, Mr. Singh. No, there's no one here to help you, no one here to hear you. We're all alone in the world, just the three of us, all alone and no one knows a thing!"

"But they do, Dr. Webster. Remember my notes. They do. It's just a matter of time. Why don't you untie us and run on out of here. You can be in California with two days hard riding. We'll tell no one." She looked at the school teacher, "Isn't that right, miss?"

The girl nodded energetically, too afraid

to utter another word.

Webster held out Rebecca's note, shoving it in her face, "Oh, you mean this note? This note? Hah!"

"Please, Dr. Webster," Rebecca's heart sank at the realization that he'd lifted it, right under her nose. She became frantic. "Please. I, I'm begging you. I want to live, I want to see my baby before I die."

He held up a hand, index finger pointing skyward. "I have an idea!" And with that, he walked out.

Rebecca held back the tears and spoke to the young woman in her calmest voice, "Will you pray with me, Mary?"

The girl nodded and swallowed the blood backing up in her throat. She wanted to vomit, and then gained control. The words still would not come. She mouthed the prayer as Rebecca recited, "The Lord is my shepherd; I shall not want. He maketh me to lie down in green pastures: He leadeth me beside the still waters . . ."

Webster burst in with a large scalpel. He looked Rebecca over clinically. "I'll give you a good look at your baby before you die." He grinned, "Always wanted to perform a Cesarean delivery."

He moved closer, preparing to make the incision, when a sound caught his attention outside. He stopped and held up a hand for both women to take heed. He put his finger to his lips, signaling for them to keep quiet. He pulled out his pistol and left the room once again. All was quiet.

Rebecca continued, tears streaming down the sides of her face, running into her ears. She worked hard to stop her quivering jaw. "He restoreth my soul: He leadeth me in the paths of righteousness for His name's sake. Yea, though I walk through the valley of the shadow of death, I will fear no evil: for thou art with me; thy rod and thy staff they comfort me." She looked down at the school teacher, sobbing and shaking, "Come now, my darling, say it with me."

Allingham burst through the door and took the deranged man's first shot, allowing Singh time to throw his chakkar with deadly precision, sinking it deeply into the bridge of Webster's nose, blinding both eyes. The maniac fell back and fired wildly in the direction of his attackers, putting a couple of slugs in the Sikh's turban. Singh remained unscathed. It would not be the first time he would dig bullets from his dastar.

Allingham was now on top of Webster, knocking the gun from his hand. Webster sat, propped against a wall, waiting for what, he did not know. Allingham called for Rebecca, looking about wildly, as he shoved a handkerchief into the hole in his shoulder wound, staunching the blood. It was not nearly as bad as what he'd suffered at Canyon Diablo. He felt no pain.

He discovered her in the next room, kissed her desperately on the mouth and covered her with the discarded dress. He worked to set her free. Rebecca stopped him.

"Help Mary first." She nodded with her head to the school teacher tethered to the wall. Allingham looked at the bloody and naked young woman. He averted his eyes and found a blanket to give her some long overdue privacy. Allingham worked on unshackling Webster's makeshift bindings. Mary was free at last.

He took a deep breath and felt the blood pound in his ears. He was wild, more furious than he'd been in his life. He swallowed hard, did his best to regain control. He liberated his wife.

Both women were free and dressed properly now. Rebecca comforted the young school teacher; she'd been abused the most of the two and for the longer time. She cried as Rebecca held her.

Singh calmly nodded to Rebecca, his countenance betraying his true feelings of relief and remorse. "Kaur, please, please forgive me."

She shrugged. "Nothing to forgive, Bapu. You've saved our lives." She grabbed him and kissed him gently on the cheek. She squeezed him with all her might. "I didn't think I'd see you again, Father. I didn't think I'd see any of you again."

Webster groaned, the pain unbearable. They looked upon him as if just now remembering the monster amongst them.

"He was building a recreation of his mother." Allingham grimaced at the memory of the partial corpse he'd discovered earlier in the day.

Rebecca smiled weakly. "Yes, and I was to be the head."

"And, I, the voice. That's why he kept me alive." The school teacher looked at her captive with hatred and disgust in her eyes. She gave her tormentor a sound kick in the legs.

Rebecca remembered something and smiled at Mary Rogers. "It was your cipher that brought us here." She looked at the two men. "But he took it, palmed it when we left to get you, Bapu. How did you know? How did you know where to find us?"

Singh looked at his companion. "Our man, Allingham. He made a rubbing of the paper under your worksheet. Your pencil marks had made an indentation and Allingham rubbed it with a lead. They emerged and we could read them clearly."

"Oh, I'm in so much pain." The doctor reached up with both hands, and carefully felt the razor sharp disc, deeply imbedded in his skull. His eyelids involuntarily blinked, the blade cutting more deeply with every movement. "Please, please help me."

"Is that what all your victims said to you, doctor? Please help me, as you savagely tortured them to death?" Allingham sneered. "You're not even a doctor, are you? A sick mortuary surgeon. That's where you learned your horrible craft; on the battlefields of that terrible war, experimenting on the poor dead. Oh, by the way, bastard, the sheriff is going to survive."

Webster looked toward the others. Allingham suddenly reached over and unceremoniously yanked the blade from the man's face as the maniac screamed out in agony, blood, brain fluid and aqueous humor freely running down his cheeks, soaking into his shirt.

"No, I'm not a physician, Allingham, not a physician. But I am a man smart enough to make you look the fool, and that arrogant ass Halsted. By the way, Mrs. Allingham, I didn't cut his throat when I had the chance. Didn't because I wanted him to see what

I'd done to you. I wanted him to regret his hubristic flaunting of his perfect daughter in the newspapers. I heard he took ads out in every major city, the arrogant fool."

He cackled, despite the intense pain, magnified every time he screwed his face up in diabolical glee. "I learned all about the big man, Allingham, that way. How he saved the day at that worthless settlement, Canyon Diablo; how he was a genius at solving crimes."

He stopped and turned his head, looking with his ruined eyes toward Allingham. "I knew, also, how much Halsted hated all that — hated you — still hates you. I could read between the lines, could tell he was ashamed of what a poor choice his daughter had made, marrying a low-down, low-life police-man, and not even a real detective at that."

He threw his head back and looked as if he might howl like some deranged wolf. He continued: "Then, then to see your picture, Lady Allingham! To learn that you even shared my momma's hair color." He became overwhelmed and would have cried had his eyes not been destroyed.

He went on, "All together in one pretty package. It was then that I knew I had to come out to this godforsaken Arizona land and work on my masterpiece." He stopped, and carefully ran his fingers over his oozing, wounded face. "The only regret I have is that Mrs. Allingham deciphered the little bitch's message. My one slipup or I would have killed at least a dozen more before my grand finale." He shrugged, "But no matter, I had the enjoyment of those first few. Oh, their screams were simply delectable." He winced in pain. "Oh, I'm dying, I need help, a doctor's help."

Allingham sneered again, "Don't worry, we'll make certain you get patched up, good and ready for the hangman. The next stop for you is the gallows."

Webster suddenly laughed maniacally. "Not so, Marshal Allingham, not so. You see, I am insane. No court in the land will hang a madman." He giggled like a child. "Look at old Daniel Sickles! You know, I met him once, at Gettysburg. Another arrogant fool. He got away with it and so will I. I'll spend the rest of my days living in a hospital. No one will touch me." He looked around with his lifeless eyes, "In fact, I think I'll make some trouble for all of you. Entrapment, cruel and unusual punishment! I imagine Mr. Singh will go to prison for using this ancient weapon of barbarity on me. No, Marshal Allingham, I think not."

"No! It is *I* who thinks not!" Mary Rogers

reached over, liberating Singh's kirpan from the sheath under his arm. The Sikh did not stop her. She plunged the blade into her tormentor's heart. "Go to hell, Dr. Webster. Go straight to hell, where you belong."

The doctor screamed again as the pain from the blade seared through his body, the teacher holding the handle firmly, feeling the beating of the evil man's heart until it faded, then finally stopped.

She looked at her companions and slowly stood up. "Will someone take me home now, please?"

CHAPTER XXXVI:
THE COMEUPPANCE

Ramon la Garza spoke quietly to his Alanza and stroked her lovingly about the ears. He looked at Pierce Hall and Old Pop and nodded his appreciation. He could do no more just now. He was speechless, as he thought he'd never see his mare again.

Hilola stepped up and spoke to the men. "So, you're my husband's protectors." She extended her hand and Old Pop blushed at being given so much attention by such a stunning lady.

"I, I don't know about that, ma'am, just tryin' to do what's right." He looked at Pierce who stood, a little self-consciously, staring at the ground. "Pierce here is really the hero; I'm just along for the adventure, and the ride."

Ramon finally found his voice and spoke up. "I am sorry about your father, and about your brother, Pierce. I know they were not the best of men. I know they were difficult to like, but they were family, and it is very hard to lose family."

Pierce looked up and thought of something that had been preying on his mind. He was a man ignorant of the protocol of such things. "Will you all be attending the hanging?" He looked back toward the center of town and the courthouse where the deed was to be carried out.

Hilola spoke for both of them. "No, mister. We've had enough of killings. It's time to start living, and I think that goes for you men, too. Seeing your brother get strung up won't do you no good." She became a little embarrassed at her own temerity, but Hilola was finding her voice, now that Ramon was by her side.

"My wife's right, Pierce." He looked at Old Pop and then back to Pierce. "We've all got ranches to run and, Pierce, I'd like to talk to you about a partnership."

Pierce's eyes widened. "A partnership?"

"Yes. Our ranches would benefit; you with your beeves and we with our horses. But we need a white man to act on our behalf," he smiled at his wife. "It would go a long way if you and Old Pop would handle the business of selling our horses in the states for us. Seems the gringos are not yet ready for us Mexicans up here. Maybe they won't be for another hundred years. Maybe won't be, ever, but we've got good horses and we can do good business. If you'll consider helping us out."

He extended his hand and Pierce shook it. He did the same for Old Pop.

"I think I can say for both of us," Pierce nodded at his companion, "Me and Old Pop would be honored to work at your side."

Old Pop arrived at the courthouse on the morning of the hanging. He insisted, and stood stiffly, resolutely, as Thad Hall cried like a little child, groping and hugging the old cowboy about the neck.

"Where's my brother? Where's my Pierce?" The old man held his tongue and his revulsion, as Thad was a broken man. He stood firm, however, and looked the blubbering man in the eye.

"I'm here for you, son. Your brother's a gentle soul, and watching you being put out of your misery would be too much to ask of him. More than you gotta right to ask."

"But I want to see him!"

"No!" He held back his anger. "Now, you listen to me, *boy.*" It was the kind of firmness Thad could have stood twenty years ago. Perhaps if he had, he would not now be facing the gallows. But that was no

360

longer here nor there. It wasn't Thad that Old Pop was comforting. It was his favorite person in the world, his man, Pierce, that he was concerned about.

Thad looked desperately at the old man. He was wilting, fading as he waited for some words of wisdom and, perhaps, forgiveness. "Ye . . . yes, sir. I, I'm listenin'."

"Now, you calm yourself and make your peace with God and talk to the preacher there. You tell him you're sorry and you hope that God will have mercy on your soul, boy. As penance, you can think about your brother and how you can spare him seeing your last moments at the gallows. That's the right thing and that's what you need to do. Your brother's a good man and he deserves that consideration. You need to tell me, right here and right now, a good message for me to take back to him."

"Yes, yes. Yer right, Old Pop."

Thad wiped his nose with the back of his hand. "Please tell him . . . , tell him I'm awful sorry for treatin' him so bad. And tell that Mexican I'm sorry and . . . just tell 'em all, that sheriff's family and all his friends, that I'm sorry. I'm sorry as I can be. Tell 'em all I'm getting what's comin' to me. Just tell 'em all."

"Okay, son. Now, go and see the preacher,

prepare to learn the grand secret and repent for all the black-hearted things you done in this world. I'll be there when you die. I'll be there and I'll pray for you." He nodded and Thad turned away, head down, crying as he'd never cried in his life.

It was a crisp morning, clear and cool and the two prisoners walked resolutely to their deaths. Thad reeled a little as he ascended the steep oak stairs to the gallows. The fresh oak's pungent odor was offensive and stomach churning. Why could they never use sweet smelling pine? He received a steadying hand from the preacher who walked behind, stone-faced, Bible in his right hand, and together, they eventually made it to the top.

The whole affair, Thad could have sworn, swayed dangerously under foot, as if they'd only tacked it together and forgot to finish the job. Thad was convinced the entire contraption would tumble them all to the ground. It made him dizzy and sick and difficult to stay upright. He held the preacher's shoulder and looked him wildly in the eye, "Please, please don't, please don't let me fall."

The minister held him firmly. "It'll all be all right, son. It'll all be all right."

The other prisoner was falsely cavalier, and bobbed to and fro as the hangman tried to place the hood on his head.

"Don't need no danged hood, want to go to my death eyes wide open."

The sheriff held him, still and tight. "Hood's not for you, son, it's for us. We don't want to see your mug any more than we have to, especially when the rope snaps your neck."

Thad looked over and cried and quietly recited the lines of the prayer the preacher had taught him. He suddenly had a severe kink in his neck, and nothing he could do would make it go away.

He stood still as the hangman tied the leather restraints around his wrists, then arms, then legs. He could remember only a few of the words, and repeated them now over and over. "I fear no evil, I fear no evil," as the black hood was resolutely pulled over his head. He felt the noose tighten the hood against his face and tried hard to breathe. His companion was not helping matters any as he began to cry like a baby.

"Oh, Jesus, I can't breathe, oh God, please, please take it off!" The cavalier man now panicked and convulsed. He began vomiting great gouts into the hood, tightly cinched about his face with the hanging rope, filling it up and filling the air with the stench of his stomach contents. The hangman and sheriff briefly considered calling the whole thing off as the man was choking and crying and making the entire surreal experience even less bearable.

But the preacher intervened and nodded for them to proceed. He was a man of God and did not condone capital punishment, but the prolongation of it would be crueler than the act itself. In less than a minute both men were swaying, necks broken, bodies relaxing in death.

Old Pop felt numb. He was not happy nor was he sad. It was his first hanging and it was exhausting. He left the courtyard quickly, away from the pungent odor of vomit and fresh oak and death. He thought he could stand a stiff drink.

Instead, he wandered through Yuma as he could not talk to anyone he knew just now, did not want to interact with anyone really at all, but still needed to be among normalcy. He needed to be among normal human living and interaction and nature and just normal things. He wandered down the street fronting the river and listened to some children playing off in the distance. He watched boat traffic on the river. He moved aside so a carriage could pass. He listened to birds sing. He needed to see and hear these things and breathe clean air and not think about Thad or the Old Scotsman, or even Donny, whose death started all this, it seemed, like a hundred years ago.

He sat on a bench and rested for a while. This was an ending, but it was also a new beginning, and suddenly he felt energized by the prospect that now, all the evil had been expunged from the ranch up north, from his life and the life of his favorite friend, his son. A new man, a good man would be in charge, and he'd be there for him, be there to guide him and comfort him and support him.

A young pretty woman walked by in a blue print dress and smiled at him and wished him a good morning. He tipped his hat and looked up at the clear blue sky and smiled back at her. She was clean and pretty and pure and, to Old Pop, likely pure of heart. It made him very happy to see her, as if God had sent her to him as some kind of sign, an Angel from heaven, sent down to tell him that it was indeed a good and beautiful morning and that it was time to start living. For a man of nearly sixty years, that was no insignificant message, as Old Pop had wanted to start living all his life. Now was his chance, now was his time, and he'd take it.

Chapter XXXVII:
A Good Soldier and Friend

Allingham lay in bed next to his wife and dared not move as he didn't want to disturb the sleep she most desperately needed. He thought about the news from their family doctor that Hobbs was dying and it made him sad. He thought back to the first day they'd met, Hobbs in his broken down bed with the scruffy dog sleeping at his feet. He couldn't believe it was more than two years ago and was surprised, really, that Hobbs was still with them after all that time. Allingham knew well enough, Hobbs was a dead man walking then, and he'd been through a lot since. Allingham had run him through the ringer and, for this, Allingham had many regrets.

But these were largely unfounded regrets. It was Allingham who'd brought them all together. It was Allingham who'd made it possible for Hobbs to find the love of his life. It was Allingham who'd made Hobbs

feel good and productive; and it was Allingham who'd helped him become a Jew again.
Because without Allingham, Hobbs would
have never known Singh, and without
Singh, he'd have never known what it was
to be with his God.

So, as always, Allingham the great detective, was blind to the most important things
in life; blind to the knowledge that he was
so pivotal in the actions of others' lives.

Rebecca finally spoke up. "Hello, my great
sleuth-hound of a husband." She kissed him
on the cheek.

"Hello."

"A penny for your thoughts."

"Oh, just thinking about Hobbsie."

"Poor dear."

"I feel like I've worn his heart out."

She sat up and rested on her elbow. "How
so?"

"Everything. All this. Just everything."

"Do you know what Rosario told me?"

"No."

"She said that Hobbs told her that the
time he'd been with us, with you, was the
grandest time of his life."

"Hmm."

She smiled at his response. "You are a
great man, darling. You have a great gift and
there is greatness about you. But this great-

ness comes at a price, and that price is an intensity of living known only to a very few. To live with such greatness, and to use such greatness, means that you must live at that level of intensity; the intensity and energy of a comet, a sun, a force that burns bright and bold. It is, frankly, exhausting to anyone who lives around it, amongst it. But those who choose to be with you would have it no other way." She kissed him. "I can attest to that."

"Hmm. Don't feel very great." He grabbed her and held her tightly, a bit desperately. He boldly ran his hands over his growing child. "I certainly bungled this whole thing. I've made a colossal mess of it. Nearly lost you."

"You did not."

"Didn't catch him until he'd done so many horrible things."

"He was diabolical, darling. He knew you, knew your methods. How could you anticipate such a thing? Wearing false teeth, wearing a false fingernail and whiskers? He played us all, darling. He was playing an evil game with a stacked deck." She kissed him again and squeezed him tightly. "And you were brilliant and clever and fearless. You beat him, darling, and there is something to be said for that."

"I don't know." He turned on his good side, as his wound ached. He pulled her close to him and wanted to cry. "I don't know what I would do without you, Rebecca. When I saw you there, and when I realized what nearly happened to you, I, and our baby, our baby. I . . ."

"Shh. Darling, stop thinking of it. It is done, and we are safe, and there is no profit in considering what could have, but did not happen. It's done. It's done."

Hira Singh smiled at Hobbs as he'd awakened from a long nap. Hobbs smiled back. It was all he could do, as he was too weak to sit up.

Singh reached over and picked up his friend's skull cap, turning it over in his hands. "It is much simpler than mine." He put it back in its spot on the nightstand next to Hobbs's bed.

"Yes, I've seen what you go through to make your turban right. What a job." He smiled weakly. "Is everyone all right, Hira?"

"All fine, my friend. All fine. Just worried over you a bit, but the baby is fine and she will be born soon. Allingham is recovering well, just another battle scar for him to add to his collection, and Halsted is over his cold. Rosario is working hard to make us all

370

fat as pigs." Singh patted his own belly and smiled.

"So, it was all over a wedding photo."

"Apparently. The evil man saw Rebecca as his mother. He schemed and planned and learned all about Allingham and knew what a great detective he is and created many false leads to throw our friend off. He was a bad man and a sick one, and spent his life and cleverness and talent to do the devil's work. And now he can spend the rest of eternity with his master."

Hobbs, with great effort, pulled his hand from under the covers, as the slightest movement was exhausting to his dying heart. He extended it and held it out for the Sikh to take. "Do you remember what Francis said to you, Hira? To you and Allingham, just before he died? That he was sure glad he got to know you?"

"I remember."

"That's what I'd like to say to you, my friend. Thank you for helping me find my God again. Thank you. Just . . . thank you for being a good friend." He closed his eyes and blinked the tears away as Singh squeezed his hand gently.

"It's been my honor and privilege to find another good soldier. And you are my good friend and soldier. And may you know that you are going on being right with God."

He stood up to leave as Hobbs was fairly exhausted. He was called back by the dying man.

"Hira?"

"Yes?"

"Rosario was reading the paper to me earlier today, and she stopped. She kept something from me and, well, I have to say, it is driving me to distraction. Please, tell me, my friend, what is it that so put her off?" He pointed to a table on the far end of the room, near the door where the paper sat folded, out of Hobbsie's reach.

Singh found the page and did not want to read it, either. He looked sadly at Hobbs, and knew now what Rosario was keeping from her husband. "I'd rather not, my friend. I'd rather not."

"Now, Hira, I really must insist. Tell me. I think I can take it. I'm a grown man, a soldier, even, by your estimation." He gave his friend a little smile.

Singh sat regarding the page for a moment, then took a deep breath and read: "Calamity Strikes San Francisco Hotel, Tragedy Touches Arizona Ranch." Hira read through the rest to himself, then he looked at Hobbs and continued. "The little girl, the child you met and were so taken with on the riverboat, the one you told us so much about. She's dead, my friend. She died of typhus while in San Francisco, staying at the fine hotel there."

"Oh." Hobbs closed his eyes again, remembering everything about her. He looked at Singh through tearful eyes. "Why does our God do these things, Hira? She was lovely. She was just the sweetest little thing you'd ever want to know. Why? Why can an old fool like me live so long and then a sweet, innocent, wonderful little girl have to die of typhus? Be plucked up and carried away before she even has a chance to live? Why? Why is that, Hira? Why?"

Singh shrugged, then slowly shook his head from side to side. He had no answer. He himself wondered at all the terrible unknowns. Why would God let Webster go on and on doing the horrible things that he'd done? The Sikh did not know.

"I'm tired now, Hira. I think I'll sleep for a little while."

He awoke and watched Rosario sleeping in the rocker by his bed. She was beautiful, even when snoring, and he worried she'd wake up with a kink in her neck, as her head rested at an odd angle on the back of the chair. Still, he dared not awaken her. He looked to the right and watched the day dawn and the light brighten around the drawn curtains darkening his room.

He'd lived to see another day and was surprised that he did not want to cry at such a thought. He remembered his dream and was happy. He decided he needed her and moved a little in bed, enough to make the frame squeak. He knew this would rouse his lover, and it did. He beckoned her to the bed. She crawled in and held him tightly.

"Oh, your feet are cold." He kissed her. "Why didn't you come to bed in the first place?" He rubbed her neck where it was often sore and knotted up from her constant work. "You're all tightened up, too." The little bit of exertion exhausted him.

"Hmm." Rosario loved Hobbsie's massages.

"I dreamed of the little girl."

She sat up and looked him in the eye and thought of Hira reading the story to him. She could not be angry at either of them. Hobbsie went on. "She is in heaven and she's a happy little girl, maybe even an angel." He stopped and was quiet for a while. He looked Rosario in the eye and gave a confident nod. "I'm not scared anymore, Rosario."

"I am glad, my darling." She tried not to

cry but couldn't hold back the tears any longer.

"Now, now." He patted her gently as he squirmed a little in bed, "This is the third time you've buried a husband. I would think you'd be used to it by now." He tried to get her to smile. His heart was not cooperating at all this morning and he felt it flutter in his chest. His vision was darkening, and he had trouble making his mouth move, to say the words he intended Rosario to hear. He slowly settled deeper into the bed. "I'm going, now, darling. I'm going on to the angels, and I just want you to know . . . I've had a good . . . life, with you."

Hobbsie was dead.

EPILOGUE

Hilola sat on the hill overlooking the hacienda; her home, her majestic, stately home was off in the distance and she suddenly looked down at the grave plot at her feet. She was alone now. She had wanted to come back and visit it alone and was happy she'd done so.

The first day he'd brought her up to the cemetery, Ramon had pointed to three places next to his father. One was for Ramon's mother, the other for him, and the final one for Hilola. She remembered Ramon kissing her gently on the cheek and saying, *But not to be used too soon.*

She lit a candle and adjusted the rebozo covering her head and nodded to the cross marking the grave. She crossed herself as Ramon had taught her. She was becoming comfortable being a Catholic. She thought that she'd like to build a little shrine here, the kind she'd seen at the local church where they could put statues and pictures and burn candles, and these would be protected from the wind and the sun and rain. It was comforting to her to see these things and to smell the scent of the wax melting; to feel the heat on her face from many little flames, captured, held and radiated from within the little enclosed spaces.

She loved the colorful statues of all the saints and the Virgin. She found the way her new Mexican family and culture dealt with death refreshing, as if it did not have to be so terribly gloomy. It did not feel so dreadfully sad. She just liked all the pretty, brightly colored statues with their calm and contented faces looking down at her, as if to say, *It is not so horrible to pass on through this life. Better things are in store for you when you've gone.*

Alanza, her newest gift from Ramon, walked up behind her and gave her a none-too-gentle push with her moist muzzle. Hilola reached back and petted her lovingly. She spoke to the marker. "Señor, I wanna say some things about your son, your fine man, and to tell you what a good man he is and how much he misses you. I'm sorry I never got to meet you, Señor, because the way Ramon talks about you, and the way he misses you and, more important, the way you raised such a fine man, means sure enough that you were a good and fine man yourself."

She looked back at the house and saw Adulio and Paulo working and they waved to her from a good distance away. She smiled and waved back and continued. "I wanna tell you, Señor, that I'm so happy and I'll do my best to make your son happy, but I'm afraid. I'm so afraid 'cause I ain't smart, and I'm old, and I just ain't up to your boy's measure. I ain't by a mile and I know it." She shrugged and tried to make her voice stop shaking. Hilola was working herself up into a fairly agitated state. Her nose ran and she sniffed hard and wiped the tears from her eyes. She went on. "But Ramon keeps tellin' me I'm fine and he loves me just as I am and he don't act like he's getting sick of me at all. And, Señor, I ain't too old for babies, I know that. And I think I'm goin' to be makin' you a grandpa soon."

She felt better saying that, as she'd told no one yet that she was likely pregnant. Saying it made it more real to her, more likely that it was going to happen, that she wouldn't miscarry or that it was just a false alarm. Hilola was certain she was going to be a mother and this made her all fluttery inside.

She stood up and arched her back and decided not to tell her dead father-in-law about her plans to build him a grotto. She'd keep that a secret and work on it with the old men of the hacienda. They'd like to help her build it and it would be a secret and would be to surprise Ramon. She thought that maybe it could even have a baptistery, and her baby could be baptized right here, right next to Ramon's father's grave. That would make it even better and now Hilola wasn't afraid anymore. She was happy and wrapped herself tightly in Ramon's mother's favorite rebozo and fairly skipped back to her home, Alanza in tow.

Rosario had endured too many funerals in her time. She'd not have one for Hobbs. Instead, she had a celebration of his life. She also had a celebration of Francis's life and there'd be a big party. She insisted the Hall ranch men and the la Garza hacienda men be in attendance.

The gambler was also summoned, as well as the school teacher, Mary Rogers, who found the attentions of Mr. Singh most appealing these days. She was falling in love, and the handsome Sikh was finding that, at nearly fifty, it would not be completely preposterous to consider starting a family with the comely schoolmarm.

They all danced and celebrated and congratulated Rebecca on the baby that was ready to come at any time. The one-armed sheriff was constantly by her side, as though he was not so much of a lawman as he was a tax collector, by his own reckoning, at least he'd taken a small part in bringing the villain, Webster, to justice. Being with Rebecca made what he'd endured — the loss of his limb, the horrific things he'd seen — a little easier to endure.

Allingham watched them all from the corner of the room. He'd made this all happen, once again, and still did not fully comprehend why or how. He thought a lot about Rebecca's words; thought a lot about how it did, in fact, always happen. He made things happen around him, and he simply didn't understand how. Halsted sidled up to him, putting a drink in his son-in-law's hand. He shuffled and coughed. Allingham did his best to ignore him.

"So, you solved it. Made everything right, once again."

Allingham looked at him out of the corner of his small eye. "Hmm."

"All because of that damned photograph

and article I sent to New York."

"Hmm."

"Damn it, man, stop saying hmm. I'm trying to apologize."

Allingham looked into his drink and then at Halsted. "Accepted."

They were thankfully interrupted by the sound of a lively polka and Old Pop and Rosario dancing with great enthusiasm right past them, and then on around the entire room. It looked like a lot of fun and Allingham thought he'd like to try it, had he been a different sort of man. Instead he stood back and watched and marveled at how lightly Rosario could dance, as she was quite round.

The Mexicana could not seem to shake Old Pop, and did not seem to mind at all. Rosario was more like a man than a woman in this respect. She'd lost too many husbands in her life to waste a lot of time on grieving. She loved Hobbsie, certainly, but, as she was not a young woman herself, was not about to waste her life in mourning. No one held it against her, as Rosario was a force unto herself and lived by no one's rules of propriety when it came to such things. She'd decide on her grieving period and decide when and, more importantly, with whom to move on.

Allingham watched them dance. He was pleased for them. He looked at Halsted and was trying his best to forgive him. Halsted was too proud for his own good but Allingham had known too much evil in his life to condone plastering his business — and his wife's business, much less her picture — all over the newspapers for everyone to see. He had never wanted it or condoned it, but hadn't protested overly much, either, as he never intended to stand as a wedge between his wife and her father. But he was a private man and knew too much of the evil out there in the world to want to let his life be revealed for the worst to see. And now he'd been vindicated, in a most profoundly horrible way, for his alleged paranoia.

If it had not been for Halsted's hubris, they'd have not been subjected to Webster's depravity. Webster would not have even known of Allingham or Rebecca's existence and he would not have been inspired to include them in his terrible plan. Webster would not have read of all the things Allingham had accomplished and would not have wanted to test his genius against the terse policeman.

He looked over at Rebecca, now conversing — holding court, really — with the pretty blonde wife of Ramon la Garza on one side, and the courtly old gambler opposite her. He could tell, without knowing any details at all, that Rebecca was mentoring the young woman, a woman actually more advanced in years than Rebecca, but with so much to learn now that she was the head of a substantial hacienda to the south.

They were both soon to be mothers, as all that practice on the river with Ramon inevitably resulted in a happy pregnancy. Hilola sat proudly, with her new and very pregnant mentor and friend, absorbing everything Rebecca could impart, as she wanted so desperately to make Ramon proud of her.

Allingham watched Mary Rogers fall in love with the practically perfect warrior saint, Mr. Singh. She doted on him and served him tea and watched him with a certain reverence in her eyes. He was her knight in shining armor and saffron turban. She'd never again be afraid as long as Singh was by her side and it was unlikely, knowing the man, that he'd ever let her stray very far.

Allingham was certain there'd be yet another baby coming along by next winter. He caught Singh watching him, knowing what he was thinking and Singh gave a just discernible smile, holding up his tea cup to

Allingham as a silent toast, a salute to his fellow lawman. The Sikh then looked at Mary Rogers, reached over and whispered something in her ear and by the school teacher's response, it was a nice thing to hear. Singh was most certainly in love.

Allingham watched la Garza and Pierce Hall, two young entrepreneurs, working diligently, chatting energetically, and hatching a business plan. They'd remain lifelong friends and partners and this was heartening to him as well. He was glad for his part, or at least the part his people had played in that little drama, as well.

Perhaps there was something to what Rebecca had said. He was a force, had a certain energy about him that made things happen, made the lives of others better. If so, then this was the greatest gift Allingham possessed. He was just now beginning to comprehend this, and it made him feel very well.

He turned and looked at Halsted and nodded his great head, "If it's a boy, we thought Robert Hira Allingham."

Halsted smiled and nodded. "That has a nice ring to it, Allingham. But, then again, so does Francis. Francis Hira Allingham."

Allingham smiled for the first time in a long time. "If it's a girl, Frances Margaret

Allingham."

The old man smiled as he watched the happy revelers. He gave his son-in-law a knowing grin. Things would be different between them from now on.

The employees of Thorndike Press hope you have enjoyed this Large Print book. All our Thorndike, Wheeler, and Kennebec Large Print titles are designed for easy reading, and all our books are made to last. Other Thorndike Press Large Print books are available at your library, through selected bookstores, or directly from us.

For information about titles, please call:
(800) 223-1244

or visit our Web site at:
http://gale.cengage.com/thorndike

To share your comments, please write:
Publisher
Thorndike Press
10 Water St., Suite 310
Waterville, ME 04901